The Dragon King's Assassin

Amy Sumida

Copyright © 2022 Amy Sumida

All rights reserved.

Legal Notice

This book is copyright protected. It is only for personal use. You cannot amend, distribute, sell, use, quote, or paraphrase any part of the content within this book without the consent of the author or copyright owner. Legal action will be pursued if this is breached.

Chapter One

It was the most important night of my life.

A month ago, I'd been hired for a job that would assure me of a place in Racul history. Granted, if everything went as planned, the kingdom's history books wouldn't record my name, not my real name. But in my line of work, an alias was necessary for survival and for keeping me out of a Talon jail cell. And with the notoriety I'd receive from this job, my alias would be whispered with respect and, even more importantly, I'd be propelled into the gold league. As in, I'd charge a lot of gold for what I did, and people would line up to give it to me.

Not that the money I made tonight was anything to turn your nose up at. Along with career-boosting potential, this job came with serious risks that required a large monetary incentive. And I had definitely been incentivized by the substantial advance I'd been given for all the groundwork I had to do. Most of which wasn't done on the ground.

For the weeks that followed my acceptance of that advance, I'd spent most of my time watching my target—learning his routine, his habits, and even what he ate for breakfast (let's just say he's a carnivore). And that wasn't all. In addition to him, I had to research all the people around him and learn their routines—where they would be and when. Especially his guards. This man had a lot of guards.

It sounds like a lot of tedious work, but I was used to it,

albeit on a smaller scale. Half my life was spent watching other people live their lives, even when I wasn't on a job. Being an assassin doesn't make it easy to form lasting relationships.

That wasn't a complaint.

As dark as it sounds, I loved my work. I took pride in quick, clean kills that left the Talons, those illustrious officers of the law, scratching their heads and chasing their tails. And if I pulled this off, the entire Talon Force wouldn't merely be flummoxed, they'd be howling in fury—some of them literally. That is, if they were even allowed to investigate. My target had his own army and an elite team of knights formed entirely of Dragons. I couldn't imagine them inviting the Talons to take a look around the crime scene.

"Fuck the Dragons," I whispered as I scaled the roof of what was technically a garden shed.

Since this shed held tools for the royal gardeners and stood at the far end of the King's private garden, it was nicer than my first home. It also happened to be directly in line with the balcony outside the royal bedchambers.

Now, when I say that the building whose roof I was perched upon was in line with that prestigious stone viewing platform, I don't mean that it was close. Nothing was close to the royal chambers. That would have been a huge fuck up by His Majesty's Guard. And since the King's Guard was made up exclusively of Dragons, that sort of fuck up did not happen. On second thought, an assassin was currently within viewing distance of the King's bedroom, and that should *never* happen. So, I guess they did fuck up.

Or I was just that good.

I took my binoculars out of one of my many pockets in my assassin's vest and focused them on the windows to either side of the balcony. Unlike other balconies gracing homes in the crown city of Mhavenna, the King's didn't have glass doors leading to them or even a window that looked directly upon the outdoor space. What was likely a security precaution was actually a fault that I'd use to my benefit. Sure, no one could see in, but no one could see *out* either. The windows were dark; the King was asleep.

I tucked my binoculars away and removed my launcher. After sliding the steel shaft into the barrel, I aimed at a spot between the posts of the balustrade and fired. The rod went flying, trailing a black cord behind it, the whir of its passage barely audible. My aim, as always, was perfect, and it sailed right between the stone posts. As soon as it hit the wall, the prongs deployed so that when I pulled the rod back to me, they hooked over the posts. I gave an experimental tug, then secured the line to the U ring I'd installed in the shed roof the night before. With sure movements ingrained in my muscles, I hooked the sliders to the cord, fastened the cuffs around my wrists, and silently crawled off the edge of the roof.

Using their forward-only function, I moved the sliders along the cord, each shove taking me a little further along the line before locking into place. For the untrained, it would have taken over an hour to cross those forty feet, but I made it in less than three minutes. Even if there had been a patrol that came through the King's garden, and even if that patrol had looked up—two things the royal knights never did (damn sloppy)—I would have crossed the distance before they spotted me.

Once I reached the terrace, I freed my wrists and crawled over the railing to land on the soles of my soft leather boots, quiet as a cat. Despite the windows to either side of the balcony remaining dark, I dropped to my belly and slithered to the solid doors. Pressing my ear to the crack between the double doors, I heard the soft sounds of even breathing and smiled. I carefully rose into a crouch and pulled the lock-picking tools out of my vest.

A few seconds later, I was opening one of the balcony doors and slipping around it. I shut it just as quickly and quietly, blocking out the moonlight to give me more shadows to hide in, then stood pressed against the wall while my eyes adjusted. I was only a human, after all. I didn't have the night vision of the other races of Racul.

When the bed came into focus, the dark mound of the sleeping king atop it, I removed my weapon. As it was with all my tools, the metal of the slim tube was blackened without gloss. It was a simple device, one that many assassins preferred for its precision, speed, and silent execution. Execution being the keyword. The problem was, it was a weapon that required proximity to your target. The barrel had to be pressed against the victim's head—anywhere on the head, but I tried to go for the base, somewhere under the chin or at the top of the spine in back—and then the pointed rod within the tube could be released. Death was instantaneous, even for an immortal Dragon. Immortal, they may be, but not invulnerable.

Did I care that killing King Tarocvar Verres would throw the entire Kingdom of Racul into chaos? That although there was some satisfaction in taking the life of one of those elitist assholes—the head elitist asshole—another Dragon would inevitably take his place. Did it bother me that this man had done some good for the kingdom and his replacement might fuck things up?

Nah. I'm an asshole too.

I crept up to the enormous bed, heading for the side he was closest to—the left. My left. The King slept on his side, curled up like a baby. Not that his position made him any less intimidating. Even asleep, the Dragon King exuded power that sent shivers down my spine. I'd studied him long enough to know his body nearly as intimately as a lover, had spent many nights watching him bathe, dress, and fuck.

I could bring an image of the King's body to mind in a second—a very detailed image of bulging muscles and golden-brown skin. Of long hair as black as midnight that gleamed crimson in the light, glittering teal eyes so bright that they seemed to glow, and a jaw that could crush rocks. But I'd never been this close to him. So close that I could smell the spice of his skin and see the cleft in his chin—a little dent, as if he had indeed tried to crush rocks with it. Damn, he was handsome. Fucking breathtaking. What a shame.

Just as I leaned forward to set the weapon beneath the royal cleft chin, those stunning eyes shot open and focused on me. The King knocked away my weapon before locking his strong hand around my throat.

A deep rumble vibrated through the air between us. "Hello, little mouse. Have you come to play?"

Chapter Two

King Tarocvar stood up, hauling me with him. Normally, I could keep my heart rate slow, even in the most tense of situations. But it seemed to have forgotten that fact and pumped as if it could break free of my chest and run away without me. *Fuck you, body; I'll take my chances without you.* I dangled from the royal grip, my hands clutching his forearm to alleviate some of the pressure on my neck. My toes didn't even brush the floor. I was strangling. Dying.

And I still looked down.

The Dragon King was nude. Gloriously naked. That perfect immortal body was slabbed with muscles that bulged as if begging to be touched. Stroked. Licked. *Oh, fuck.* The guy looked as if he'd been carved from stone and polished for pleasure. Shoulders wide enough to carry an ox, pectorals big enough to bench press a unicorn, and thighs strong enough to thrust for hours. Speaking of thrusting, that piece of man-flesh between those thighs would fill me as I'd never been filled before. Long and thick, but not massive. Perfect.

Oh, fuck, was I really getting turned on while he strangled me to death? Some people liked that, right—being strangled in bed? Did this count as that?

When I lifted my gaze at last, I found the Dragon King looking down, his stare focused on my crotch. I didn't have to look to know that my erection tented my pants. Maybe I'd die of embarrassment before he killed me.

The King set me on my feet but didn't release my throat. "Is it being strangled that has aroused you, or is it me?" He eased up on his grip so I could answer.

Panting, I looked down his body again. My cock twitched. I mean, at this point, why not be honest? What was he going to do, kill me twice?

"I see," he said, his tone amused. "You've come to kill me, but now you want to fuck me. How interesting." He leaned in and inhaled deeply, his nostrils flaring, then straightened and let me go. "What's your name, little mouse?"

"Locrian Mahvis, Your Majesty." I bowed and hoped it didn't look mocking. My heart still beat wildly, probably because it, like me, couldn't figure out what the fuck was happening. "Lock, if you like."

King Tarocvar slid his gaze down my body. "I just may. Turn around and we'll see."

"What?" I squeaked like the mouse he labeled me.

"Turn. Around."

I turned in a circle.

"Take off your mask. Let me see your face." He flicked a finger and the logs within the fireplace to my left caught fire.

I flinched but did as ordered, pulling back my hood before pushing down the mask that hid the lower half of my face. I smoothed my hair and licked my dry lips as I waited for the King's verdict. He was silent for several nail-biting minutes, his gaze roaming my face and body. And my stupid cock remained at attention for him the entire time.

At last, the King stepped away from me and left the room

through a dark doorway. I gaped after him, then took a step toward the window.

"Do not make me hunt you, little mouse," the King called from the other room. "I have your scent now; you cannot hide from me." He came back into the bedroom wearing a pair of loose pants. "And I'm not in the mood for a chase." He grinned. "Not tonight."

I stood still as he circled me, one hand sliding over my chest, down my arm, and across my ass. He paused and squeezed one cheek. My teeth ground together to hold my groans back. *What was happening? Was he going to fuck me before he killed me? Was I opposed to that?* My cock twitched as if to say no.

The Dragon King stepped in front of me. "Who hired you to kill me?"

"I don't—"

"Do not lie to me!"

I flinched back from his sudden fury. "I'm not lying, Sire. No assassin knows who hires them; it works best that way for both parties."

"Then how are you hired? How are you paid?"

"Through an intermediary, a broker."

"A broker?" he said it as if it were ridiculous. "And who is this intermediary?"

"I don't know that either. When they have a job for me, they seek me out in a local bar I frequent, and they're always cloaked and masked during our meetings."

"How did you hire this person, to begin with?"

"They were referred to me by my old mentor, who is now dead."

"Great blasts of fire!" the King roared. "If you have nothing to give me, you are worthless."

With that, my erection finally deflated.

"I could find out," I hurried to say. "And until I do, I could protect you."

"*You* think you can protect *me*?" He laughed even as several guards came running into the room. He waved them off as he held my gaze. "I think I've proven that I do not need protection. Not yours, nor theirs." He waved a hand at his knights. "Although I expected the King's Guard to perform better."

"Sire, is this an intruder?" one of the soldiers asked.

"Is this an intruder, he asks," the King drawled. Then he turned to the knights. "Get out! And don't fucking return. You're all dismissed from my service!"

"Your Majesty?" another knight dared to ask.

"I said, get the fuck out! You're all fucking useless!"

The knights fled the King's fury. I wished I could go with them. Instead, I'd use their incompetence to my advantage. Again.

"I slipped past those men twice," I said, pointing after the knights. "*Twice*, Your Majesty. Yes, you woke up in time to defend yourself, but what if you hadn't? I made it past them, right into your bedroom, and this was after I'd conducted surveillance while on the palace grounds. And if I did it, someone else could too. Maybe the next assassin will have better luck than me. Three seconds, Your Majesty. That's all I would have needed to kill you. Three. Seconds."

The Dragon King crossed his arms and regarded me with a narrowed stare. "Why did you accept this job?"

"Honestly, it was a lot of money and it would have made me famous. I have nothing against you. It's just a job."

He chuckled and it had a wicked sound to it. "Just a job? All right, Locrian Mahvis, I will give you a chance to earn your life back. You are now *my* assassin." He stepped closer, close enough for his breath to brush my face. "You will obey my commands unfailingly. If I tell you to kill, you kill. Without hesitation. And you will protect my life as if it were your own. Better even than that. If needed, you die for me. Understood?"

"Yes, Sire."

"If you try to kill me again, I will eviscerate you and eat your fucking heart."

"I will not betray you. I swear it."

"Good." He stepped back, grabbed a pillow from his bed, and tossed it at me. "Choose a door and sleep in front of it—balcony or hallway. You start your new job tonight. Anyone enters this room before morning, kill them."

"Yes, Your Majesty." I tossed the pillow down just inside the balcony doors and went out onto the balcony to remove my grappling hook and untie the line.

As I stood, I watched the Dragon King settle onto his side, this time facing the balcony. He grinned at me, closed his eyes, and went back to sleep. Just another night for the King of Racul.

Chapter Three

After I took care of the hook, I set a chair in front of the bedroom door, locked the balcony doors, and then stretched out in front of them. It wasn't the first time I'd slept on the floor, but it was the first time that I was unsuccessful at it. I lay on my back, listening to the Dragon King breathe as I tried to settle my stomach and heart. Neither seemed to understand that we had survived the King's wrath. As for King Tarocvar, sleeping in the same room as an assassin—an assassin who had just tried to kill him—didn't bother him in the least. He was so confident in his superiority and my obedience that it didn't occur to him to worry.

I, however, was worried enough for both of us.

What had my dick gotten me into this time? To be fair, if King Tarocvar hadn't noticed my erection, he probably would have killed me. So, I guess my dick saved my life. That alone was mind-blowing. But then the King accepted my offer and now I was sleeping on the floor of his bedroom, basically enslaved to him until I figured out who had hired me. *If* I could figure it out. And *if* he freed me after I did. He hadn't exactly been clear about that. And I wasn't about to wake him up and ask.

I don't know when I fell asleep, but exhaustion eventually took over. I woke to the sound of chair legs scraping over wood. Pulling a dagger from my vest, I shot up and dashed across the room to the hallway door. Even though the fire had burned down to embers, sunlight seeped through the windows, so there was no missing the boot that wedged between the door and the jamb, pushing the chair out of the way before kicking the door open. Silently, I lifted my knife and slid behind the man who entered the room. Then I noticed that he was carrying a tray laden with food. Not too many assassins use breakfast trays as their weapon of choice.

"Sire, are you awake?" the man called softly. "I have your breakfast."

"I am, and I believe you'll have to announce yourself in the future, Reginald. You were seconds away from a very violent introduction to my new assassin."

"Your new *what*?" The man looked over his shoulder, saw me, and let out a startled yip. Luckily, his grip tightened on the tray instead of loosening. "Who the blazes are you?"

"Locrian," I said as I sheathed my knife. "Did you see this food prepared?"

"Did I *what*?" The man scowled at me, then carried the tray to the bed, flicked its legs down, and set it across the King's lap. "He's your *assassin*, Your Majesty?"

"Yes, newly hired. He'll need..." He looked at me. "What will you need?"

"A place to keep some things. That's all."

"How big does this place need to be?" The King started cutting into his breakfast, the sheet bunching at his waist and baring his chest. It was ten times as glorious in the sunlight. "Lock?"

"Yes?"

"How much space do you need? An entire room, or will a

chest do?"

"A chest?" My gaze went right back to the smooth, hard curves of his pectorals.

The King's lips twitched; they were firm too. "A *wooden* chest. Would that be enough space for you to keep your things in?"

"I . . . don't need a chest; I have one."

"Very well. Fetch my assassin a sleeping pallet with linens and pillows and the like."

"A pallet, Your Majesty?"

"Must I explain every word that leaves my lips?"

"No, Your Majesty!" Reginald bowed and hurried out.

"Hey, hold on!" I called after him.

He paused in the hallway.

"You didn't answer my question. Did you see this food prepared?"

"No, of course, not," he huffed and hurried away, muttering under his breath about crazy assassins.

"Damn it." I hurried to the King. "Don't eat that, Your Majesty."

The King lifted a brow.

"It could be poisoned." I waved at the bite of steak on his fork. "May I?"

"You want me to share my breakfast with you?" He looked as if he couldn't decide whether to be amused or annoyed.

"Just a bite of everything. Choose the bites randomly, if you please."

The King just stared at me.

"Dragons can be poisoned, correct?"

He sighed heavily and started placing little bites of his breakfast on the tray. I picked up the pieces and ate. Once I was finished, he started to lift another forkful.

"Your Majesty, please!" I held out a warding hand. "Some poisons take a few minutes to work."

He went still. "You truly think the food could be poisoned?"

"Yes, of course."

"And yet you didn't hesitate to eat it."

"You said I should be prepared to die for you."

The King spent the next few minutes staring at me in a very unnerving way. At last, he asked, "Is that long enough?"

"Uh, yes." I cleared my throat. "I think you're safe to eat it. From now on, we'll need someone to watch your food be prepared, then taste it in front of you."

"If they watch it get prepared, why would they need to taste it?"

"To ensure that they aren't poisoning it."

"Huh. Very well. I will assign Reginald the task." He began to eat.

"I need to go home and fetch my things," I said.

"Stop by the kitchens and get some breakfast on your way out."

"They won't know me."

"Oh, believe me, the whole castle will know who you are within ten minutes." The King chuckled.

"Yes, Your Majesty." I headed for the door.

"And Locrian?"

Damn, but he even made my name sound sexy.

"Yes, Your Majesty?"

"Do not tarry. I expect my assassin to be beside me throughout my day—a shadow, silent and watchful. My enemies could be anywhere."

"I think the label will confuse people, Your Majesty. Perhaps, bodyguard would be better?"

"But you are not a bodyguard, Locrian, are you?"

"No, Sire. I am an assassin who happens to be guarding you."

"Then that is what I shall call you. I do not believe in masking the truth. You are a killer, but, as a dragon, I can respect that. Besides, I like the sound of it—the Dragon King's Assassin."

"Yes, Your Majesty." I bowed and left the room before my smile betrayed the fact that I liked the sound of it too. Maybe I'd make a name for myself after all.

Chapter Four

The King was right. No one stopped to question why I was walking the halls of the Royal Palace. The servants drew back from me with wide eyes and the Palace Guard glared. I'd hoped that King Tarocvar would cover up who I was and protect me from some of the negativity I'd doubtless receive from his people. But with that one word, he'd made sure they all knew I had tried to kill him, making a mockery of the King's Guard, if not the entire Palace Guard, and destroying the sense of security everyone else had been enjoying. In short, I wasn't going to make any friends there.

When I stopped by the kitchens as instructed, one of the kitchen boys rapidly grabbed a fresh custard bun and shoved it in my hands before rushing to the other side of the room. The cook wouldn't even look at me. But the custard bun was delicious, far better than I'd expected to get, and I was content with that. I took my wins where I found them. I was alive and eating better than I had in weeks; that was enough to put a smile on my face.

And it was a good thing that I enjoyed myself while I could, because that contentment didn't last.

If there were an assassin's motto, it would be to expect *and* prepare for anything. That motto, more than any skill I possessed, saw me through the next few minutes. When someone came rushing out of a doorway I had just passed, I wasn't surprised. I had, in fact, caught a whisper of movement when I walked by the dark room. Dark despite the hour of the day. The movement and strange lack of light were enough to inspire me to slip on a lightning glove and quickly activate it with a few rubs against my thigh. A silent spark let me know it was ready for use. Just in time.

As soon as the knight's hand landed on my shoulder, I spun toward him, going into a crouch to slam the flat of my gloved hand into his belly. Light exploded between us, crackling tendrils crawling over the man as he went flying backward. His two friends gaped at their fallen comrade's twitching body before coming at me together. I didn't wait for them to reach me but instead picked one and ran for him, dodging the blow the other sent my way as I passed by.

Going low again—it's a good tactic with a taller opponent—I used my momentum to drop into a slide, my feet arrowing into the space between my target's boots, bashing them apart as I shot between his legs. And while I was down there, I grazed his balls with my gloved hand.

He grabbed his sparking balls and toppled over, knocking into a pedestal to bring a massive, empty vase—what the fuck is the purpose of a vase that you don't put flowers in?—to the ground with him. The vase shattered with an impressive amount of noise, but the knight's screams were even louder.

I came to a stop beside a servant girl who had flattened herself against the wall. She gaped at me as I jackknifed to my feet. I didn't bother to say anything witty to her or even wink; an assassin knows better than to get cocky in the middle of a fight. Instead, I ran for my final opponent, recharging the glove along the way.

But this one had gotten wise to my charged glove and my tendency to go low. I noted the downward arc of his hand and knew he was going for my wrist. Since he was a dragon-shifter, he'd likely break my bones with one blow. But again, expecting anything saved me. In a fight, I'm rarely the biggest, baddest opponent, but I knew my strengths and how to use them. I was smart, observant, and really fucking fast.

I switched my trajectory just before I reached the knight and jumped onto a long, narrow table set along the wall. My landing dislodged a stone head on a stand (I think it's called a bust, though I can't imagine why), launching it at the knight—a man who I recognized from the night before as a member of the disbanded King's Guard. The bust headbutted the ex-guard, and as he reeled back, I kicked him in the chest. He fell to the ground. I landed atop him and pushed off with my gloved hand. I would have slapped him just for the fun of it, but I couldn't use the glove while in contact with him or I'd be fried too.

Panting, I took a quick look up and down the hallway. A few servants were peering out of doorways, but there were no more knights to be seen. Discharging the remaining lightning with a sharp flick of my hand, I started to run. My assassination plan hadn't included entering any part of the palace beyond the King's bedchambers, but I had *prepared* for it just in case. The palace map had cost me more than I'd wanted to spend, but it had been worth every penny. Because even though this was my first time *inside* the Royal Palace, I knew exactly where I was and exactly how to get out in the fastest way possible.

My boots silently hit the marble floor as I fell into an easy lope, conserving my energy in case I should need it. Although I was fleeing the palace, I am ever the observer, and I cataloged the fine art and furnishings that spotted the hallways as well as the craftsmanship of everything from the gilded moldings to the elaborate doorframes topped with carvings of lounging dragons and, of all things, flowers. The prosperity of the

Dragon Court of Racul was well known, but now I'd seen it firsthand.

And, as the poor often do, I found fault with the wealthy.

All that space and luxury used by so few. All those expensive trinkets and elaborate gardens admired only by the members of the Dragon King's Court, nobles handpicked by the King himself. And none of them, except the King, of course, were even Dragons. The Dragons of Racul didn't live in the Royal Palace. Dragons, unlike some of the other shapeshifting races, aren't pack people. Oh, they'll band together to defend the kingdom and, especially, their king, but they don't do well living together. Too many alpha types.

So the only Dragons in the Royal Palace, again, other than the King, were the knights—sons of noble Dragon Houses, sent to serve the King for a required number of years as a tribute. Those knights I'd just laid out, the ones I'd gotten fired the night before, would be going home to their prestigious families in shame. Another thing Dragons don't tolerate well.

Which meant that if I kept to the main halls, I'd probably be attacked again. The King's Guard had consisted of eight knights and only three had attacked me. Five more to go.

I ducked into a room. It turned out to be some kind of music room, with a piano in one corner and a harp beside the fireplace. I didn't give a shit about the instruments; the only thing that interested me was the window. I opened the dual panes, slipped out, and shut them behind me. With a glance, I oriented myself to the grounds, then dashed to the cover of some trees. The wall I'd scaled to enter the grounds the night before was only a few yards away. Hopefully, no one had discovered my climbing gear.

The continued silence behind me was a good sign. It

meant the other dismissed knights were still lying in wait for me instead of searching. Perhaps the palace servants were helping them, bringing word of my whereabouts. Whatever the case, they'd be waiting a while. Because there was my rig, hooked right where I'd left it. My luck was holding.

I climbed the wall, pulled my rope up after me, unhooked the gear, and shimmied down the other side. In a few minutes, I was lost in the morning crowd that filled the busy streets of Mhavenna. I pulled up my hood, hunched to hide my face, and headed home.

Chapter Five

Safe in my one-room apartment, I changed out of my professional clothing and into a more casual outfit, though still discreet. Black was perfect for night work, but to blend into the background at the Royal Palace, I'd need something less stark. I chose a pair of brown pants and an indigo tunic. A glance in the mirror over the dresser had me grimacing. Even in my nicest clothes, the palace servants would be dressed better than me. Oh well, no sense in lamenting something you can't change.

Despite the outfit change, I still needed my assassin gear. So I slipped my vest on and covered it with a light jacket. I went with a pair of brown boots, but the heels were just as flexible as my black ones, and I filled the secret slots running down the sides of my calves with more of my tools. After a quick splash of water on my face, I packed a small trunk with clothes, tools, and a few necessities, then tied some rope around it to form two straps. Sliding my arms into the straps, I settled the trunk on my back like a traveling pack.

"Now, to get back inside," I said as I headed out.

I knew I couldn't go through the front gates. The avenging knights would snatch me up before I got anywhere near His Majesty. But they hadn't found my rig, so I felt confident in retracing my steps.

Around me, the city of Mhavenna had come fully awake.

Its inhabitants strolled the streets, going about their business, most of which was legal at this time of day. Not a single one of them paid me any mind, even with a trunk strapped to my back, and that made me grin. I loved this city. I loved the congestion that many people hated. The press of bodies that I could get lost in. Several races called Mhavenna home, but as a port city, it also played host to some very exotic travelers who brought very exotic things to sell. The air was laced with the scent of fine perfume, roasting meat, sea salt, and a hint of sweat, and full of a cacophony of carriages, hawking merchants, and, depending on where you were in the city, either birdsong or the call of ambitious whores. After midnight, the mist rolled in from the Vevaren River and crept through the streets like a sorcerer's spell. It was paradise.

I bought a sausage from a street vendor and stood across the street from the Royal Palace, pondering. I wasn't contemplating running. I knew that the King had spoken the absolute truth when he said he could find me by my scent. Dragons were renowned for that ability. You know, on top of breathing and controlling fire, flight, and the whole turning into enormous, winged lizards thing. They had magic in addition to the control of fire, but no one knew exactly what it was. Secretive bastards, those Dragons.

I finished off my sausage, licked the grease from my fingers, and strolled across the street. The Royal Palace didn't have curtain walls like a castle. Those walls were around the city itself, with proper battlements and wall walks that could be patrolled by the Horns—soldiers in the Dragon King's army. Not like these shorter, narrower walls that were more of a reminder to the rest of the city of who lived within them than a true barricade. Everyone knew that if you went beyond those walls, you'd be faced with either Dragon knights or the soldiers they had trained. Only a fool would cross that border. A fool or an assassin.

It was trickier during the day. No shadows to hide me, plus I was carrying some extra, bulky weight. But the route I'd chosen was the least populated, down a side street that was less used. I walked slowly, waiting for the single pedestrian—a water-dwelling Neraky, fresh from the river at the end of the lane—to pass by me before I approached the wall and, with a quick movement, launched a grappling hook over it. Those pretty iron horns that topped the walls, both decoration and warning, were the perfect size for my hook to grip. In seconds, I was over the wall and dropping back onto the royal grounds.

I didn't go into the palace but instead crept around it, sneaking alongside high bushes like a thief, hiding whenever I heard footsteps. Finally, I made it to the King's garden and the very shed I had climbed the night before. My U ring was still in place with the cord attached to it, dangling down the front of the building. I drew the rope up, affixed a new grappling hook to the end, and set up my launcher.

Once more, I found myself shimmying over the garden, this time I crossed above a patrol who entered the area when I was halfway across. I didn't stop, that would have been foolish. I figured if they saw me, so what? I'd be in the royal bedchambers before they could do anything about it. And if they had the balls to bust into the King's bedroom, they could explain to His Majesty why they were hunting his assassin. I nearly laughed at the thought, it was so absurd. But, as luck would have it, the idiots kept to their routine and never looked up.

I crawled over the balustrade, dropped silently onto the balcony, slipped my trunk onto the floor, then used my lock-picking tools to unlock the doors that I had locked the night before. I suppose I could have just knocked, but that would have alerted the soldiers below, and I was having too much fun evading them.

Just as I was reaching for the door handle, it turned and one of the doors swung open. I stared up the impressive length of King Tarocvar Verres, who stared back at me with a lifted brow.

"What are you doing, little mouse?" he asked.

I grinned and stood. "As you said, Your Majesty, the palace was made aware of my new position here before I left the building. Unfortunately, that didn't work out in my favor."

"Yes, I heard about what you did to those three Dragons." His lips twitched, then gave up the fight and spread into a smile. "As upset as I am that they attacked you after I dismissed them and made it clear that you are now mine, my pleasure for your proficiency is greater. Well done, Assassin. I am impressed."

"Thank you, Your Majesty."

"But you didn't need to creep back into my bedroom. The knights have been escorted from the palace grounds and your welcome has been made known to all."

"Made known to all but me, Sire. Besides, it gave me some added insight into your security."

"Did it?"

"Yes. In short, it sucks ass."

The Dragon King laughed and the sound went straight to my groin. At least he was fully dressed now, though not in the royal raiments one might expect. Instead, he wore a simple pair of black pants, boots, a crimson silk tunic that matched the sheen of his hair, and an unadorned belt. His hair was braided back, making his features seem even sharper than they were, and his crown was absent. I wasn't surprised by the outfit; I'd seen him dress this way often enough to have gotten over His Majesty's lack of pomp. But seeing him in his casual attire up close did strange things to me. For example, I had a terrible urge to grab his braid and use it to pull his mouth down to mine.

"I'm glad you returned. I was wondering if you'd try to run."

"I failed at my job, and that should have meant my death, but you gave me another chance. I owe you, and I gave you my word. I'm here until my debt is repaid."

The King stared at me for a minute, then said, "Come inside, Lock." He turned and strode across his bedroom, waving at his closet as he passed it. "You can put your things in there for now."

I grabbed my trunk, went inside, set the trunk in his closet—wait, no, make that his dressing room—then followed the King out of his bedroom, down the hall, and into a small dining room. Three people sat at the long table, all Dragons, distinguishable by their angular features, and all finely dressed, more so than the King. One of them was a woman, which meant that these were not soldiers. Dragon females did not fight; they were excused from such duty. Not because they were incapable of it, far from it; the females were often more terrifying than the males. But as the gender that bore those precious Dragon babies, they couldn't be risked in battle. So, who the fuck were these people, and what were they doing at the Royal Palace?

King Tarocvar took the most elaborate chair at the head of the table and waved a hand at an open seat beside the dark-haired woman. She slid a green gaze my way, looked me over, and dismissed me. Did I mention that the females knew they were valuable and tended to be even more egotistical than the males because of it?

"This is Locrian," the King said. "My assassin. Lock, these are my advisers. Balahar,"—he waved at the only blond in the room—"Sha,"—his hand moved toward the woman—"and Mikbal."

"Please, tell me you're at least going to kill him after he helps you find those who hired him," Mikbal drawled.

My stare met the King's.

He smirked at me, then at Mikbal. "Not unless he does something worthy of execution."

The breath left me in a rush.

"Attempting to kill you isn't worthy?" Sha asked.

The King's lips twitched before he said, "It's just a job, Sha. Nothing personal about it."

I bit my lip to keep from laughing and lowered my gaze. Who would have thought that the Dragon King had a sense of humor?

"This is ridiculous," Balahar said. "He's human, for fuck's sake. What can he possibly do for you? How can *he* protect *you*?"

"Physical strength isn't everything, nor does a person have to be immortal to achieve wisdom," the Dragon King said. "Locrian got past the palace guards, including the King's Guard."

"Then your knights are incompetent," Sha said.

"I agree. Which is why I dismissed the King's Guard."

"You did what?" Balahar leaned forward and gaped at the King. "The entire Guard?"

"They were incompetent, as Sha said." The King waved

a hand toward the lady. "And when three of those guards, ashamed over their dismissal, ambushed Locrian on his way out of the palace, my assassin prevailed, leaving those knights unconscious on the floor. Not only did he make it out of the palace unharmed, evading the other five knights lying in wait for him, but he also crept back into my bedroom without alerting a patrol of knights directly beneath him."

Three pairs of Dragon eyes shifted my way.

"Impressive," Balahar admitted. "How did you do that?"

"Trade secrets," I said with a straight face.

The King chuckled at Balahar's sour expression. "He's cunning, Bal. And quick. No, I don't need his protection, but I think I could use his eyes and,"—he paused to look me over—"skills."

Balahar cleared his throat. "Sire, this is—"

"Enough, Balahar," the King said. "I've made my decision and come to an agreement with him. Locrian is *my* assassin now. I like the thought of having a killer under my command, a man who doesn't follow the rules. As the King, I must obey my own laws. But Locrian will remind the people of Racul that they are *my* laws, and *I* decide who is worthy of the protection they offer. He will be my vengeance against those who wrong me, justice made flesh."

"You have the Talons to enforce your laws and investigate those who break them. They will arrest whoever hired this man and take him to the Courts of Teeth to receive punishment. That is how you get your justice, Your Majesty," Sha said. "Not like this."

"The Halls of Talons and Courts of Teeth are bound by my laws and that is a good thing, Sha. I can't have my enforcers, advocates, and judges breaking the very laws they have sworn to uphold. Locrian is not a soldier, an officer, or even a lawyer. But he can be all three of those for me—Horn, Talon, and Tooth. He will investigate, present his findings to me, and then carry out my sentence."

"An assassin in the employ of the King," Mikbal tested the words. Then he looked at me. "I hope you're up to the task, human. Our king is expecting a lot from you."

The Dragon King motioned to me. "Tell us why my knights are so terrible at guarding me. Prove to my advisers that you are up to the task."

"I will need to do a full analysis of the palace to determine where the weaknesses are in your security, but I can tell you what I've observed so far," I said, then I told them.

And they listened.

Chapter Six

If I was disliked and distrusted before that meeting, I was outright reviled afterward. The King's advisers agreed with my assessment, so the King ordered the Captain of the Palace Guard to allow me access to all areas of the palace, as well as answer all my questions, and implement all the changes that I recommended.

I spent the next few days analyzing the walls around the palace, the palace itself, and the routines of the Royal Guard. Then I spent another week working with Captain Vettan and his knights, going over all my recommendations. The Captain, who never stopped glaring at me, endured my presence only because the King was always nearby. I had a feeling that if the King hadn't insisted on me attending him at all times, quietly conducting my meetings with Vettan to the side of whatever meeting he was in, the Captain would have skewered me with his sword.

But the King did insist—guarding him was the main part of my job after all—so the Captain's sword remained sheathed, and the changes I recommended were made smoothly. Despite my status as the palace pariah, I was not attacked again. Again, I think this was more due to the King's presence than any restraint on the part of the palace knights.

Since I'd never had a lot of friends, I wasn't bothered by the lack of warmth. Frankly, I didn't give a shit what the people who lived and worked at the palace thought of me. I was there for one man, and that man ruled them all. So, I ignored the nasty looks and focused on His Majesty.

I quickly fell into a routine with the King. I'd get up, check his entire suite as he awoke more slowly, then we'd eat breakfast together. By this, I mean that he ate his breakfast in bed, naked (gods damn him), and I munched on something in between using the bathroom, getting dressed, and determinedly ignoring his nudity. Then I'd watch over him as he attended meetings, functions, and the like. At midday, we'd have lunch—him at the table and me standing, then more meetings or visits, dinner, sex, and sleep.

Just to clarify, his daily sexual activity did not include me. I would wait on the balcony while he entertained his chosen paramour, then, after they were dismissed, I could come inside and sleep on my pallet on the floor. This was the most excruciating part of my day, and I eventually came to dread nightfall. Standing just outside his bedroom, listening to his lovers moan and scream and go on about his prowess, was a form of torture for me.

The first night, it had been a woman, which disappointed me on two counts. First, that she was a she and second, that she wasn't me. I knew I had little chance of ever being invited to the King's bed, but if he were straight, my chances dove into the negative. The second night, however, he brought a man to bed, and I experienced the odd sensation of relief combined with envy. Since then, the envy had grown into bitterness.

"Oh, fuck," tonight's lucky man moaned. "Fuck, that cock is magnificent."

"Yeah, yeah, he's got a nice dick." I crossed my arms and glared into the shadows of the garden. "So what? Lots of men have nice dicks."

There weren't as many shadows out there now that the lampposts I'd ordered had been installed, but I made sure to inspect the few unlit areas that were left. It's not as if I had anything better to do.

"Oh, yes, Your Majesty! Please, fill my ass with your royal cum!"

I swung a horrified look toward the balcony doors. "Royal cum? For fuck's sake. Does he have to fuck such morons?"

The King's deep grunts were all the response the courtier received.

"He's probably trying to ignore the guy so he can get off," I muttered.

"Oh, fuck! Oh, fuck! Ohhhhh fuuuuck!" The man screamed.

Then there was the whimpering that always came after, well, after they came. It had only been two weeks, but I'd made a mental outline of His Majesty's fucking. Through the conversations—if you could call them that—he had with his lovers, their exclamations of delight, his grunting, the general sounds of sex, and my previous surveillance of him, I'd been able to work out the King's routine. The man's whole life was a routine, so why not his sex? And damn was it all boring.

I almost felt sorry for him. He chose someone new every night, as if a new lover might make a difference. I mean, he couldn't have someone new every night, he'd run out of courtiers, but I'd yet to see the same person twice, so he must have them on rotation. Anyway, if he were dining with the court that night, he'd motion at the lucky bastard or bitch, just a little come-here curl of his finger, and they'd follow him— or us, rather—to his bedchambers. If he decided to dine alone (with me standing to the side) in his suite, then he'd summon someone to him.

Once his chosen courtier was there, I'd go outside, and then they would undress him while complimenting his body. "Oh, Your Majesty, your chest is magnificent," that sort of thing. The courtier would then perform oral sex on the King, he would grunt through it in a very unimpressed manner, and then they'd get on to either vaginal or anal sex.

From what I'd heard, the King did not pleasure his lovers beyond the act of penetration. They were there for *his* pleasure and it sounded as if he didn't enjoy performing oral sex. Perhaps he kissed them or played with their bodies—I couldn't tell by sound alone—but it generally went fairly quickly. The King would penetrate his lover, they would moan, he would grunt, they would orgasm (or fake it), he would grunt more, they would whimper while his thrusts sped up, and then the King would make one last grunt that sounded more like relief than pleasure and be done with it. The lover would leave without protest, and I would go back inside with an aching dick.

Yes, despite the uninspired fucking and the distinct possibility that the King was a three-pump pony, I still wanted the guy. Listening to him fuck other people was giving me indigestion and blue balls.

But did it have to?

I looked down at the bulge in my pants, then around at the empty garden. No one was there. The doors behind me were solid wood. I was essentially alone. Why not?

I undid my pants enough to slide my hand inside.

The slap of flesh on flesh echoing out to me grew faster. The man's whimpering turned into the harsh panting of air forced from lungs by the thrust of powerful hips. I closed my eyes and imagined it was me. That I was on my knees on the royal bed, with the royal cock slamming into me, about to fill me with that royal cum. The smacking sound grew louder; His Majesty was close. Oh, fuck, so was I. I'd been listening to this man fuck for two weeks now, all while wanting him, and I hadn't been given the time or opportunity to relieve myself like this. So it didn't take much to send me over.

I bit my lip to hold back my cry but a soft sound escaped as my hips locked up, and I came hard, shooting my release through the posts of the railing and into the garden below. The orgasm was so violent that it made my ears ring, and it took me a few seconds to realize that His Majesty had come with me. As I panted and set myself to rights, I heard the King's lover get dressed and leave. I stretched my shoulders and neck, smiled at the stars, and sighed. Finally, I could get a good night's sleep.

"Assassin!" the King called as he did every night, but this time, there was an edge to his tone that didn't bode well.

I went inside the dimly lit room and locked the doors behind me. I always slept in my clothes, my weapons nearby, so I only removed my boots before I went into his dressing room to fetch my pallet. I set it up before the balcony doors, then hung a bell over the inner door's handle, all without even glancing his way. It wasn't until I was on my way back to my pallet that the King broke our routine.

In a voice full of claws, teeth, and cock, he said, "I smell you."

I froze. "I'm sorry, Your Majesty. I didn't realize I was overdue for a bath. I will—"

"I smell *your cum*," he cut me off. "You pleasured yourself out there. You touched yourself while you listened to me have sex."

Fucking Dragons and their fucking super senses!

I cleared my throat and faced him as blood rushed to my face. "I did. You know I'm attracted to you—that was clear from the first night—and I've had to listen to you fuck for two weeks now. I'm sorry, but I needed that. If you have a problem with it, let me go into another room while you fuck your annoying, idiot lovers so I don't have to listen to them blather nonsense about royal cum while you grunt through your orgasm."

"Grunt, do I?"

Oh, I was on a roll. My reason and sense of self-preservation seemed to have spurted out of me with my cum, allowing my mouth to spew all the frustration I'd been feeling. "Yes, grunt. Did you even enjoy that? For fuck's sake, it sounds as if you follow a list. One, get dick sucked; two, put them on all-fours; three, stick dick in them; four, wait for them to come; five, orgasm. Done."

The Dragon King, one knee bent and the other leg straight before him as he sprawled against his headboard, lifted a dark brow. "You think I have a formula for fucking?"

"Your whole life is scheduled, even the sex, so yeah, I think you fuck by formula."

"And you think you can do better?"

I paused, my brain finally catching up to my mouth. *What the fuck was I doing? And what was he really asking? Oh, fuck it.*

"Better than those morons you mindlessly screw? Yeah, I *know* I can."

"Take off your clothes."

"What?" my voice broke.

"Take off your clothes, Lock," he said more slowly. "I want to see what you have to offer before I accept."

Accept? Had I offered something? Was he really talking about . . . ? I started throwing off my clothes as if they were on fire.

The Dragon King chuckled softly as he watched me. The sound went straight to my dick so that when I dropped my pants, it was saluting its monarch. His gaze went slowly down from my face, over my chest, and lingered on my cock. He licked his lips, briefly looked over the rest of me, then tossed back the covers to reveal his erection. Let's just say it was far more impressive than mine.

"Well?" the Dragon King prompted.

Holy shit, this is happening.

I went to the bed and climbed up on the foot. Holding his stare, I crawled up to him, straddling his body as I went. The King straightened his bent leg, brushing my calf as he settled it between my legs, and I shivered from that single touch. His brows lifted.

I ventured further, not stopping to touch him, not yet. I waited until I was over his hips, our cocks aligned, and then sat myself down atop that thick, hard body and leaned forward to press us together gently, not giving him my full weight just yet. The Dragon King sucked in a breath as I began to rock against him, rubbing our shafts, torsos, and even parts of our legs together. He exhaled with a moan.

Encouraged by the sound, I went for it. I slid one hand up his throat, weaving my fingers through his hair—the silkiest hair I'd ever felt, and held his head still as I brought our lips together. He didn't shut his eyes. I could feel him watching me, but then I nipped at him and licked the seam of his mouth playfully. He opened his lips, closed his eyes, and I plunged into him.

Broad chest expanding, lifting me, the Dragon King moaned. It was the first time I'd heard such a sound from him, and I may have gotten cocky because of it. I twirled our tongues together as I ground against him, taking the time to draw his tongue out, into my mouth. To suck at him and explore the feeling of our kiss before allowing the passion of it to take over.

But the King wasn't having that. I'd woken a sleeping dragon, and the beast was hungry. With a growl, he wrapped his arms around me and pulled me closer. His tongue stabbed into my mouth, nearly gagging me, and his lips slashed over mine as if he could merge our bodies into one if only he applied enough pressure. I groaned into his mouth and writhed against him, cocks sliding along each other, and balls brushing his base. He tensed, clutched me tighter, and started to roll me onto my back.

I jerked back. "Oh, no, you don't."

The King blinked up at me in a daze.

"We're not doing what you just did with that idiot," I said. "I promised you something better. Now, where's the oil?"

"I . . ." He looked to the left. "There."

I shifted off him to grab the bottle of oil from the bedside table, then went right back to straddling his waist. As the Dragon King watched with wide, glittering, blue-green eyes, I poured a little oil into my palm, stoppered the bottle, then tossed it to the foot of the bed. Our dicks were pulsing and twitching together but I shifted down a little to disengage. The King made an angry sound.

This time I lifted my brow at him. "Patience, Your

Majesty." I coated him in oil, then massaged it in, rippling my fingers up and down his shaft.

"Fuck!" He threw his head back and clenched the sheets in his fists.

I smiled to myself, hardly believing that I had the Dragon King's dick in my hand and intending to make the most of every blissful second. But I wouldn't suck it. Especially not after he'd been fucking some other man. No, I would be different. He'd remember this, even if it was our only time together. I would stand out in his memories as the one man who made him moan and didn't have to suck his cock to do it.

I lowered my other hand to his balls and gently worked them as I thumbed the opening at the top of that blushing tip. Then I formed a ring with my thumb and pointer finger to slide over him. Up and down. Up and down. Fast, then slow. Tight, then gentle.

"You're driving me mad!" King Tarocvar lifted his head and grabbed my hips. "Get on with it, Assassin."

"No." I brought our cocks together, using both hands to rub them as if they were one shaft.

This time, when the King moaned, I cried out with him. Our hips moved together, pushing hard, slick flesh between my clutching fingers. Shoving and retreating. Pumping together as if we were fucking someone else at the same time. His large hands tightened on my hips and his tongue flicked out to lick his lips. I bit mine as I watched him. He'd never been so beautiful. Dark hair glinting red, eyes like precious jewels, wet lips plumped by my kiss, and that glorious body writhing for me.

"Better?" I asked.

"This is nice. But I'm waiting for more, Assassin."

"As you wish, Your Majesty." I let go of my cock and took a firmer grip on his.

Raising to my knees, I positioned myself over him, then eased down and took him into my body at last. I couldn't hold back my moans as his oiled shaft speared me, stretching my hole little by little as I worked myself onto him. Rotating my hips, easing my muscles open, my body began to welcome his.

The King started to pant. "Hurry."

"Easy now, Dragon. I will have my pleasure too."

He bared his teeth at me, but then I slammed down, taking all of him. The Dragon King's eyes closed at last, and his head rolled against the headboard. I leaned forward, took hold of his shoulders, and began to ride him like a fucking stallion.

I knew then why all his lovers sounded stupid. That fine dick of his fucked the sense out of your head. Three pumps, and I was moaning and writhing in such sublime pleasure that I couldn't think straight. My cock wept so much it dripped down to my balls and tingles bubbled up from my ass, tickling my insides and tightening my nipples. Suddenly, screaming for him to fill me with his royal cum didn't seem like such a bad idea. But then I met his stare.

As soon as our gazes collided, his caught fire. I mean that literally. Those teal orbs started to glow as if he burned within. They cast shadows over his handsome face, tinting his skin a strange greenish-blue as if he were underwater. And that was when I saw his dragon.

Something shifted within those eyes. Below that fine skin. Something woke. It stirred and rose. Stared back at me.

With a rumbling snarl, the Dragon King pushed up, gripping me in a tight embrace as he launched himself forward. He took me down to the bed and started pumping like a wild thing, his face an inch from mine. I couldn't tell if he were furious or fervent in his desire. So I nipped his chin, right over the cleft. The King bared his teeth again with a snarl, then covered my mouth with his. His tongue lashed at mine, a savage thing set loose. One powerful arm slid beneath my right knee and lifted so that my leg angled outward and my ass opened further to him.

With a triumphant growl, King Tarocvar thrust deeper, hitting places that rarely got attention. I moaned into his mouth and wrapped my arms around his waist, roaming his broad back with my palms. The muscles tensed and released beneath my fingers, teasing me. I needed more. I moved a hand to his ass and squeezed, urging him even deeper. I was near as lost as he was to desire, grasping at something I couldn't name.

The Dragon King lifted his head, breaking our kiss abruptly, and roared.

It wasn't an orgasm, more of a triumphant cry. An *at last!* He kept pumping wildly, the muscles in his neck bulging and his jaw stretching on the primal sounds that rolled out of his mouth. My hands couldn't be stilled. I brought them forward, sliding them over those spectacular pectorals, over his shoulders, up that tight throat, then grabbed his face and pulled him down to me.

Eyes still alight, the Dragon King stared at me as if he'd never seen me before. As if he were surprised to find that it was me there, beneath him. Then he kissed me; a kiss full of passion but also something else, something intense. Something like that roar. I tasted blood and wasn't sure whose it was. The King growled and sucked at me. Slammed into me. That oiled dick became a rod of fire, branding me. Searing its way into my soul. It felt as if he were fucking every cell of my body and making them all his.

My dick couldn't take it. With a wild shout, I emptied

between us. With the touch of that warm release, the King sped up. Something tore beside my face. I turned to see the sheet in shreds, his fingers dug into the mattress. The slap of flesh became so rapid it was nearly one long note. The massive bed trembled and creaked. The whole world condensed down to the two of us. No one else existed.

My body shivered through the aftermath of the most brilliant orgasm I'd ever had, clutching the King's cock as if it refused to let him go. But the King's will could not be denied. He lurched back, onto his knees, pulling his cock free, then gripped it and angled it over me. As I trembled and panted, he painted me with his hot desire. And it was hot, nearly too hot. I flinched, then moaned through the searing lashes, but couldn't look away from him. His stare held mine captive as he emptied himself over me. Again and again, his hips jerked forward, and his cock shot through his hand, releasing streams of cum. An insane amount. It striped my chest, whipped my stomach, lashed my thighs, and then, he gave one last shudder and coated my cock.

The King's hand opened as if it had been locked around his dick and ached from the effort. Our ragged breaths were all that could be heard as we stared at each other. I felt as baffled as he looked. I thought he would send me away then. Tell me to get the fuck out of his bed. But he didn't. With the oddest, almost tender, expression, he laid his palm on me and began to rub his cum into my skin.

Where his hand went, my skin tingled. Like bubbles bursting between us. I moaned and began to writhe beneath his touch, my cock rising again. He didn't touch me there. He looked at my hardening shaft but otherwise ignored it. Instead, he methodically massaged his desire into me, sending those tingles deep into my flesh. Kneading my muscles and pinching my nipples. Zings of pleasure shot into my skin like lightning to awaken my whole body. Then I looked down and saw that the cum, his royal cum, was disappearing. My body was absorbing it.

"What's happening?" I whispered.

"Lift your legs for me," his voice was even deeper now, the sound of rocks grating in a deep cavern.

I grabbed the back of my knees and lifted them, exposing myself to him. He'd finished rubbing all but the cum on my cock. My erection twitched, my balls lifting. It was all on display for him, even my tightening hole. At last, the Dragon King grabbed my dick and worked his cum into it as I had done to him with the oil. Then, before the cum had fully absorbed, he lowered his hand and pumped a finger into my ass.

I came all over myself and promptly passed out.

Chapter Seven

I woke up on my pallet, naked and crusted with my own cum. I knew it was mine since his had been absorbed. It had fucking sank into my fucking skin! I shot upright, my heart racing, and through the dim light seeping past the curtains, saw the Dragon King sleeping peacefully on his bed.

Had that really happened or had it all been a crazy dream? Had I undressed and come in my sleep? I rubbed a hand over my belly and remembered the strange tingles. No, that was real. I didn't know what the fuck it was or what it meant, but it was real. It happened. Maybe it was a Dragon thing. He was the first Dragon I'd ever fucked, so I had nothing to compare him to. Maybe they had tingling cum that absorbed into skin. That would be nice. He could come inside me all he wanted, even with that crazy amount, and I'd never be uncomfortable.

If we ever had sex again.

I got up and crept out of the room, then down the hall to the guest bedroom where I kept my things. The attached bathroom was for my use as well. It wouldn't be appropriate for a human assassin to share the Dragon King's shower or, gasp, his toilet. Gods forbid my ass touch the same seat as the King's.

I went straight for the shower stall and turned on the hot water. I needed to bathe before I did anything else. I smelled . . . musky. Not in a bad way. In fact, it was rather nice, like expensive cologne. The scent of Dragon sex perhaps. As nice as it was, it was a clear sign that I needed to bathe. That and the dried cum on my belly.

As much as I wanted to luxuriate in the hot water, I hurried through my shower and dried off just as rapidly. In a few minutes, I was dressed in a fresh set of clothes and back in the King's bedroom. Thank all the Gods of all the races of Serai, King Tarocvar was still asleep. I rushed to the balcony and popped outside, checking that all was well out there before I went in and opened the curtains. Sunlight painted the Dragon King in burnished copper and gold, and I allowed myself a second to admire him and maybe shiver a little as I remembered the night before.

I wasn't stupid enough to think that it had changed anything. I was still indebted to him, and he was still the Dragon King. I had to prepare myself for the possibility of increased indifference this morning and a new courtier in his bed that night. So I let go of the memories and went about my morning routine, heading to the suite door where Reginald would probably be waiting with the King's breakfast tray. I could think about the sex later, when he was fucking someone else. It would make me feel smug and satisfied to hear him go back to his formula, knowing I had been different. I had broken his pattern and made the Dragon King roar.

Yeah, that was enough for me.

"Is His Majesty awake?" Reginald asked as I let him into the suite.

"If he isn't, he should be anytime now." I went ahead of him to open the bedroom door and yank the nearby cord that activated the enchanted globes within the chandelier. I only pulled it once, so that they came on at their brightest. Then I took my plate off the tray—a custard bun with two sausages—

and went to lean against the wall near the balcony as I ate.

"Sire?" Reginald hesitated by the bed.

The King was on his side, facing me, his eyes closed. He opened them suddenly, his stare latching onto mine, and the skin around his eyes twitched. He sat up, stretched, and waved Reginald away. "Take that to my dining room, Reginald. I need to bathe first."

Reginald blinked, then backed up as the King shifted his bulk out of bed—his naked bulk. He strode past Reginald and into the bathroom without another word.

I took a bite of the bun to cover my grin. The King always bathed at night, just before he summoned a bed partner. And he never worked up enough of a sweat to need a shower afterward. Not until me.

"Well, I . . . yes, Sire," Reginald said even though the King was gone, the bathroom door already shut. He took the tray down the hall to the King's dining room.

With a grin and a deep breath, I opened the balcony doors and went outside to set my plate on the railing and lift my face to the sun. I felt amazing. I couldn't remember when I'd last felt so alive. So fit. I could have climbed down the palace wall and done laps around the garden. And my mind felt sharper, more focused. Within a minute of being outside, I had a plan for the day. And it didn't involve the King. Sometimes, all you need is a good fuck to clear the cobwebs.

"Assassin," the King called.

"Yes, Your Majesty." I strode back inside, set my empty plate down on a table, and followed the King out of the bedroom, down the corridor, and into his dining room.

I took up a position near the door as the King sat down at

the table. Reginald had removed everything from the tray and set them out nicely on the table. He'd even filled a dainty cup with coffee and left the cream and sugar nearby for the King to use. But he didn't know what to do next, so he stood to the side of the King's chair, back against the wall, clutching the tray to his chest like a shield.

"You may go, Reginald." King Tarocvar waved the servant away.

"Thank you, Sire." Reginald hurried off before the King could do something else out of the norm.

"Why did you become an assassin?"

My gaze shot from the window to the King. "Pardon me?"

"Why did you choose to kill people for money?" He lifted his cup and stared at me over the rim as he sipped.

"No one's ever asked me that." Then I snorted a laugh. "Probably because I don't tell anyone that I'm an assassin."

"Not even your lovers?"

"Especially not them." I grinned. "Many a man has been brought down by a tongue loosened with sex."

"So I'm the first to know what you do?"

I blinked. "Yes. I suppose you are."

"Then answer my question. Why this career?" He started cutting into his meat—he always had steak for breakfast.

"Why this?" I repeated. "I don't know. It's not as if I grew up with a desire to sneak into homes and kill people." I thought back, really considering his question. "My family was poor. I've always lived in the Broken."

"The Broken?"

"Yeah, the Broken. You've never heard it called that, have you?" I snorted in the way that everyone from the Broken does when some rich fucker says they've never heard of the place. Not that people from the Broken meet a lot of rich fuckers.

"No, I don't know what you're speaking of." He set his utensils down. "Where is this place?"

"It's the poorest part of Mhavenna. The southeast section along the wall. Bracken Road curves around it, separating it from the rest of the city and the difference between one side of the road and the other is really fucking obvious. One side is Bracken where people eat regularly and the other is—"

"Broken," the King finished. "Where they don't."

"Yes." I lifted my chin as if being from the Broken was something to be proud of. "I'm not surprised you've never been there. It's not a place fit for royalty."

"As the King, I know all of my city. I have been to the area you call the Broken. I just didn't know it had a name."

I lifted my brow again, this time in surprise. He had been to the Broken? When? A visit from the King would have been noted by, oh, everyone.

"I assure you, I have seen the derelict buildings and shanties," the King said to my look. "I have even sent the Scales to offer assistance to the residents. But they were turned away every time."

I snorted. "Yeah, social workers aren't welcome in the Broken. It's a funny thing, the pride of the poor. You have to be *really* desperate before you take a handout. We'd sooner steal."

The King shook his head. "I don't understand that. I can't

help people who won't accept my help."

"I didn't know you sent the Scales." I stared at him for a second, wondering if I would have done anything differently. Or if I would have tried at all. Honestly, I was impressed that he even knew the Broken existed. "That's . . . well, it's good that you tried. Maybe you should send them more regularly. There are some people desperate enough to accept their help. Though, usually, those people will go to the Halls of Scales to seek charity instead of waiting for it to come to them."

"Yes, so I've been told." He scowled down at his steak a second before looking up at me. "You were telling me of your family."

"Yes, uh, we couldn't afford any of the vocational schools. I've been working since I was, oh, five years old. I'd do odd jobs. Whatever I could find. We struggled but got by. Then . . ."

"Then?"

"You don't want to hear this." I looked back at the window. "It's a common enough story and not suitable for breakfast entertainment."

"I'm not looking for entertainment," he said softly. "I want to know what brought you to me."

Brought you to me. The words seemed intimate. Enough that I looked back at him. He lifted his brows as if daring me to answer.

"All right," I said. "But it's not a pretty story."

"As long as it's the truth, I want to hear it."

"My family died in the Ricarri Riots."

"The Ricarri Riots? That was ten years ago. From what

I recall, the Ricarri were protesting the unsafe working conditions in a light orb factory." He motioned at the chandelier above him. "Something about spells misfiring. The protest got out of hand, and the factory was destroyed, but I was told that no one was hurt."

I grimaced. "No one *important* was hurt. We lived in a tiny apartment above that factory, along with several other families. The Ricarri used their metal magic to bring the building down. I wasn't home. I was working, doing some carpentry for a rich man who didn't want to pay the price a professional would demand. But my family was there, all of them. They were crushed to death along with many of our neighbors."

"I'm very sorry, Lock."

"My mother, two sisters, and younger brother. All gone dying while I hammered nails."

"What about your father?"

"He left when I was six. I don't know what happened to him, and I don't give a fuck."

The King's brow furrowed. "How old are you?"

"Twenty-six."

"Sweet Ensarena, you were sixteen when that happened?"

"That's a grown man in the Broken." I shrugged. "I came home to a pile of rubble that night, and I remember feeling this deep, aching grief, but also a horrible relief. I had no family and no home, but I also had nothing tying me down. I didn't have to provide for them anymore. Didn't have to worry that they had enough to eat every day. And I didn't have to abide by my mother's rules. She wasn't there to insist that I do the right thing. So I didn't. I started working for the people she warned me about. Got in good with a Raltven gang, so good that they made me one of them. Then one day, someone told me there was money to be made for someone with the skills of a thief and the stomach for murder."

"And you had the stomach for it?" He took a bite at last and chewed as he watched me.

"The stomach and the talent. What the fuck did I care about some rich asshole who stole from the wrong people?"

"I didn't steal from the wrong people."

"Maybe you did."

"Excuse me?" He set his utensils down again, this time with a click.

"I'm not calling you a thief, just trying to tell you how some people view kings, especially Dragon kings. I'm all for order. I wouldn't want to live in a lawless city. And I think you've done a lot of good for this kingdom. As far as kings go, you're not so bad."

"Then why kill me?"

"I told you why I took the job. I don't know why I was hired, or why they chose to offer this job to me, but I can tell you that most of the poorer population of your kingdom see you as a figure of authority who is forced upon them. Even though they secretly appreciate the laws as much as I do, you are at best, someone unconcerned with them and at worst, a tyrant to be endured."

The King surprised me by saying, "I don't enjoy hearing that, but I understand it. I've tried to do right by my kingdom and the people who inhabit it, supporting not only the Horns in my army but also the Talons who patrol the city streets, the Teeth who punish criminals, and the Scales who help the abused and downtrodden. I work hard every day to maintain order in this kingdom. But I must rely on the Horns, Talons, Teeth, and Scales, those extensions of myself, to do what I cannot, and I know it is never enough." He ran a hand through his hair and sat back. "It's never enough."

"It is enough," I said firmly. "People will complain even in the best of situations. Do I wish the Broken was a better place to live in? Sure, but what you said is true; you can't help those who won't accept help. The point is that you try. I knew you were a good king even before I learned about what you do for your kingdom. It is enough, Your Majesty. But that will not change the perspective of many people. You are the King. Whether you are good or bad, there will always be those who are against you."

King Tarocvar snorted. "That is more true than you know."

"But I wasn't hired by a poor man." I crossed my arms, brought one hand to my face, and tapped my lip in thought. "The advance I received was more than I make in a year. Your enemy is wealthy, so I need to figure out why a rich man would want you dead. Then I'll be closer to finding his *or her* identity. And I'm going to start my investigation today."

"Are you, now?"

I nodded. "I'll let Captain Vettan know that I'll be out today and have him assign you—"

"You are not leaving my side." The King leaned forward, his hands clenching into fists on the table. "You are supposed to be watching over me."

"I can't investigate from here. You do want me to find out who hired me, don't you? I thought that was part of my job?"

The King stretched his neck, sharp pops coming from it. "I do. Very well. You have two hours."

"You're going to restrict me to two hours? I won't be able to—"

"Two hours!" He slammed his fists onto the table.

I flinched, my body shivering and tingling, reminding me of the night before. "Yes, Your Majesty. May I go now?"

The Dragon King waved a hand toward me, shooing me as if I were a great annoyance. I rushed from the room without a backward glance.

Chapter Eight

I started where I'd last seen my broker—the Shrieking Ghost. The Ghost was a Raltven bar in the Broken. It was not a place where nice people went to have a cocktail. But if you were a criminal of any sort, it was a great place to find work, especially with the Raltven. Raltven were some of the shadiest people on the planet of Serai, and I mean that in all definitions of the word.

Despite the early hour, the bar was open and full. Once inside, it was hard to tell what time it was, what with the lack of windows and the light globes set to low. Raltven liked the dark, all the better to blend in. Literally. I passed a table of them, most in solid form since they recognized me. The two who were unknown to me went transparent, the misty outlines of their bodies vanishing in the dim light while their dark clothing merged with the gauzy fabric that draped the walls and hung from the ceiling to form partitions between tables. Their friends leaned over and whispered something, and the Raltven went solid to nod at me.

They didn't know exactly what I did for a living, but I'd run with their kind long enough for them to know that my work was outside the Dragon King's laws. In the Shrieking Ghost, that made you welcome and worthy of a certain type of trust. I may be a killer, but I wasn't an undercover Talon looking to make a quick arrest. And in that room, everyone was a killer. The only difference between them and me was that they didn't get paid for it.

Which meant I had to tread carefully.

I could have gone straight to the bar at the end of the room and spoken to the barkeep; a barman was a font of information. But that information flowed in the direction of money. If he talked to me for a price, he'd share our conversation with someone else for the same amount of coin. So, instead of going to the bar, I veered right, sweeping aside a length of black gauze. The fabric was the clearest indicator that this was a Raltven hangout. Not only did it give every table a sense of privacy, but it also put the Raltven at ease. Sort of like a security blanket for really dangerous children.

"Hello, Tengven," I said to the only Neraky in the place.

"Lock." Teng grinned, flashing his pointed canines.

Tengven had been watching me cross the room through the gauzy fabric, just like everyone else, so he wasn't surprised by my greeting. He only jerked his head toward the empty chair beside him, then huddled over his steaming bowl of soup. He stirred the broth, the opalescent fish scales on his hand glistening in the light of the lantern above. A tentacle floated to the surface, and Teng scooped it up with his broad spoon, then slurped it into his mouth. Iridescent green eyes closed in bliss as he chewed, their nictating membranes shutting a second before the outer lids.

"I need some information," I whispered.

In addition to being the only Neraky in the Ghost, Tengven was also the only man there who knew what I did for a living. Because Teng wasn't just one of my few friends, he was also the only man I trusted in the whole damn city now that Gren was gone.

Tengven slid a look my way, then quickly around the

room. "About?"

"The Hood."

Tengven shifted toward me. "I thought you didn't want to know about the Hood?"

"Circumstances have changed. It's become imperative that I find him."

"The only man who knew the Hood's identity was Gren."

"I know."

"And he's dead."

"Yes, I know my mentor's dead. Thank you."

"I can make some inquiries but it will take time and coin."

I pulled out a small pouch of coins and passed it to him under the table. "Teng, my life is on the line."

He blinked slowly—the inner membrane, then the outer lid. "Who?"

"*Him.*"

Tengven cursed, straightened, did some facial acrobatics, then leaned back toward me. "You got caught?"

"He woke up just before I finished him."

Teng gaped at me.

"He let me live." I lifted my motioned at myself. "Obviously. But to keep living, I have to find the man who hired me."

"Fuck me," Tengven whispered. Then, in a stronger voice, "I told you not to take that job!"

"I know."

"But you were so certain you could do it."

"I know."

"Him?! *He* caught you?"

"Yes."

"Fuck."

"Yes."

"Jingtin damn you," Tengven muttered. "Fine, let me finish my soup."

"Thank you, Teng."

"Yeah, yeah. Just don't mention my name to *him*."

"I may be an idiot, but I'm not an asshole."

Tengven snorted, then started slurping.

Chapter Nine

The main docks of Mhavenna were just within the western river gate, closest to the Fresian Sea, but there were many docks along the broad Vevaren River that crossed the city, some more secure than others. Tengven docked his ship near the eastern river gate for two reasons; the river was cleaner there, having just entered the city from the mountain end, and the Neraky underwater city of Fei-Sha was just outside the gate, in the center of Sungla Lake. The fact that it was within walking distance of the Shrieking Ghost was just a bonus.

I stood on the deck of Teng's ship, the Lu-Ken, staring toward the eastern gate. The portcullis was raised for the day, and boats were already sailing in. Most of them would be carrying honest merchants, unlike my friend, who only masqueraded as one.

"Come inside," Tengven said.

He led me past the skeleton crew lazing in the sun. In between jobs, Teng's men had it easy. They maintained the ship and guarded it, but that was done in shifts of small groups, with the rest of the crew free to come and go as they pleased. But Tengven was no pushover. He gave them such leeway because he expected so much from them when they did work.

A lot of pirates earned a reputation for themselves;

sailors would see their ships approaching and try to flee. But the Lu-Ken was known only as a merchant vessel. and that was a far greater accomplishment. He could sail up to any ship, and they wouldn't know they were in jeopardy until the very last moment. I don't know how he did it. If Tengven had a no-survivors policy or if he was simply exceptional at masking his ship and crew—and I didn't want to know.

We went into the captain's cabin, a room at the end of the main deck, beneath the quarterdeck. The most spacious room on the ship, it was also the most airy, with little windows that had been flung open to emit the breeze. To one side was a built-in bed, to the other, a dining set, and in between, was a sitting area with a full-sized couch, two armchairs, and a trunk for a coffee table. Teng called out for tea, shucked off his heavy coat, then sat down in one of the armchairs.

"I could sail you out of the kingdom," he said. "The crew's ready for another job anyway."

"He'd find me." I shook my head. "He has my scent."

"Fuck, Lock. You really messed up this time."

"I am aware."

One of the crew brought in a tray with tea and tiny cookies, managing to look intimidating despite his dainty, elegant burden. He set it down on the trunk between us, nodded at his captain, and left, his thick boots thudding on the expensive rug. The rug and tea set weren't the only fine things in the room. One look around Teng's cabin was all you needed to know that he was good at what he did. From the crystal lanterns chained above us to the bottles of expensive liquor set within a wall bracket, everything was the best quality money could buy.

"All right." Tengven stabbed a cookie with one of

his long, pointed nails and popped it in his mouth. After swallowing, he went on, "I'll start with the whores and the thieves. They should know something. Someone has to have seen the Hood leaving the Ghost at some time. I need you to tell me everything you know about him, no matter how small a detail it may seem. Then I need you to think back to anything Gren may have said or done in regard to the Hood. Any references to social standing or facial features. Quirks. Anything at all."

I started to go over every memory I had of the hooded man who was my intermediary with my anonymous customers. Every little detail, and then everything I could remember Gren saying about him. This went on for much longer than I'd expected, and I was shocked by the number of things Tengven recorded in a little notebook. By the end of it, my stomach was rumbling.

"Shall we break for lunch?" Tengven asked.

"Lunch?" I frowned. *Why did that alarm me?* "Oh, fuck! What time is it?"

"Uh." Tengven looked toward a clock near the bed. "12:30. Why?"

"Fuck! I have to go." I jumped up and rushed for the door.

"Lock?"

I paused. "Is that enough to get started?"

"Yes, of course. But what's—"

"He told me to be back in two hours. I've gotta go, Teng."

"Yes, yes, go!" He waved me off.

I bolted across the deck of the Lu-Ken and then across the boarding plank. At this time of day, carriages actually ventured into the Broken and one happened to be passing the docks. I shouted and ran for it. Thanks be to all the Gods, it actually stopped for me.

"The Royal Palace!" I said to the driver as I jumped in. "And hurry!"

The driver straightened in surprise, snatched up the reins, and slapped them down. Jingles sounded as the carriage lurched forward over the cobblestone road. I sat back against the rear wall, panting, trying to calm my racing heart. It was only half an hour. Surely, he wouldn't notice that I was half an hour late. He'd have to have checked a clock right as I was leaving. As I had done. Either that or have some kind of internal timer. No, I was fine. I could make an excuse. Except that Teng's dock was a good twenty minutes away from the palace. That would make me nearly an hour late.

"Fuck!" I slammed a fist on the seat and jiggled my leg anxiously. The horses were already going at a fast clip, I couldn't demand more speed. I'd just have to—

The sound of screaming horses accompanied the sharp creak of straining wood and the driver's alarmed shout. The carriage came to an abrupt halt, sending me to the floor. I was still picking myself up when the door was yanked open.

"Son of a bitch!" I snarled as I lifted my head . . . and stared straight into the eyes of the Dragon King. "What the fuck are you doing here?"

"I said *two* hours, Assassin," the King stepped back, revealing a line of palace knights behind him. "You are late."

"I got tied up with the investigation." I remained in my half-crouch, staring at him, trying to process the fact that the King of Racul had come out of his palace to hunt me down for being half an hour late. "It's only thirty minutes."

"You would have been even later by the time you arrived."

"Yes, but at this moment, I'm still only half an hour late."

"Are you going to get out of the carriage or crouch there arguing with me?"

"Uh." I looked at the knights, then at myself. "Right. Yes."

I got up and jumped out. The Dragon King didn't back up for me which meant that when I straightened, he was mere inches away. I stared up the length and breadth of him, swallowing past the dryness in my throat his nearness brought on. He looked even larger out there, on the street, where I could see him around normal people. And those normal people were frozen, watching their king as warily as I was.

"I'm sorry for my tardiness, Your Majesty," I said.

He lowered his face to mine and snarled, "Get in the fucking carriage, Lock."

I was confused for a second and glanced back at the carriage I'd just exited.

"Not that one! *My* carriage!" The King's arm shot out, one imperious finger pointing at the royal carriage a few feet away.

"Yes, Sire!" I ran for the carriage and leapt inside.

The King followed more slowly, first paying the driver of my carriage before waving his knights back to their mounts, then striding to his carriage. He had to practically bend in half to get through the doorway, then sat in the center of the bench opposite mine. Someone shut the carriage door, and we started moving.

"I was trying to do my job," I said. "I had to go to the

Broken to find—"

"When I tell you to do something, you do it," the King cut me off. "And you do it within the time limits I give you. Now, shut the curtains."

"What?" I squeaked.

"The curtains over the windows." The King jerked his head toward the left. "Close them, Assassin."

Oh fuck. This didn't bode well.

The windows to either side of the King were already covered, and the door was solid. That left the little windows to either side of my bench. I stretched to one side and then the other, drawing them shut. The filtered light shadowed the Dragon King, making his expression even more menacing.

King Tarocvar spread his legs. "Kneel."

I looked at the floor between the King's feet.

"Yes, there. Kneel, Assassin!"

I lurched forward and fell to my knees between his. My whole body trembled, and I couldn't figure out if it was in excitement or fear. My stare lowered, focusing on the edge of his seat, noting the pale stitching on the dark leather cushion. But then movement caught my eye and brought my gaze up another inch. He was hardening, his pants tightening around the bulge. My breath lodged in my throat.

"Undo my pants and suck my cock," he said.

I wanted to. Damn all the Gods of Serai, but I wanted to suck him and taste his release. I wanted to know if it would tingle on my tongue as it had on my skin. But not like that.

Stomach clenching, I met his stare. "No."

"What?" The Dragon King's jaw dropped.

"I won't let you ruin this for me. Later tonight, if you want me in your bed, I'll suck your cock magnificently. I'll wrap my lips around it and deep throat you until your eyes roll back in your head. But I'm not doing it when you order me to."

He grabbed my throat, nails extending into claws that dented my skin but didn't draw blood. Not yet. "You have disobeyed a royal order! I was being kind to punish you thus. Any other man would be whipped!"

"Then whip me."

"What?" He released my throat, his hand falling away as if his muscles had suddenly stopped working.

"Whip me." I moved backward and shifted up onto my seat. "Make it a public whipping if you want. Let the whole damn palace know that I fucked up, and you're punishing me for it. But I'm not letting you take this from me!" I pointed at his dick as if it were mine. Ridiculous and so very stupid. I don't know why I said it. But I did and now I had to commit. "We were fantastic together. It was the best sex of my life. So fucking good that I refuse to taint it with this. I will not make this memory with you. You need to punish me because I lost track of time? Fine. *Do it*. But not with sex."

The Dragon King was the one trembling now. His hands shook so badly that he clenched them, forgetting that his claws were extended. He instantly cursed and opened his hands, revealing deep wounds that began to bleed over the carriage floor.

"Damn it!" I went back to my knees and grabbed his wrists. "Fuck! What have you done?" I took the hem of my shirt and ripped it off, tearing it into two strips of fabric. I rapidly wrapped one of his hands with a strip. "Put away your fucking claws!"

His claws retracted.

I folded his fingers over the bandage and started dabbing at the wounds in his other hand. "Hold still." I propped his arm on his leg to steady it. "Of all the idiot moves." I shook my head.

"Locrian," the King's deep voice rolled over me.

"Just let me do this and then you can yell at me."

"Lock, look at me."

I looked up at the Dragon King. His stare wasn't furious or even stern; it was tender.

"Your concern and ministrations, though touching, are unnecessary. I'm fine."

"You're not fine." I went back to wiping the wounds.

"Look." He took the fabric from me and briskly wiped off his palm. "I'm a Dragon; we heal *very* fast."

Sure enough, his wounds were already closed.

"Oh." I started to back away.

The Dragon King tossed aside the bloody cloth, grabbed my upper arms, and hauled me upward. Once I was in a half-crouch, he shifted his grip to my thighs, lifted me again while he shut his legs, and set me over his lap. I groaned as his erection bulged beneath me, the hard line of it wedging between my ass cheeks. Before I could speak, his mouth claimed mine, that hot tongue splitting my lips and then slashing at mine. I grabbed him by the shoulders and kissed him back.

Those big hands went to my ass, squeezing and kneading, pulling me forward to grind against his cock. I reached between us, undid his pants, and pulled him free. Long and glorious. Hot and hard. And that scent, the same scent that he'd left on me, rose to fill my nose and send my mind reeling.

Precum dripped from his tip, and I rubbed it down him, massaging him with his own liquid desire. The Dragon King moaned deeply, arching into my grip, and broke our kiss to bite his way along my jaw.

"I cannot let you defy me, Assassin," he whispered in my ear. "If you do it now, I will forgive you."

I went still. I'd backed the King into a corner. He had made a threat and couldn't retract it now; it was either I suck him off or be whipped. But he didn't want to whip me. So he'd made the punishment into a pleasure. The question was, did I go with it and allow him to get away with this or stand by what I'd said? What would it do to us if I bent to his will now? And what if I didn't?

I leaned back to look at the King and that's when it hit me; I wanted him. More than just a one time fuck. More than sucking his dick in a carriage. I wanted to be his. Not his assassin, but his lover. And I wanted him to be mine.

That wouldn't happen if I let him rule me as he did everyone else. I had to be special. As different with him out of bed as I was in it.

"I'm not trying to defy you, Your Majesty. I'm trying to keep something for myself." I tucked him back in his pants and buttoned them, all while he stared at me. Then I scooted back onto the opposite bench, met his stare, and said, "I will take the whipping."

The Dragon King roared and kicked the door. It went flying off its hinges, startling the horses. They reared before clattering down on the stones. Luckily, we had just entered the palace courtyard and were nearly to the main steps. So the King didn't have far to go when he exploded from the carriage and strode toward the palace.

"Assassin!" he shouted over his shoulder.

Everyone gaped at me as I jumped out and ran after the King. I tried to keep pace with him, but his legs were longer and his stride furious. I had to start jogging so I wouldn't be left behind. He didn't speak again, nor look at me, but when we were within ten feet of the doors to the royal suite, he shouted at the knights on duty there.

"Fetch me a whip!"

The knights looked at each other with wide eyes, then one ran off to do the King's bidding. I stumbled, my legs suddenly weak, but kept following the King. I had asked for this, near demanded it, and I couldn't back down now. I was as bound by my words as he was by his.

What the fuck had I done? I had never been whipped in my life, but I was pretty sure it was a horrible experience. And, damn it, I had a nice back. My lovers always complimented it. Shit. Now I'd have to explain why it was covered in scars.

The Dragon King went into his library and kicked a chaise lounge out of the way. It skidded into a shelf-covered wall, bunching a rug beneath it and dislodging several books that fell onto the cushions. The behemoth fireplace was cold, but heat radiated off the King as he continued to push the furniture toward the sides of the room, clearing a space before the menacing mantle of rearing dragons.

I waited in the doorway, watching him until the knight appeared with the whip. "Give it to me."

The knight handed me the whip with an almost sympathetic look and hurried away. Dragging strips of leather behind me, I stepped into the room and shut the door. Something tinkled as I went to the King, and I glanced down to see that there were metal barbs affixed to the ends of some of the strips. Holy fuck, they'd tear the skin of my back open, maybe even my muscles.

Suddenly, I realized that I might not survive this. All because I wanted to make a point. So fucking stupid, but I was a child of the Broken and too proud to back down, even when I knew it could save my life. As the Neraky say, only a pussy dips his toe to test the water; real men jump in. It was time for me to jump.

The King stood in the center of the space he'd cleared, chest heaving. He removed his belt, then shrugged out of his tunic as I approached. I stopped before him and waited as he tossed those aside. Then I calmly handed him the whip. He just stared at me.

Holding his gaze, I removed my assassin's vest, then my tunic, and went to the nearest couch to lay them there. I returned to him and waited.

"Brace yourself against that column." The King nodded toward the right column that bordered the fireplace.

I did as he said, leaning my torso against the cool marble and wrapping my arms around it. I heard him move behind me, heard the whip jingle. Seconds went by. Minutes. My face was pressed against the column, but I could see him moving in the corner of my eye. He was fiddling with the whip. Procrastinating.

I didn't rush him.

"Locrian Mahvis, I find you guilty of disobeying a direct royal order and sentence you to three lashes."

Three. Fuck. I braced myself.

The whir of the whip came and then the sting of it landing. I jerked and clenched my teeth against the bite, but it wasn't nearly as bad as I'd expected. I felt no barbs cutting into my skin, nor the strength that I knew he could have put into it. He was holding back.

Even as another blow landed, and I grunted inadvertently from the pain, I rejoiced. I had won. As horrible as this was, it was a step forward for us. A step I doubt he'd ever taken before. And I intended to make it as large a step as possible. In short, I was gonna milk this for every drop of guilt I could get.

When the last blow landed, I cried out as if I'd been stabbed, and released the column to crumple to the floor.

"Lock!" the King shouted and rushed over to me.

I groaned, biting my lip to hide my grin, and then hissed in pain when he lifted me.

"Damn you for a fool!" the Dragon King snarled as he carried me to the closest couch and laid me upon it.

I moaned when he accidentally laid me atop my vest, and he shot forward to remove the clothing and settle me more gently onto my belly. I let my arm fall limply to the floor as he rushed to the door and flung it open.

"Bandages and healing ointment!" the King shouted. "Now!" Then he hurried back to me and knelt beside the couch. "Lock?"

"I'm all right, Your Majesty. You don't have to fret over me. I've learned my lesson. You win."

"Fucking humans," he growled but when he set his hand on my head, his touch was gentle. "You idiot."

I let out a small whimper. My back felt as if it were on fire so it wasn't all acting, but the heat and pain quickly turned into a dull throbbing. So when his breath caught and his other hand went to my hip, I grinned into the cushions.

"Sire?" someone said from the doorway.

"Bring it here!" The King held a hand out for the tray of medical supplies.

"Would you like me to tend to—"

"Get out!" the King roared.

The man went running.

It was all I could do to not start laughing.

But then came a terrible sting, and I shouted, "Fuck! What the fuck is that?"

"It's antiseptic, you damn imbecile. Even though these are only welts, I need to clean them. You fucking humans are so vulnerable to infection. Fuck!" He dabbed at my back. "What was the purpose of this? To prove something to me? You're such a fool."

"No, to prove something to myself." I lifted my head to look at him. "You may own me but there are certain things, parts of me, that you will never have unless I give them to you."

The Dragon King paused, his hand hovering over my back. "Very well, Lock. Keep those pieces of yourself. I hope they're worth this."

He began ministering to my back again, and I lowered my head to the cushions but as I did, I caught a strange look in his eyes. Shock, I think, though I wasn't sure. His hands hesitated several times, almost as if he couldn't believe what he was seeing.

Whatever he applied to my back worked like magic. Maybe it was magic. He slathered some ointment on me, then had me sit up so he could wrap the bandages, folding himself over me as he brought them around my chest. By the time he was done, I felt immensely better.

The Dragon King tossed the remaining bandage onto the tray and stood. He didn't look at me but at the mess he'd made of the room.

I stood up. "Thank you, Your Majesty."

He flinched.

Then my stomach rumbled.

The Dragon King snorted a laugh, shook his head, and looked at me at last. "You are stubborn, childish, and foolish. You wouldn't last a day in my army."

"Then it's a good thing that I'm not one of your Horns, Your Majesty." I stepped forward and took his hand, opening it to run my fingers over the healed palm. "I'm your assassin, but you've given me the duties of a bodyguard, so your safety is all that matters to me."

I let go of his hand, and he lifted it to my face, cupping my cheek as he stared at me.

"You are also amusing, handsome, and very good at what you do, Lock. Both in and out of bed. I think I shall keep you for a while." He looked down at my rumbling belly. "Which means I should feed you. Come along." He dropped his hand, turned, and left the library without bothering to put his shirt back on.

I followed the King but before I reached the door, a glimmer caught my eye—a pile of metal barbs on one of the side tables.

Chapter Ten

Throughout the meal—one I spent standing—the King grew more and more distant. I didn't push him or try to regain his interest. I knew better than that. He'd said some nice things to me, perhaps too nice. I was human, after all. Dragons rarely took a human lover. There was that whole immortality thing to consider—namely, his. I wasn't asking for forever; I wasn't asking for anything. Still, a line had been crossed. He had revealed his interest and now, it looked as if he were regretting it.

By the time we retired to his bedchambers, the King was a different man. I went to check the rooms of his suite, leaving him to prepare for bed. When I got back to his bedroom, he had a visitor. A woman.

I may have prepared myself for his aloofness, but I hadn't expected him to go this far. I paused in the doorway, watching her run her hands possessively over the man who, just hours earlier, had ministered to my back after whipping it. Because I wouldn't suck his cock. The King lifted his head and met my stare, his expression almost belligerent. Not taunting but aggressive, as if he expected a fight. Maybe even wanted one.

Well, I wasn't going to give it to him. I set my gaze on the floor and stepped past him.

"Where are you going?" the King asked.

I stopped and glanced back at him, only a glance to be sure that he was indeed speaking to me. "To the balcony so you may have your privacy."

"I don't need privacy. I need you to do your job."

The woman didn't seem bothered by this. Since she was a Shanba, I wasn't too surprised. The forest folk fucked in public all the time. Nature was their bedroom and all that bullshit. She flicked her large, rounded, brown eyes my way, gave a sniff from her flattened, fawn nose, and slipped out of her robe. A lean, lightly muscled body was revealed. Small breasts sitting high on her long torso and patches of darker skin spotting her pale flesh. Those spots were coveted among the Shanba, so I knew immediately that not only was she a beautiful woman, but she was also an exceptional example of her kind. Doubtless chosen by the King to be a courtier for that very reason.

As I watched, she went to her knees and started unbuckling the King's belt. This wasn't her first time with him.

"I can do my job better on the balcony," I finally said. "Where I won't be distracted."

"If sex distracts you, you aren't fit to guard me."

Right. So, not only was he retreating behind the line he'd crossed, but he was also daring me to challenge him on it. If I did, it would give him a reason to push me even further away. The problem was, if I let him push me too far, I'd end up hanging from a noose.

"As you wish, Your Majesty." I checked the balcony, locked the doors, and went to fetch my pallet from his dressing room.

The sound of fellatio followed me, the Shanba's wide mouth amplifying everything. The lights were dimmed, but

I could clearly see his cock moving in and out of her mouth as I passed by them. He had undressed while I was gathering everything, and once I was settled on my pallet—feeling a bit like the single audience member at a sex show—my stare was immediately drawn to his magnificent body. At first, I tried not to look but then I thought, fuck it. He told me to watch; I might as well get something out of it. So I looked. I really stared at him, at all the places I'd been too busy to fully enjoy while I was fucking him. The dark, hard nipples. The indents at his hips. The corded muscles of his forearms. Even his damn toes turned me on.

Then I happened to glance up and my stare collided with his. He'd been watching me watch him. I flinched, but lifted my chin and refused to look away.

The King's eyes twitched. He pushed the woman away. "Get on the bed. On your hands and knees."

"Step two," I mouthed at him.

She climbed onto the foot of the bed, facing the head.

The King glared at me and snapped at her, "No, across it. Face the balcony."

I nearly groaned.

The woman repositioned herself and lowered her head to the bed so that her ass rose high for the King's pleasure. He went to stand behind her, not even bothering to kneel on the mattress, gripped her thighs, and pulled her closer so that her calves hung off the edge. Then he pushed her hips down until she was at the perfect level for him. With a groan, he sank into her, and she began to make delighted gasps.

"Oh, yes, my king," the Shanba cried as he began thrusting. "That big cock has made me so wet!"

The King grunted and pulled out, a look of irritation on his face. She only had a moment to look over her shoulder at him in question before he slid back into her.

"Oh! Sire, you've split my ass in twain!"

He grunted again and sped up, holding my stare. I had to lean against the balcony doors to keep from falling over. My whole body was going limp with feverish desire. Not because of the moaning woman or the way he pumped into her. Not because of her dirty words, begging for more, or his primal grunting. Not even because of the way his body gleamed in the low lights. It was his eyes. The way he looked at me as if the only reason he was able to fuck her was that I was sitting there, watching him. His eyes held wild desire but also fury, and a flash of fear speared through my lust.

But then it was over. The King skipped step four entirely, pulled out, and grunted as he came on the floor. Taking the hint, the woman quickly faked her orgasm. No sooner had she "come" than the King was dismissing her with a curt nod. The beautiful Shanba scurried off the bed, slipped into her robe, and left, casting her wide gaze from him to me before she shut the door.

And still, he didn't move. King Tarocvar stood beside the bed, cock limp and chest heaving, as he stared at me. After a few minutes of this, I laid down and pretended to fall asleep. But I was still awake when he stormed into the bathroom and slammed the door.

Chapter Eleven

"I need to go out again today," I said as I watched Tarocvar eat his breakfast in bed.

"No." He kept eating.

"You're going to have to let me leave the palace if you want me to find out who hired me."

The King stretched his neck as if needing a moment to seek patience, lifted his breakfast tray, set it aside, and climbed out of bed naked. I looked and didn't try to hide it. I figured I had a right to look after he'd forced me to witness that . . . whatever the fuck that was last night. But I didn't get aroused by his magnificent body this time; I was too annoyed with him. I might have even sneered a little.

"Where will you be going?" he asked as he headed into his dressing room.

"I need to pick something up for you."

"Pick something up? I can have someone else do that."

"No, I need to choose it."

The King went silent for a few minutes, then stepped out of the dressing room, fully clothed and looking spectacular. He had put on a pair of leather pants—damn his fine ass—a thin, cotton tunic that clung to him in all the right places, knee-high boots, and a wide belt to emphasize his narrow waist. His hair was pulled back in a loose ponytail, and he stood in the doorway, glaring at me.

"What is it?" the King demanded. "What is so important that you must select it in person?"

I let out an irritated huff of air. I might as well tell him. Preparations would have to be made to care for the animal, and I'd need money to buy it. "A vanrussa."

The Dragon King's scowl vanished into blinking, then he shook his head as if to clear it. "A dog? You want to buy me a dog?"

"I want you to have another reliable layer of security. The Ricarri train those dogs to be some of the greatest companions on the planet—loving and protective. They see everything and what they don't see, they smell. A vanrussa would be able to warn you if anything was wrong, maybe even before I could. I'd feel safer leaving you for a few hours if you had one guarding you."

"So this is about leaving me?" He crossed his thick arms.

"I . . . you . . ." I stuttered, trying to get past the oddness of that question. "I need to investigate, and you're crippling that investigation by keeping me here, Your Majesty. Why won't you let me do my job?"

"Your job is to guard me. I released my entire King's Guard because of you. You are their replacement."

"Which is why I want the vanrussa. You also ordered me to find out who hired me."

"I never ordered you to investigate."

"What? Hold on, you don't want me to find whoever hired me?"

He made a sort of rumbling grunt. "I do. I just never gave you that order."

I rolled my eyes. *What was with this childish runaround?* "You implied it. And, correct me if I'm wrong, but you also implied that my life depended upon me finding this person."

He grunted, his face twitching, but didn't dispute it. "Very well. I will accompany you to purchase the dog."

"You want to go dog shopping with me?" I asked, not sure how I felt about it.

"He will be my dog, correct? I should pick him out."

"Her," I said absently.

"What?"

"A bitch will bond with you better. You will take the place of a mate for her."

The King's expression became horrified. "You want me to mate with a dog?!"

I burst out laughing, then laughed harder when he growled at me. The kind of laughing that went into wheezing and coughing. Double-over, knee-slapping laughter. Finally, I held up my hand to ward off his anger, caught my breath, and said. "No, of course, I don't want you to fuck a dog. That would be animal abuse on top of disgusting. I'm saying you will hold that level of importance for her. She will not have a mate; she'll have you instead. You will be her master but, hopefully, she will also love you."

The King's gaze went intense. "Is it possible for someone to love their master?"

I went still.

He prowled over to me and grabbed my chin. "Well? Answer me, Assassin."

"Yes." I paused, my heart thudding so strongly that it felt as if it were fluttering my tunic. "I'm sure it is possible."

"Did you enjoy watching me last night?"

I jerked my chin out of his grip. "With all due respect, Your Majesty, fuck you."

The look on the Dragon King's face was one I'd remember for the rest of my life . . . which might not be that long. *Fuck, why did I say that?* I've always been one to run my mouth, and it's gotten me into some serious trouble in the past. But you'd think I would know better than to say that shit to the King of Racul.

Then he burst out laughing, and my heartbeat started to slow.

When the King finally settled into a smile, he said, "I suppose that was cruel of me."

"Not at all, Your Majesty. I have no expectations of you. In fact, I wasn't surprised when you summoned another lover last night, not after witnessing you take a new partner to your bed every night before me. It was *your* expectation of *me* just now that I took offense to."

"Meaning?"

"I am your assassin. Bid me kill, and I will without hesitation. Order me to watch over you, and I will do my very best. I will even stand guard while you fuck your courtiers, all of them if you wish. But do not expect me to enjoy *any of it*. I agreed to obey you, but you cannot order me to like watching you fuck someone else, especially when you do such a poor job of it."

The Dragon King grabbed me with a growl, spun me around to face the opposite direction, and forced me to the bed with his hand on the back of my neck. Once there, he bent me over the end and gave me one last shove so I'd know to stay put. With my head turned, I saw him step over to the bedside table and open the bottle of oil.

He looked over at me as he unlaced his pants. "Pull down your pants, Assassin. We'll see how poor a job I do with you."

"Yes, Your Majesty." I turned my face into the bedding to hide my grin, and quickly undid my belt, then my pants, shoving everything down to my knees. My cock was already twitching to life.

The King made a pleased sound as he stepped behind me, it went well with the wet strokes of his hand on his cock. "Now spread your ass and hold yourself open for me."

I bit my lip to hold back my excited whimpers and reached behind myself to pull apart my ass cheeks for him. Cool air hit my hole and made it pucker, but then an oiled, thick finger circled it, rubbing the oil in until my muscles relaxed. With an appreciative sigh, the King slipped his finger past that loosened ring. I cried out, then moaned while he worked me open, taking his time with me as he hadn't with the Shanba the night before. Then I heard him move, felt the brush of his body, and nearly came off the bed when something wetter and warmer than his finger slid into me.

The Dragon King was tonguing my asshole!

The warm skin of His Majesty's face pressed between my ass, his cheekbones digging in, and as he worked his tongue as deep as it could go, he groaned in what sounded like pure delight. It was all I could do to hold still for him. My cock ached and wept between my stomach and the bed. I wanted to grind it into the mattress, but even more than that, I didn't want him to stop. So I held my hips still, allowing myself only a few shudders and moans. As soon as he heard me, he withdrew and stood up. I finally gave in to the urge to grind myself against the bed, not caring one bit that he'd see me do it. But I went still when I felt the tip of his cock press against my dripping hole. He pushed gently. It popped its way inside, and we both made eager sounds.

"Is this what you call poorly, Assassin?"

"No, Your Majesty," I panted.

"Do you want me to stop?"

"Oh, fuck, please don't."

He slammed into me, and my grip on my ass cheeks tightened. That wondrous cock began rubbing all the best places inside me, making my body twitch with zings of pleasure. Primal sounds—growls, snarls, and grunts—came from the King, but they weren't like the noises he made with his other lovers. These were the wild cousins of those tame sounds, made by the savage beast inside him.

My hands were suddenly squished as he laid on me, slid his arms beneath me, and brought them up my chest to grab my shoulders. Using his grip as leverage, he pulled me onto his dick even as he pumped, and went so damn deep that it made my eyes roll back in my head.

"Are you bored, Assassin?" the King growled in my ear. "Shall I stop my pathetic attempts at fucking?"

"You have yet to be pathetic with me, Sire. Only with the others." I turned to look at him over my shoulder, his face only inches from mine. "Why is that?"

King Tarocvar bared his teeth, shoved himself up onto his hands, and slammed into me ferociously. "Because you infuriate me!"

"Then I hope I never stop!" I cried out just before my hips lurched forward, and I came all over his beautiful bedding.

The King made another of those bestial sounds and followed me into pleasure. This time, he didn't pull out. Instead, he filled me, pumping so much cum into me that I thought it would surely leak out around his cock. But, just as I'd suspected, the hot liquid vanished, sinking into my body as it had with my skin. When he pulled out at last, my channel tingled but was utterly empty. I'd never felt anything like it.

And I couldn't wait to feel it again.

The Dragon King stood up, slapped my ass, and said, "Get up, Lock. I wish to see the dogs now."

Chapter Twelve

From the direction we were heading in, turning left on Fangrier Road—known to all Mhavennians as Fang Road since it passed in front of the Courts of Teeth—would take you to the Vevaren River. Going right would lead to the largest shopping district in Mhavenna. The royal carriage went right.

We drove for a bit, pedestrians inclining their heads respectfully at the carriage since the King could be seen through the windows. I worried about that. An arrow could be shot through the window, and a professional could easily hit him in the head—a kill shot, even for a Dragon. But the King was smiling—had been since I'd pulled up my pants and followed him out of his suite—and I didn't want to ruin his good mood. Plus, we had an escort of mounted soldiers both in front of and behind our carriage. I hoped that would deter an assassin. Plus, no one knew we'd be going this way, even the knights hadn't known until we were leaving the palace. We should be fine.

The carriage pulled over to the sidewalk a few minutes later, stopping directly in front of a solid door. To the left of the door, a small plaque read; *If you don't know what we sell or can't afford it, go away. All others should announce themselves upon entry.* It was one of the few shops in the district without a window displaying its wares or even a sign with a name that hinted at what was sold. As far as I knew, it didn't have a name, and it wasn't entirely a shop.

I got out of the carriage before the driver could get down and waved him off as I looked up and down the street, then up at the windows on the higher floors of the surrounding buildings. Once I was certain the King was safe, I motioned him out.

"This way, Your Majesty." I led him to the door. But when his knights attempted to follow us, I held up a hand. "Nope. You will not be welcome in there."

"I don't give a shit if we're welcome or not; where he goes, we go," Captain Vettan said.

Yes, the fucking Captain himself had insisted on joining us. If he'd put this much effort into protecting the King at the palace, I may never have made it onto the grounds. But I didn't say that to him.

Instead, I voiced the very thought that had prevented me from mouthing off, "You will only cause unnecessary trouble."

"You're not walking into some strange, unmarked shop alone with the King."

"I will be fine," King Tarocvar said with a wry grin. "Guard the door." Then he opened the door and went in before I could stop him.

"Aw, fuck!" I hurried in after him, calling out, "He's the King, don't attack him!"

Even though the King only had a three-second head start on me at most, he was already surrounded by snarling dogs and four hulking Ricarri. They were mountain people, but the Ricarri did well in cities, far better than the forest-dwelling Shanba. Probably because the Ricarri had an affinity for metal—magic which these Ricarri were currently showing off, twirling swords that hovered above their hands, ready to launch them at the King. Even had they opted to wield the weapons with their hands, the threat would have been enough to make most men wet themselves. Muscles larger than the King's bulged against their clothing and the metal deposits in their skin caught the light, giving the illusion that they were weapons themselves. They kinda were.

"Stand down!" one of them said as he stepped between the dogs and us. "That's Lock. Lower your weapons!"

Great, it was my face, not the shouted warning that the Dragon King stood among them, that stilled their hands. But then, he wasn't the Ricarri King, was he? Only a Dragon who happened to run the kingdom their mountains were in. Most of the races of Serai had their own monarchs, but they gave their allegiance to the Dragon who ruled their kingdom above all others. Even their monarchs did. Not so much with the Ricarri.

It was one of the reasons the Ricarri Riots had happened. No other race would have dared such a thing, especially not in a crown city with the King in residence. And yet, even after the riots, King Tarocvar allowed the Ricarri to live in his cities. I don't know what reparations the Ricarri had made, but I did know that other kings had banished Ricarri to the mountains for less. Conclusion, I seriously doubted that it was a Ricarri who hired me.

I stepped past the King and extended my hand to the man in charge. "Bracaro, it's good to see you."

No, I didn't hold a grudge against the Ricarri for my family's death. They had probably thought the same thing the King had; that the factory was empty. Plus, Brac hadn't been a part of the riots.

"You too, kid." He shook my hand as the other Ricarri withdrew, their dogs following. "Now who the fuck is this? There's no way the Dragon King would ever be in your lowly company."

The King cleared his throat, lifted a brow, and stared at Bracaro as if a look alone would prove his status.

"Don't get offended, brother." Bracaro slapped Tarocvar on the shoulder. "You do look like him. You even got his glare down."

"Um, Brac?" I held up a cautioning finger.

"But the Dragon King's got gray eyes, everyone knows that."

"Do I, now?"

"Oh-ho! You're really into this, eh? You an actor?"

"Bracaro! This *is* His Majesty, King Tarocvar Verres," I said with as much pomp as I could manage. To the King, I added, "I'm so sorry. He just can't believe that you'd be with me. Which, granted, is fair."

Bracaro frowned. "Okay, that's enough, Lock. This isn't funny anymore."

"No, it isn't. It's not a joke. Brac, this really is the King. If you don't believe me, step outside. You'll see his knights and carriage. Look at him, he's obviously a Dragon. Do you think *any* of them would go slumming with me?"

"You're so full of shit, Locrian." Bracaro snorted as he went to the door, his dog, Fire, keeping pace with him. He opened the door and stood there, frozen in place. Finally, Fire whined, and Brac slammed the door shut. He rushed back to us. "I beg your forgiveness, Your Majesty."

I lifted a brow at that. I'd expected surprise and an apology, but not that kind of deference.

"It's all right. This was very amusing," King Tarocvar said. Then he cocked his head at the dog-breeder. "Why did you think I have gray eyes?"

Brac grimaced. "I made that up to get you to admit that you were an impostor."

"I'm relieved to hear it. I thought perhaps there really was someone impersonating me."

"Not that I'm aware of, Your Majesty. And may I just say how grateful all of us are that you allowed us to stay after the riots."

"You had a valid complaint." The King glanced at me. "And, at the time of my ruling, I was not aware of the loss of life."

"Loss of life?"

The King looked back and forth between Brac and me. I subtly shook my head at him. The last thing I wanted was for Bracaro to feel indebted to me for something other Ricarri had done or, even worse, pity me.

"People were living above that factory," the King said. "I've only recently learned of their deaths."

"Fuck," Brac whispered. "Aw, fuck me. I had no idea. Do you know who they were? The Ricarri who were involved will want to make amends."

"I have handled it. The survivor wishes to remain anonymous."

"I see." Brac glanced at me. "I shall inform my people. This will never happen again."

"That promise has already been made to me by your council member."

"Yes, Sire, I know. But now it means more, and I shall ensure that all of my people know it."

"Very good."

There was an odd silence, so I cleared my throat and filled it. "Hey, Fire. How you doing, girl?"

Brac's dog yipped and flashed her metal-capped canines at me—a gift from her master.

"May I offer you . . . aw, fuck." Bracaro grimaced. "I don't know how to entertain a king."

"I'm not here to be entertained. I'd like to purchase one of your dogs," the King said.

"You . . . you want one of my dogs?"

"He needs an elite. Your best female," I said. "One that will look after him as if he were her mate or even her pup. A fierce protector."

Bracaro nodded. "That's a wise decision, Your Majesty. My dogs can sense things even your Dragon knights can't, and they can see in utter darkness. A caverns breed, they are."

"I've heard good things." The King glanced my way again.

Bracaro looked at me with wide eyes, but I shook my head at him this time. I didn't want to explain how I'd come to be in the King's employ. It would mean exposing my profession. Not that it would remain a secret for much longer, what with the King telling everyone I was his assassin. Shit. I hadn't thought of that. If the kingdom found out who I was, I'd never work again, as an assassin or otherwise.

"Well, I've got my best bitches separated from the others," Brac said. "Please, come this way, Your Majesty. We'll see which of them takes a liking to you."

"Takes a liking to me?"

"You can choose whichever dog you wish, but it's always best if you let the dog choose you. Then you'll know that she'll bond with you."

"So, it's good that I've joined Lock today?" the King shot a smug look my way.

"Oh, yes."

"I didn't think it was an option," I grumbled. "Frankly, I'm still surprised you're here."

"Here we are." Brac unlocked a door and took us into a courtyard garden.

Another Ricarri was lounging on a collection of boulders set against one wall, a fluffy dog perched beside him. The dog's long fur was nearly the same shade as the gleam of the Ricarri's skin, so that the two of them blended in with the boulders, becoming one with the background. Or they would have, if the dogs—all of them, not just the one sitting beside the Ricarri man—hadn't started running for us, yipping happily.

"Hello, my beauties!" Bracaro declared as he went to his knees and opened his arms.

These were not small dogs, the top of their heads would come to my waist at least, but Ricarri were not small people. Brac held his own under the onslaught of gray fur and pink tongues. Laughing, he stroked each dog, then affectionately pushed them away and stood up.

"Lock!" the man on the boulder called as he climbed down. "You finally get enough gold for a dog?"

"No, I've brought the King to select one."

The man burst out laughing. "Sure. The King. Let me just fetch my girlfriend, the Queen of Fuck-You-Lock, and they can have a tea party together."

"Trinsane, this *is* King Tarocvar," Brac said. "Please, don't repeat my mistake and call him an impostor. His carriage and knights are outside; I've seen them. Trust me, this is him."

"Holy fuck!" Trinsane gaped at Tarocvar. Then he flushed. "I mean, um. Sorry 'bout all that, Your Majesty. Only joking. Uh, welcome to our, uh, here. Do you want some tea or something?"

"I only drink blood," the King said.

Trinsane paled.

The King started laughing.

Bracaro and I exchanged glances. For a second there, I hadn't been sure if the King was joking, and from the look on Brac's face, neither had he.

"Oh, ha-ha," Trinsane said weakly. "Well, we're honored to have you in our shop. These are our finest females. Any one of them would make an excellent companion."

"May I?" Tarocvar waved a hand at the dogs.

"Of course," Trinsane said and bent at the waist as he swept his hand toward the animals.

Once the King stepped past, Brac moved closer to Trinsane and whispered, "What the fuck was that?"

"A bow. We're supposed to bow, right?"

"I don't fucking know!"

The dogs started to follow Brac, but with a motion of his hand, they sat.

"I'll teach you the hand commands, Your Majesty," Brac said. "They're very simple, and most of the time, your dog will sense what you need before you command her." He waved the dogs toward the King.

The King crouched. With his motion, several of the animals paused, their sharp eyes watching him, checking for signs of danger. Three kept coming. Out of those three, one—a pure white female—stepped up to Tarocvar and sniffed his face.

"Hello, sweetheart." The King held out his hand. "I'm Taroc."

The dog set her paw in his palm and, laughing, the King shook it. When he let go, the dog made a soft sound and dropped to the ground to roll on her side, exposing her belly.

"That was fast," Bracaro said as he stepped over to them. "She likes you."

"I like her." Tarocvar—Taroc to his dog, evidently—said as he stroked the dog's head. "Would you like to come home with me?"

The dog rolled to her feet and circled the King, sniffing him as she went. With a soft sound, almost a mew, she nudged the cleft in his chin with her nose.

"I'll take that as a yes," he said and stood.

The dog settled into place on his left.

"Well, shit," Trinsane said. "I wanted to keep her. She's rare; such a pale gray that she's practically white. Been a long time since I've seen one like her."

"She has excellent taste," the King said with a smirk. "What's her name?"

"Her name is Renraishala. It means, 'moonlight upon water.' But you may change it, of course. I can teach her a new name to respond to, only take an hour or so."

"It's beautiful. Will she respond to Ren?" Tarocvar asked.

Renraishala yipped.

"Yes, as you see, we train them to know all versions of their names. In a dire situation, you may not have the time to speak the entirety of it."

"Then I shall keep her name. How much is she? I assume she's more because of her coloring."

"There's no charge for Your Majesty. It's our honor to provide you with your first vanrussa."

"That is generous, but I cannot take such a precious animal for nothing."

"Please, I insist."

"Then allow me to thank you properly. The Rite of Ensarena is in a week. There will be a celebration at the palace. I'll send you and your team an invitation to attend."

"Thank you, Your Majesty. That is yet another honor," Bracaro said.

"And feel free to bring your dogs."

"Now, I really like you." Brac grinned.

Chapter Thirteen

Ren sat at her master's feet on the carriage ride back to the palace. A packet of care instructions, commands, and additional training advice sat beside me on the bench across from the King. He couldn't stop stroking her, and she was eating it up.

Fuck, was I seriously jealous of a dog?

"You've done well, Lock," the King finally spoke to me. "I'm greatly pleased with Ren. This was a good idea." He grinned. "I've never had a pet."

"Only people you treat like pets," I muttered under my breath.

"Ren is not the only one with excellent hearing." Tarocvar chuckled. "Do you want me to treat you like a dog, Lock? Or are you judging the way I interact with people? *Again.*"

"To be absolutely honest, I think it's a little of both." I laughed at myself. "You adore her already and all she's done is sniff you and nudge your chin. I can do that too."

"You've done much more, and I stroked you for it as well, didn't I?" His grin grew sensual.

I swallowed past my suddenly dry throat. "Not in the way I would have liked, but I suppose you did."

"Oh?" He lifted a brow. "You'll have to show me how you like to be stroked."

"I will. If Your Majesty sees fit to invite me back to his bed."

The King made a pensive sound and looked back at his new dog. "I suppose you should be rewarded for today."

I knew better than to mock him for labeling sex with him as a reward. If I were absolutely honest with myself, I'd admit that it was true. Even that fast fuck before we left that morning had been amazing. If he were a whore, I'd impoverish myself to have him. But he wasn't a whore. As far from it as he could get, even though he sort of acted like one.

I snickered at the thought.

The King lifted a brow at me.

"Sorry. I was just thinking about Trinsane's face when Bracaro offered you the dog for free. I thought he was going to shit himself."

"How much do these dogs go for?"

"Brac's dogs start around five gold."

"Five?" His eyes widened. "That's more than this carriage is worth. With the horses."

"Yup. And that dog there is the best of the bunch, with her rare white coat. I wouldn't be surprised if he had expected to get eight gold for her. Maybe even eight gold and twenty silvers."

"Well, fuck. Now I feel like an asshole for just offering them an invitation in return."

I burst out laughing. "Those guys would never have seen

the inside of the palace any other way. Your invitation is worth more than gold to them. Plus, if they show up with their dogs, and you're there with Ren, they'll have rich customers lining up to buy their animals. They'll make up their loss in no time. Brac was smart to give you the dog."

The Dragon King grunted. "I suppose. Still, I'll try to inspire interest in his dogs."

"Just bring Ren to the festivities. Trust me, that's all you'll have to do. You're the King; everyone will want a dog like yours."

"You hear that, Ren?" He focused on the fucking dog again. "Everyone will want you. But if anyone gets too close, bite them."

Ren yipped.

"Good girl."

Chapter Fourteen

Another week passed by smoothly. A week of dog bonding and preparations for Ensarena's Rite. A week in which the King summoned no one to his bed. Because I was there. The man was adorable with his dog; he was definitely the type who craved constant affection. I wasn't the type to give it, especially not when I had to be focused on the King's safety. So I was glad Ren filled that void, while he filled my void, as it were.

Despite Ren's exemplary behavior and the passing of every test I gave her, Tarocvar refused to let me leave the palace again. This was particularly frustrating because it had been more than long enough for Tengven to gather some information for me. But no matter how hard I argued with him, the King refused. He kept putting me off, saying after the rite, he'd think about it. That everything was too hectic at the palace and with all the unknown people coming and going —craftsmen, bakers, musicians, and the like—he needed me there. I guess he had a point.

The King did, however, allow me to leave his side as long as I stayed on the palace grounds. So, after inspecting the room, where the celebration would be held, I made one last walk-through of the main gardens where the rite itself would be conducted.

People scurried about, seeing to all the last-minute touches. I passed some Shanba gardeners using their nature magic to guide plants into artistic displays, most featuring yellow sunbursts to honor Ensarena. Their nimble fingers curled and coerced flowers into blooming to the perfect degree as well as in the proper place. None of them looked suspicious or interested in anything other than plants.

Then there were the carpenters, most of whom were human. They were conducting their final inspections of the platform and altar they'd been working on for several days. The sun icon, brought over from the palace's temple, was getting one last polish and a carpet was being rolled out for His Majesty to stand upon. I glanced up at the sky; the rite would be held when the Sun reached its zenith, a time that could only be determined by the court's high priest.

Damn Dragons and their complicated gods. Not that humans were much better. And not that I knew much about any gods—Dragon, human, or other. I'd never been to any sort of religious rite. Perhaps that's why I was nervous. I had gone over the schedule the High Priest had sent to the King, so I knew basically what would happen, but when you're dealing with the divine, it's impossible to anticipate everything.

I circled the carpenters, peering in their tool boxes and looking over their tools. Several of the men looked at me askance, but I didn't explain myself. The entire palace now knew who I was; if these men didn't, they could ask around. I didn't have time for niceties. I inspected the men as intently as their gear and finally determined them to be exactly what they presented themselves to be.

Moving on, I went to the gathering of priests and priestesses who were preparing their holy jars and spells and what-not under the High Priest's critical stare. They knew me but bridled at my inspection, sending me disdainful looks. No, they didn't have to say anything. They were all Dragons, and I wasn't; that alone was enough to confirm their superiority. But these were holy Dragons, and that took it to another level. That a lowly human who made his money by killing people would dare to question their loyalty was repugnant and outrageous. I was only being tolerated because His Majesty had made it clear that I must be.

I didn't give one holy shit about their pride. This was about King Tarocvar's safety and after a week in his bed, I was more inspired than ever to do my job properly. I know, I shouldn't let myself be led around by my dick, but fuck it. The man already owned me, why not become obsessed with him? He was worthy of my obsession. At least when I was in bed with him.

I smirked and turned away from the sanctimonious Dragons. They didn't have anything in their possession that could hurt the King. I mean, other than themselves. I'd watch them during the ceremony just as I'd watch everyone else, but I didn't think they were a threat.

I headed for the musicians, and that gave me a few seconds to think about how different Taroc—he said I could call him that in private (yes, I'd been awarded the same privilege as Ren but since she couldn't speak, I viewed myself as a smidgen higher)—was when he was in bed with me. And I don't just mean different from how he fucked others. The bed had become a neutral zone for us. I felt like his equal there, a lover free to say anything. But once we left his bed, or wherever we'd been fucking, he went back to being the King.

And that's what worked for us. I've always been a bit casual with him but if I had pushed that further and become overly familiar with him in front of others or acted in any way as if I expected to be treated differently, he would have ended things with me, perhaps fatally. I was walking a very dangerous, fine line, but I was an assassin. This was normal for me. In fact, I thrived on this sort of excitement. And the brilliant part was how well the King treated me because I didn't expect it of him.

And word had gotten around.

I'd overheard the gossiping, so I wasn't surprised when people of the palace, both staff and courtiers, began to treat me more respectfully. Even the Dragon knights eased up a little in their glaring, though they didn't go as far as nodding to me politely, as the musicians did when I approached.

Unlike the carpenters, the musicians were well informed and knew exactly who I was and why I was peering so closely at their instruments. They went as far as to hold out their guitars, violins, and harps for my inspection without my asking. I grinned at them as I looked everything over, not at all surprised by their insight. Musicians were even better than bartenders when it came to gossip. They heard it all and offered it for free. It was getting them to keep a secret that was the problem.

Wait a second... musicians. Gossip. Huh.

I motioned to the group. "Gather around, if you please."

The musicians shared a curious look, then formed a circle around me.

"Have any of you heard gossip about someone wanting the Dragon King dead?"

"That's some dangerous gossip," the flutist said.

The musicians shared another look, this one far heavier than the last.

I lowered my voice even further to say, "You *have* heard something."

"There are always such rumors floating about a

kingdom," the harpist said. "Any kingdom."

"I don't care about the other kingdoms. Tell me what you've heard *here*."

"Not in the open like this," the violinist said brusquely. "Later tonight. Find me after the festivities."

"Tell me something now," I insisted. "There will be hundreds of people here soon. You may know something that could help me focus on the right ones."

"Look to the upper class," the harpist whispered.

"Yeah, I've already figured that out. Anything else?"

"Rumor has it, this isn't political," the drummer said. "They're not after his crown."

"So, it's someone he's angered," I said. "This is personal?"

The musicians nodded.

"Anything else?"

"Not here," the violinist said again. "I may have seen something to help you, but—" he glanced over his shoulder and went still when he saw one of the knights staring at us. "Not here. Later, Assassin. Meet me at the fountain in the south garden at 2 a.m."

I grimaced at the title and his paranoia but agreed. "All right. Thank you. I'll let His Majesty know how helpful you've all been. I'm sure there will be something extra in your pay tonight."

They all grinned at that.

Then I hurried away. The guests would be arriving soon and before they did, I needed to speak with the King.

Chapter Fifteen

Ren saw me first and yipped a welcome. Then Taroc turned, dislodging several attendants who were seeing to his elaborate ritual robes.

"There you are," the King said and shooed his attendants away. "I can handle it from here."

As they left, I approached the King. He met me halfway, a small smile twitching his lips, and took my hand.

"I have to talk to you," I said.

"First, I have something to show you." He led me out of the room, Ren trailing behind us, and down the hall, to the guest room I'd been using.

The dressing room within that bedroom wasn't nearly as grand as his, but it was still larger than I needed. Frankly, I could have slept in there and been perfectly happy. My meager wardrobe didn't fill even an eighth of the space available. But when the King flung open the dressing room door, the space was half full of clothing, shoes, belts, and other accessories.

My first thought was, *someone has been in here!*

I stepped inside, my gaze going instantly to the trunk of my belongings. I had half of my arsenal on me, but the things I'd left in that trunk were priceless to me. I had used my tools so long that my hands knew the feel of them, every notch and bump. I could use them in complete darkness and that's not something you can replace easily. I went past the racks of clothes and opened the trunk to make sure everything was still there.

"Lock, do you not see your new wardrobe?" the King demanded.

"Huh?" I turned to look at him, then at the clothes. "This is for me?"

"Who else would it be for?" his tone softened. "I can't have my assassin walking around looking like . . ." He waved a hand at me.

"Me?"

"Looking as if I don't pay you enough."

"You don't pay me anything."

"That's beside the point."

"What is the point?"

"The point is that I've commissioned an entire wardrobe for you, and you've yet to show me any appreciation!"

"Ah, I see." I went to him and dropped to my knees.

When I started to unbuckle his belt, he slapped my hands away with a snort of laughter.

"Get up, you idiot. You know that's not what I meant."

Lips twitching, I stood. "You said you wanted me to show you some appreciation. That's usually what you mean."

"It is not. And are you pleased with the clothes or not?!"

I went to a rack and ran my hand over the fine fabrics, then selected a tunic and admired the subtle embroidery around the neckline. "I've never owned anything this nice." I turned to look at him. "Thank you. Truly, this is . . . hold on, how did they know what size to make these?"

"I gave the tailors a set of your clothes to use as a guide," he sounded really pleased with himself. "Now choose something to wear today. Hurry, the rite is starting soon."

He turned to leave, but I called after him, "Wait. I still need to talk to you."

"I don't have time to talk now, Lock." He motioned at himself.

"The person who hired me is likely going to be among your guests today. Do you understand that, Taroc?"

"Yes. And?"

"And?!" I gaped at him. "And I've just spoken to the musicians. Musicians know all the best gossip."

"And?"

"*And* they said that the person who hired me didn't do it for power; they did it because they want you dead."

"I assumed they wanted me dead. That's rather the point of hiring an assassin."

"You're not listening to me." I grabbed his upper arm. "This is *personal*. You angered someone so much that they hired someone to kill you."

"Well, I already knew that this wasn't about my crown."

"What?" I dropped his arm.

"Only a Dragon can claim my throne, and then, only after they've won the crown tournament."

"The crown tournament?"

"I won my throne with strength and skill, Lock. I had to fight fifty-six other Dragons who believed they'd make a better king than I. And I killed every last one of them."

"You killed fifty-six Dragons?" I blinked. *Shit, that was a bigger kill tally than mine, and he'd done it all in one go.*

"A crown tournament is to the death. It's meant to dissuade those who are not dedicated to ruling."

"So, there is no one in line for your throne? No one who would immediately become King?"

"No. If I died, the kingdom would be run by my advisers until a tournament could be held to determine the next king."

"Your advisers, eh?" I lifted a brow.

"They wouldn't be allowed to make any major decisions. They'd merely be caretakers until the next king was crowned."

"Oh."

"So, this cannot be about my kingdom."

"You could have fucking mentioned that earlier."

He shrugged. "I thought it was common knowledge."

"Fine. We've established that this is personal. You must know who you've angered so badly that they'd want you dead. So, who is it?"

"I am a king, Lock." He lifted his chin. "I anger many people."

"Not to the point where they pay a lot of fucking money to have someone murder you. Come on! You must have some idea."

Taroc grimaced, rolled his head back, and stared at the ceiling.

"It would be someone wealthy," I prompted. "Someone who doesn't care about your throne. This isn't about replacing you. This person has no political agenda."

"Most of the people I've angered have a political agenda."

"Good. Who doesn't?"

He lowered his head to glare at me. "I don't know!"

"For fuck's sake, Taroc, how many wealthy people without an interest in kingdom politics have you pissed off?"

"Honestly? All of them."

"What?"

"I told you, I'm a king. I have to make hard decisions nearly every day. Those decisions often upset those with high social standing. It's impossible to please everyone, and, frankly, I am not a man to cater to the wealthy. I always do what's best for the kingdom as a whole and the majority of its people. And the majority is formed by the lower classes. *They* are my priority; the rich can take care of themselves. So, yes, I give more time and consideration to the council members who speak on behalf of their people than I do to merchants and nobles. And that, as you say, pisses off a lot of people."

The tension drained out of me, and I just stared at him. This was the man I tried to kill. A man I had disliked merely because of his race. I'd seen the things Taroc had done for the kingdom, I knew what he said was true, and yet it hadn't sunk in. Tarocvar was a good king *and* a good man. Usually, the two contradicted each other. To be a good king, you had to be a bit of a scoundrel. To be a good man, you couldn't do the terrible things a king must sometimes do. But Taroc had the balls to be both. He did what was right for his people without compromising his morals and fuck everyone else. No catering to the wealthy to get their approval, no turning a blind eye to the criminal things they did. Even other Dragons were held accountable to King Tarocvar's laws.

That was how he'd angered someone enough to hire me and yet had no idea who that person could be.

I grabbed him by the back of the neck and yanked him down into a kiss. He stiffened for a second, then melted against me, his arms sliding around my body and tightening as his tongue twirled with mine. When the moaning and stroking were done, we were both breathless and grasping at each other.

"What was that for?" Taroc whispered.

"For being who you are. I'm sorry I didn't see it sooner. You're as rare as your dog, Your Majesty. Maybe rarer."

"How so?"

"You're a king with a conscience."

Chapter Sixteen

I stood to the side of the platform with Ren as the King participated in Ensarena's rite. Although I wore a new outfit, no one noticed me, and I preferred it that way. I tried my best to blend in with the shadows and, thanks to years working with Raltven thieves, I was pretty good at it. All eyes were on the King.

"Ensarena, we thank you for the gift of life and warmth. For the first Dragons, who you formed from your fire and set upon this world to rule it," the King intoned.

I grimaced at the ruling bit. Fucking Dragons, they literally believed they had a divine right to rule the world.

"Our ancestors settled Serai. They fought the wars that led to worldwide peace, and we thank you for guiding them and giving them the strength they needed. On this, your holy day, we offer you a tribute of our flame in honor of the spark of life you put inside all of us!" the King's voice rose with those last words and became a roar.

The guests—all Dragons (the only members of other races allowed to attend the ritual were the musicians and me)—added their roars to the King's. I suppose I should have felt excited to witness the holy rite that very few non-Dragons were permitted to see. But I only felt anxious. With all that was happening, all the distractions, it would be easy to kill the King, especially with him front and center. So, when the

Dragons lifted their hands and shot flames into the sky—fucking streams of fire—I winced. Even Ren cringed.

As the air above me burned, I kept my stare focused on the ground. Or rather, the *people* on the ground. My eyes twitched, every cell in my body telling me to *look at the fucking fire, you idiot!* But I ignored the heat pummeling me from above, driving sweat down my brow, and scanned the crowd. The musicians, those poor people, had to start playing at that very moment, and I was impressed that they didn't miss a beat. But I only glanced their way to be sure that every hand was busy, playing an instrument. The Dragons in the crowd were all engaged as well, their hands directing their magic. That didn't mean they couldn't lower one to lob something at the King, but I needed to watch everyone. So I looked away from the crowd and focused on the priests and priestesses of Ensarena.

They glided toward the platform stairs behind me, all of them holding hollow glass objects that were rounded at their centers and tapered at both ends. All except for the High Priest, that is. I turned to watch the priests and priestesses ascend the stairs, then stepped back so I had a better view of them on the platform. Ren stayed close to me, her ears perked and nose sniffing. I tensed when the holy people surrounded the King, and Ren started to growl.

"Hold," I said to her. "Not yet."

She sat down but remained alert.

The High Priest started chanting words I didn't understand, then he raised his arms and all his minions lifted their glass objects. The flames above swirled as the High Priest motioned, directing the fire into those glass containers even though they had no openings. In seconds, the sky was clear and the objects were full of blinding light. The receptacles were set within iron stands upon the altar, and then all the Dragons went to their knees. All but the King.

"We give our fire back to you, Goddess!" King Tarocvar spread his arms to present the jars. "An offering of magic and love."

As I mentioned earlier, I'm not a very religious man, so I didn't expect anything to happen. I especially didn't expect a glow to encapsulate those glass containers. I flinched, and Ren froze as that glow brightened. I didn't want to close my eyes; I tried to keep them open, even tried turning away to watch the crowd, but it became too much for me, and I was forced to duck and cover my eyes, not just close them. When the light faded and I opened my eyes again, the fire-filled vessels were gone.

"Holy fucking shit," I whispered.

"She has accepted our offering!" the King said.

"Did that just happen?" I asked Ren.

She whimpered.

The Dragons cheered and surged to their feet, several openly weeping. For once, I felt no scorn or resentment, no urge to mock them. In fact, it was all I could do to keep from crying myself. And I had no idea why. It could have been magic combined with sleight of hand. The High Priest might have summoned that light and whisked the jars away while everyone was blinded. But I knew that's not what happened. I knew it as I knew it was air I drew into my lungs and soil I stood upon. The knowledge was in my bones. That had been a divine presence. A fucking goddess had been right there, a few feet away from me.

"No wonder they act so superior," I muttered.

Ren yipped.

"Fuck, you're right." My stare shot around the gathering.

"I got distracted."

Thankfully, I didn't see anything amiss. But that fuck up was exactly what I needed to steady myself, to scare me into focus. Someone could have killed Taroc while I'd been musing about gods. And I wasn't the only one in awe of Ensarena. Fuck. One second, that's all it would have taken. One second to shoot an arrow in the King's head while everyone was distracted.

Then I processed that. The Dragons were all in attendance, and they had all passed up the perfect opportunity to kill their king.

"It's not a Dragon," I whispered. "Whoever Taroc pissed off, they're not a Dragon."

Chapter Seventeen

"Yes, thank you, I'm very happy with her," the Dragon King said for the fourteenth time.

Or fifteenth, but who's counting?

"Her name means 'moonlight on water.'" he went on.

"And the breeder is here, Your Majesty?" the merchant, a highborn Argaiv, with his membranous wings tucked away beneath a silk cloak, asked.

"He's right there." Taroc indicated Bracaro and his group, all of them with dogs. "The finest breeder of vanrussas in the city."

Yes, he'd been laying it on thick, but that only made me like him more. The King felt indebted, and he was a man who paid his debts. Brac and his team were already surrounded by a crowd of potential buyers, but when he noticed the King waving toward him yet again, he paused in his discussion, turned toward Taroc, and bowed deeply, acknowledging that they were even.

Taroc grinned and nodded.

Then a Shanba lord said, "I'm more interested in your human companion."

I met the man's stare but saw no threat, so I dismissed

him and continued scanning the massive hall where the post-rite celebration was being held. Although the rite was reserved for Dragons, the party afterward was open to all. And that meant hundreds of people from all the races of Racul—and even some guests from outside the kingdom—were milling about His Majesty. I couldn't waste a moment on whatever insult this man was about to give me. Fuck him, Taroc could deal with his bullshit.

The Shanba cocked his head, the gilding on his impressive rack of antlers catching the light and flashing in my peripheral vision as if fighting to regain my attention. "I've heard that he's an assassin."

"You've heard true," Taroc said, absently petting Ren.

"How thrilling. And he's handsome as well. For a human."

Ugh, why did they always feel the need to add that caveat? Every time someone from another race complimented me, they added, *for a human* on the end. As if there were a separate rating scale for us because it wouldn't be fair to compare us directly with an immortal. I resisted the urge to tell him to go fuck himself and continued to scan the room.

"You know," the Shanba's tone turned musing, "I'm still awaiting payment for the wine you ordered, Your Majesty."

I froze.

"And?" Taroc's voice sharpened.

"Lend me your assassin for three days, and I'll consider it paid in full."

Slowly, I turned to look at the Shanba. His wide, brown eyes slid over me and the thin nostrils in his flat nose widened on a deep inhale. A quick lick of his lips concluded the show, making it obvious that he didn't want me for my professional talents.

The King chose to ignore those signs. "You expect me to loan you my assassin to kill someone for you?"

"Oh, great Tareth, no!" the man declared. "I would never expect you to condone criminal activity, Sire. I merely want to fuck him. I expect he knows some dirty little bedroom tricks, being such a naughty man."

The other men in the group made sounds of amusement. All but His Majesty.

"You want to fuck *my* assassin, Lord Crushei?" now, the King's voice was frigid and sharp.

Lord Crushei should have taken the warning. Ren certainly did; she stood up and started to growl at the Shanba.

"He's not your lover, is he?" Lord Crushei asked. "I can't imagine that you would ever bed a human."

"I bed whoever the fuck I want." Taroc bared his teeth.

"Oh, my," Lord Crushei drawled. "He *is* your lover. How fascinating. I apologize, Your Majesty. I meant no disrespect. He gave me a look that I interpreted as interest."

Taroc swung his head toward me. I shook my head, and that was all that he needed. His focus went back to the Shanba.

"He is guarding me," the King said. "I'm certain he did give you a long look, but it was not one of interest, not sexual at least. He was determining if you were a threat to my safety, but I think it's the other way around."

"Excuse me, Your Majesty?"

The other men took a step back.

"You have precisely five minutes to leave my palace or I will release the beast inside me who is currently roaring to be freed. And, just so there is no miscommunication between us, I have no sexual interest in you either."

"I . . . are you asking me to leave?"

I leaned forward and said, "No, he's telling you to *run*."

As if to confirm it, the King growled.

The Shanba lord spun on his heels and fled. I watched his antlers bobbing above the crowd as he made a beeline for the exit, feeling a deep satisfaction at the sight. Once he was gone, I glanced at the King, intending to shoot him a secret smile, but wound up doing a double-take. I expected to find him smirking. He was not. His look was hot, but I, unlike the Shanba, knew better than to misinterpret it. That heat was not sexual, it was pure rage.

King Tarocvar didn't bother to make excuses to the group he'd been speaking to. He just stalked away, leaving me and Ren to hurry after him.

Chapter Eighteen

The Dragon King stormed into an empty room. Everything was cream and gold, from the velvet drapes to the fabric on the furniture. Within it, Taroc became impossible to ignore, though I suppose that was the case in every room he entered. This time, however, he was especially so. Granted it could have had something to do with the fact that as soon as I shut the door behind us, he grabbed my tunic and shoved me against a wall.

"Did you do it?" Taroc demanded. His cheeks were flushed, his eyes narrowed, and his teeth bared. That look said he was thinking of adding some splashes of blood-red to the decor.

Ren ran to the other side of the room and hid under a couch.

"Did I do what?" I tried to twist away, but he only tightened his hold.

"Did you flirt with Lord Crushei?"

"Are you fucking kidding me?!" I shoved at his chest. "Let me go right the fuck now, Taroc."

"Did you?!" he roared.

"No!"

The King just stared at me, nostrils flaring.

"Why would I do that?" I took his face in my hands and gentled my tone. "First of all, he was a prick. Second, you fuck like a wild thing. Third, you keep choosing me to fuck. Conclusion, I would never risk that by flirting with some skinny asshole with antlers. I mean, he can't even suck dick. Those things would get in the way."

Taroc blinked. His lips twitched.

I dropped my hands. "Go on, you can laugh. I won't tell anyone."

The King released my shirt and shook his head. "You truly didn't encourage him?"

"Again, why the fuck would I do that? No, I didn't flirt or encourage his interest in any way. The guy was obviously baiting you. Which leads me to the question, is he one of the people you've angered?"

His face shifted into epiphany. "Fuck. Yes, he is."

"Well, there you go."

"You think he's the one who hired you?"

"I didn't say that." I held up my hands. "I think it's possible. It would certainly explain his interest in me. He could have been testing me, not you; trying to see if I knew his identity. But I don't know that for certain. All I'm saying is that he had a reason to fuck with you, and when he was presented an opportunity, he went for it."

Taroc grunted pensively, and Ren crept out from beneath the couch. She ventured over to us and stared at her master, waiting.

"Renraishala," Taroc said gently and crouched. "I'm

sorry. I didn't mean to scare you."

"She's trained to kill; you didn't scare her."

"You're trained to kill, and I scared you." He scratched the dog's head and stood.

"I'm slightly smarter than a dog."

"Are you?" He cocked his head at me, his lips twitching.

"Ha-ha."

"So you're saying it's smart to be scared of me?" The King sidled closer and skimmed my hips with his fingertips.

"Uh, yeah."

He chuckled and moved even closer. "So if Ren wasn't scared, why did she hide?"

I cleared my throat. "She knew you were upset and didn't want it to transfer to her."

Taroc lowered his face to mine. "She didn't want to displease me?"

"Correct."

"And you?"

"I'd rather not displease you either."

He leaned down, brushing my lips with his as he nuzzled my face, then down my neck, breathing in deeply. "You do not displease me."

"Maybe not now, but you were sure quick to doubt me earlier."

He lifted his face to mine. "Must I remind you of how you came to be mine?"

Mine. The word sent a shiver through me.

"So you're never going to trust me because of that?"

"You did try to kill me."

"It was just a job," I huffed.

The King grinned, then said, "It's been a long time since I've taken a lover for more than one night."

I went still. *Oh, shit, oh fuck. He's opening up. What do I do? What do I say? Be casual, Lock.* "Oh?"

"Is that not enough trust for you?"

Breathlessly, I said, "For now."

"Yes, for now. We have only started this relationship, Lock. Don't get impatient with me. I've given you more than you know."

"Sorry. It's a human thing. We move faster than you immortals since we don't have as long to live."

The King made a neutral sound and stepped back. "Apology accepted. And the antlers don't get in the way."

"What are you talking about?"

"A Shanba's antlers don't prevent them from sucking cock," he said wryly. "In fact, they serve well as handles." He put his fists in the air to either side of his crotch and moved them as if directing someone toward his dick. "They're convenient."

"You're an asshole," I said dryly and left the room.

The King's laughter followed me out.

Of course, I couldn't go far since I was guarding him. I just stood in the hallway, grimacing while he laughed. Then he stepped out, saw that I was standing guard, and his laughter simmered into a smile.

"I thought you had run away, Assassin."

"Not from you, Your Majesty. I have a job to do." I waved down the hall, toward the sound of revelry. "Would you care to return to the party?"

"I suppose we must. Come, Ren." He stepped past me, went a few feet, then added, "Come, Lock."

"Not funny," I grumbled as I followed the King and his dog.

"Lock, heel!" He pointed at the floor on his left.

"That's *really* not funny," I said as I stepped up beside him.

Smirking, he said, "It worked."

"Such an asshole," I muttered and quickened my pace to scout ahead.

"You're far better at obeying commands, Ren," I heard him say behind me. "Yes, you're a good girl."

"As if that's something I should be ashamed of," I said over my shoulder.

"You just said that you didn't want to displease me."

"I meant, *in bed*." I reached the hall's arched entrance and stopped to survey the gathering.

Taroc stepped up behind me, grabbed my ass, and whispered in my ear, "Then it's a shame you don't have antlers."

As I sputtered in indignation and searched for a witty

response, he swept past me. I swear, that damn dog gave me a smug look as she took my place on the King's left.

Chapter Nineteen

It was so damn bright in that room, all the lights turned up to honor Ensarena, and I guess that was a good thing. There were no shadows to hide in. I saw everything. But after a while, it began to strain my eyes. It was the oddest thing. My focus would suddenly sharpen, then blur before settling. I rubbed my eyes over and over but nothing helped.

And the celebration seemed endless. The King had to speak with every guest there since he was the host. This meant countless conversations that threatened my focus, not because they were fascinating but rather the opposite. I could have fallen asleep on my feet listening to the sly requests the city's elite slipped into their speech, dropping hints that a child could pick up on. And then there were Taroc's practiced responses, rebuffing them without actually saying no. Those people had so much and yet they wanted more. And they wanted it from Taroc.

And I'm not just talking about money and goods.

I had to stand just behind Taroc and watch as several people, both women and men, flirted with him. And in that, they were blatantly obvious. A dock whore had more subtlety than some of these highborn assholes. The one bright spot was that whenever one of them tried to touch him, I got to step in. Like this bitch.

"Forgive me, my lady, but please do not touch the King." I

speared an arm between the King and his latest admirer before she could come in contact with him.

I didn't touch her, just barred her way, but she acted as if I'd slapped her across the face.

"How dare you!" the lady drew herself upright, then drew back her hand to strike me.

I knew I couldn't defend myself against her. She was a noblewoman; if I even started to raise my hand, just to block my face, she could twist it to her benefit. So I kept my arm where it was and my stare locked on hers.

As the blow fell, the King's hand shot out and snatched the lady's wrist. She gasped as he twisted and shoved, giving me just enough time to yank my arm out of the way. The men to either side of the lady pretended not to notice her stumble and didn't even try to catch her. In fact, their lips twitched as the woman fell to the floor in a rustle of way too many skirts. Then they feigned shock and concern, crouching to help her up.

Even as she gripped the offered arms and stood, the woman kept her horrified stare on the King. "Your Majesty?"

"Lady Helveisa, do you know that interfering with a royal guard in the course of his duties is a crime?" Taroc asked casually.

The woman blanched.

"And attacking such a guard while they are protecting me is an even greater offense. Treason, in fact. I could cast you straight into my dungeon, then strip you of your holdings and title."

"He assaulted me!" She pointed at me.

"You act as if I wasn't standing right here." Taroc waved

at the floor. "Inches away. As if I didn't witness the whole altercation. I saw it all, and my assassin never touched you."

"He is a killer, Your Majesty, and I am not accustomed to being around such people. If you say that he never touched me, I, of course, believe you, but it seemed to me as if he did. I must have been so frightened by what he's capable of that I imagined the assault. But that is not my fault."

"Every Dragon on this planet is a killer, Lady Helveisa, especially us kings. And yet, you would have touched me without fear."

"You do not kill for money, Your Majesty. You kill out of necessity."

"Do not presume to know me or my motivations." Taroc lowered his head toward her and that single motion had more menace in it than a drawn sword. "There are many reasons why I kill. One is presenting itself to me right now."

The woman fainted.

I bit my tongue to keep from laughing as she plummeted back to the floor, no dainty faint for her. No, this was the real thing, not a practiced ploy for attention. She fell gracelessly, smacking her head on the floor hard enough for us to hear it. One of the men scooped her up as he apologized to Taroc, then fled with her in his arms. The other people in the group attempted to appear unaffected, but when Taroc moved on, they deflated in relief.

As the King strolled over to the next group—a gathering of four men who looked less than excited to receive him—I whispered, "That's the second person you sent running tonight, Your Majesty."

"Technically, she wasn't running."

"No, she wasn't." I snorted a laugh. "Thank you."

Taroc stopped and looked at me. "For what?"

"For interfering. You didn't have to. Thank you for not letting her strike me when I couldn't defend myself."

"Did you think I would publicly and aggressively claim you as my lover, then allow someone to hit you in my presence? You are mine, Lock. If I had permitted her to abuse you, it would have reflected poorly on me."

"Right. It was about you, not me. Got it."

"Good. I'm glad you understand." He started for the group again. "And you may always defend yourself, Assassin. Be they male or female, highborn or low, you have the right to protect yourself."

"Even against you?"

"Well, let's not get carried away."

Chapter Twenty

I only had time for a quick check of the royal bedchambers before the Dragon King insisted that I attend him more intimately. I intended to get up once we were finished, but he was exceptionally randy and then cuddly. When I tried to slip away, Taroc clutched me tighter and told me to stay right where I was.

He wanted me to sleep with him. It was such a grand development, and I was so damn tired of sleeping on that pallet, that I just snuggled back into his arms. I almost forgot about the violinist and our meeting, but, thankfully, Taroc had a small clock on his bedside table, and its ticking reminded me. I glanced at it just before I fell asleep, noted it was a quarter to two, and jolted awake.

I climbed out of bed carefully. I may have been awake, but Taroc was not. Ren got up, though, leaving her warm cushion by the fire to nudge me.

"Watch over him while I'm gone," I whispered to her.

She climbed up on the bed, turned in a circle three times, and settled into the warm spot I'd left.

With a soft snort, I got dressed and snuck out of the room. Beyond the royal suite, the castle was just settling down for the night, but there were still Dragons on patrol, ensuring the King's safety. I nodded to one as I passed him, on my out to the south garden. He barely lifted his chin, but it was something, and he didn't try to stop me or demand to know where I was going, just to be an asshole. That was an improvement.

The south garden was lit with lampposts, just as every section of the palace grounds were now. Still, there were many shadows to hide in, especially with the large trees that grew there. My hand dove into a pocket and withdrew a lightning glove. Slipping it on as I continued to scan the area, I felt a tingle of unease go up my spine. Damn it, I hadn't bothered to get the man's name.

"Violinist?" I whispered.

The fountain was up ahead, its water gurgling as if trying to calm me, but no one sat upon its wide, stone rim or even stood to the side of it. It had to be 2 a.m., or very close to it. I stretched my neck, rubbed my glove on my thigh to charge it, and took a seat on the basin's rim.

A footstep came from behind me, but I turned toward it too late. I had one second to see a shape loom up, and then everything went dark.

When I came to, my face was in the grass and the lightning in my glove had started to disperse. It was the latter that told me less than fifteen minutes had passed. That was how long it would have taken for full dispersion of lightning. With it just starting to leak away, it had probably been around five minutes.

"Fuck!" I lurched to my feet and started running. As I ran through the palace, I called to the knights on duty. "To the King! He's in danger!"

Men fell into step behind me, and I silently thanked the Gods that they didn't question me, just pulled their weapons and ran. By the time I reached the doors to the royal suite, I had a group of over fifteen knights with me, enough to make the knights on door duty straighten in shock.

"Open the fucking doors!" I screeched.

They yanked open the doors just in time for me to go barreling into the royal suite. The sound of a dog barking echoed down the hallway.

"Taroc!" I shouted as I burst into the bedroom.

I didn't bother to pull the cord for the lights. Despite the darkness, I could see Ren across the room, lunging for someone with her steel-tipped teeth. I launched myself in their direction. One of the knights who entered after me pulled the light cord, and I had to squint in the sudden glare but kept going. Taroc was getting out of bed, and I knew simply by the way his shoulders bunched that he intended to help Ren.

"Get the King to safety!" I shouted over my shoulder as I rubbed the glove on my leg to recharge it.

Behind me, I heard the King arguing with his knights.

"Damn you, get out!" I yelled at him as I looked back. "He's after *you*! Go now!"

Taroc cursed and allowed himself to be herded out the door.

A whimper whipped my head back around, and I finally got a good look at my replacement. He was an Argaiv, his wings folded but ready for flight. I couldn't see his face or hair due to the hood and mask he wore, but his eyes were such a pale blue that they were nearly colorless. That color wasn't common for his race, and I wouldn't have known he was an Argaiv if he'd thought to put away his wings. Despite that mistake, I knew he was good at his job.

I knew it because he held Ren in an elbow lock across her neck, lifting her to expose her belly. The knife in his other hand was already making its descent. Even as her capped teeth snapped at him, he'd gut her. A few minutes, maybe a little more, that's all it had taken for him to overpower a trained vanrussa. But Ren had done her job and given her master enough time to flee. This was her purpose. She'd been trained to sacrifice her life for his.

So why the fuck did I launch myself between that blade and her belly?

I'd wonder over it later. *If* I survived. At the moment, I was too busy breaking the Argaiv's hold on Ren and taking the blow meant for her. I couldn't hit him with my glove or it might kill Ren, and then I would have taken the wound for nothing. So, as the blade sank into my back, sliding into the tender spot just beside my spine, I flicked out my gloved hand, dispersing the lightning, and simultaneously went for the dagger on my belt with my bare hand. I couldn't hold back my scream as the Argaiv's blade severed important muscles, but even though the pain was mind-numbing, I had trained even harder than Ren, and my body knew what to do without my brain directing it.

With my gloved hand, I twisted the Argaiv's wrist, breaking it and his grip on the dog. With the other, I drove my knife into his chest. The man cried out and fell back, releasing his knife, which remained lodged in my back. Just as he stumbled onto the balcony, Ren's snapping teeth driving him back, the knights rushed forward to help.

Those fuckers had waited to see if he'd kill me first. Ren and me.

The Argaiv's creepy eyes widened above his mask as he fell backward over the railing. Ren started to give chase but with the last of my strength, I grabbed the scruff of her neck and fell, face forward onto her. The last thing I saw was the knights rushing past me as the assassin flew away.

Chapter Twenty-One

I woke up in the King's bed. It felt as if someone were holding down my eyelids, but I finally managed to lift them and slide my stare around. Since I was on my stomach, with my face turned sideways on the pillow, the sliding didn't go far. And since the King was lying in my direct line of sight, I didn't want to move it far anyway. I shifted my gaze down enough to discover what was pressing against my hip—that would be Ren—then returned it to the King. My lover. He had called me his lover, so I could use the term too, right?

Taroc was on his side, facing me. His stern features were softened in sleep, but there was a new line between his eyebrows. I tried to lift a hand to touch it but my arm was even heavier than my eyelids. I groaned and gave up.

The King's eyes popped open. "Lock?" He laid a hand on my cheek. "Are you all right? Should I summon the physician?"

I tried to speak, croaked instead, wet my lips, and tried again, "I'm fine. Everything just feels really . . . tired."

"You're not in pain?" He sat up, making it harder for me to see him.

"I don't think so." I mentally scanned myself. "Did someone drug me?"

"No. The court physician saw to your wound, but you were already passed out. He injected you with a healing potion but wanted to wait until you were awake to administer pain medication."

"I was fucking stabbed!" It suddenly came back to me and the knowledge jolted through my body, thrusting my muscles into action. I rolled onto my back and sat up. Then I frowned down at myself. "Why don't I hurt more? How the fuck am I sitting up right now? I know he cut my back muscles."

"As I said, the physician injected you with a healing potion, directly into the wound. I have the best doctors in Racul in my employ. They have magical potions that they use in combination with traditional medicine."

I scowled at him. "I've never heard of magical medical potions."

"Because you can't afford them."

"I can't afford a vanrussa, but I know they exist.

Ren yipped and resettled across my legs. She laid her face on my thigh and stared at me with her ice-blue eyes. Not as pale as the Agraiv's but close.

"Oh, you like me now, eh?" I asked her. "All I had to do was save your life and take a knife for you."

"You did what?" Taroc asked.

"I know; it was dumb. She's just a dog. She was doing her job. But I couldn't let him kill her." I stroked Ren's head. "She's a good dog. So, I ended up protecting the animal who was supposed to protect you. Go ahead, call me a fool."

"You are ten times a fool," the soft tone of his voice caught my attention.

I turned to look at him and found him staring at me with

a tender smile. "Look at you. You're happy I saved her."

"Yes, of course."

I snorted. "It's only been a week and already that dog is more precious to you than everything else."

"Not everything. I'm happy because you're *both* alive, but had you died, I would have been very displeased, Assassin. This animal is precious, but she is still only an animal. You are worth far more to me. Do not take another blow on her behalf again." He smoothed back my hair, then pet Ren.

I tried to ignore the similarities in his gestures, how he pet me like his dog, but then his words caught up to me. "I'm worth more? So I'm property, eh?"

"You're more than property; I think you know that."

I froze as he lowered his lips to mine. *What was happening right now? Did the Dragon King just say that I was someone important to him? Was he kissing me as if he meant it? As if there was something more than sex between us? Was there?*

Then I grabbed his shoulder and a small ache reminded me that I'd been stabbed. I flinched, and he jerked back.

"Fuck, did I hurt you?"

"No, I hurt myself. Just a twinge when I reached for you."

"That's it; I'm getting the doctor." He flung back the covers, got out of bed, and headed straight for the door.

Normally, the King slept naked, but he was wearing the same leather pants from the night before. I blinked at that, then groaned when Ren jumped off the bed to follow her master.

"And just like that, I'm cast aside for the Dragon King," I

muttered. "Not that I blame her."

I heard the King's footsteps, then the distant sound of his voice. After a few minutes, he returned.

"Can I get something to eat?" I asked.

He spun in the doorway and left again. Ren turned and followed. I grinned and leaned back against the pillows. The King was waiting on me. Teng would never believe it. Then I frowned and slid my hand around to the bandage on my back. It really should hurt more than it did.

"Don't touch that!" a man snapped at me as he entered the room with Taroc. He was Neraky, with dark green hair braided back from his face, and a pair of blue eyes that were narrowed at me.

"Sorry, Doc!" I held up my hands in surrender. "I was just wondering why I wasn't in more pain. What was in that potion you injected me with?"

"Venom from the srapa serpent."

"Oh, all right." Then I processed. "Wait, what?! Those things kill sharks!"

"You are not a shark," he said crisply. "For one thing, you don't breathe water. Now roll onto your stomach so I can inspect the wound."

I looked from the doctor to Taroc, who shrugged. Right, he didn't know shit about humans and our fragile anatomies.

"Fine," I grumbled and rolled.

The physician removed the bandage and made a strange sound.

"What is it?" I looked over my shoulder to see him

exchange a look with Taroc.

"Nothing," the doctor said and cleared his throat. "You're nearly healed."

"Nearly healed?" I tried to see my wound, which was, of course, impossible. "Shit, your potions really are magical."

"Magical?" the doctor asked.

"Yes, I told Lock about the *magical* potions you use to speed healing," the King said in an odd tone.

"Oh. Yes. *Those*," the physician said. "I don't think of them as magical, but, yes, my potions have amazing healing properties. The process of creation is detailed and the ingredients are a secret."

"I guess that's fair. You don't want everyone to know how to make your potions."

"No." The doctor cleared his throat. "No, I don't want that."

"So, can we leave off the bandage?"

"Yes, I believe we can," he murmured as he poked around my back. "Any pain?"

"A little, but it's inside and more of an ache. Like an overworked muscle."

He made another strange sound.

"Words, Doc. I need words," I said.

"I can give you a light pain medication to take if the pain increases, but you should be fine by tonight. Until then, I want you on bedrest."

"Bedrest, eh?" I looked over my shoulder again, this time

at Taroc. "Well, if you insist."

Taroc grimaced at me. "I will not be joining you in bed, Lock."

"And how do I protect you if I'm in bed and you're not?"

"I will have to appoint a new King's Guard."

"Ugh! Don't do that. Dealing with them will be more painful than this wound."

I should have told him about the way they'd stood aside while I fought the other assassin, but I was with the Wraiths long enough to hate snitches too much to ever become one. I'd have to deal with the knights myself.

"You can sit up now," the physician said.

I rolled over, sat up, and glared at Taroc as the doctor pulled a bottle out of his bag and set it on the side table.

"Take one spoonful no more than once a day if you're in pain," he said. "I will check on you tomorrow."

"Thank you, uh, who are you?"

"I'm Dr. Chisuren."

"Thank you, Dr. Chisuren. You're a miracle worker."

"Yes, well, uh, you're welcome." He collected his things and, with one last strange look at the King, left.

As he walked out, a servant walked in carrying a tray of food. Following her was Captain Vettan. I glared harder at Taroc.

"You are supposed to be working with the palace knights anyway," Taroc said as the woman flicked out the tray's legs and set it over my lap.

"Thank you," I said to her. Then, to Taroc, "Fine, just for today, but I don't want them in here."

"If we had been in here last night, you wouldn't have that wound," the Captain said.

"What the fuck are you talking about? You *were* in here; you all followed me in." I was about to say fuck it to the whole snitching thing and call him out on his little *stand to the side and see if Lock gets killed* trick, but then I remembered something. "Oh, right, *you* weren't with them. So you don't know shit."

"My soldiers gave me a full report. And what I meant was that if they'd been in the royal suite while you were off doing whatever you were doing in the middle of the night, you wouldn't—"

"Fuck," I interrupted him and jumped out of bed.

Taroc growled and pushed me back down.

"The violinist! I went to meet the violinist!"

"What violinist?" Taroc and Vettan demanded together.

"The musician, remember?" I said to Taroc, ignoring the Captain. "He had more information for me, something he wasn't willing to talk about in public. I was supposed to meet him in the south garden at 2 a.m., but he wasn't there."

"Maybe he was just playing with you and didn't know anything," Vettan said.

I continued to ignore him. "He wasn't there, but someone else was, and that person hit me over the head and knocked me out."

"Are you sure it wasn't the violinist?" Vettan drawled.

"I suppose it could have been, but that would mean that the violinist had been hired by the same person who hired me."

"To lure you out in the middle of the night," Taroc finally spoke.

"Yes," I said. "Lure me out, bash me over the head, and send another assassin to kill you while I was out cold in the fucking garden. *That's* why I came running back here. I knew there could be only one reason to get me out of the way."

"Captain," was all Taroc said.

"I will have this violinist to you in an hour, Sire." Captain Vettan turned and started to leave.

"Hold on!" I called after him. "How the fuck did that assassin and whoever hit me over the head get past your knights?"

Vettan snarled as he spun back toward me. "If my knights had been allowed in the royal suite, that assassin wouldn't have made it this far."

"What the fuck kind of answer is that? How could a team of knights posted in here have stopped an assassin *from getting here*? He shouldn't have made it into the palace at all! Where were the patrols I told you to set up?"

"They were patrolling!"

"And were they looking in *all* directions as I advised? Or did they forget to look up, as they did the night I got past them?"

"They did their job!"

"If they had done their job, that Argaiv wouldn't have gotten in this room, and I wouldn't have been knocked unconscious!"

"Enough!" the King roared.

We both went quiet.

"You two will work together and you will do so in a civilized manner! You don't have to like or even respect each other, but you will be polite henceforth. I am the only one allowed to shout. Is that clear?"

"Yes, Sire," the Captain said.

At the same time, I said, "Yes, Your Majesty."

"Good. Now, Captain, my assassin does make a good point. How did the Argaiv assassin manage to get past you?"

"We brought in several Horns from the army to fill our ranks for the celebration, Sire. I'm afraid some of them were not as well trained as others. Still, I believe the assassin entered the palace with the guests and hid somewhere until he was able to sneak into your chambers."

"He entered through the balcony doors," I said. "They were open when I got back."

"That doesn't mean he didn't exit the palace somewhere else, perhaps on an upper floor, then fly over to the balcony," the Captain said. "He is an Argaiv after all."

"Yeah, all right, that's possible. Have you checked all the rooms for signs of his passage?"

"We did a sweep but with all the palace staff, guards, and guests traipsing around last night, it's hard to tell who disturbed what."

"I injured him. He must have left a trail of blood."

"Not one that we found. Probably because he was flying," he said the last bit dryly.

"Fuck! An Argaiv would take a while to heal a wound like that. He's holed up somewhere."

"And how does that help us?" Taroc asked.

"I have no idea. Let me eat. I think better with a full belly."

"Very well. Find me that violinist, Captain. It looks as if he may be our only lead."

"Yes, Sire." The Captain bowed and left.

As soon as he was gone, I said, "You're going to have to fuck me gently today."

"I told you, I'm not getting into bed with you, and I'm certainly not having sex with you. You're on bedrest; that means you need to *rest* in bed."

"That's why I said the bit about being gentle."

"I'm not fucking you today, Lock."

"Are you sure?" I asked in a sing-song tone as I waved my sausage at him—the one from my plate, not my dick.

Taroc snorted. "Of course, sex would be your main concern."

"As if it isn't yours?" I lifted my brows and took a bite of the sausage.

"No, it's not."

I stared at him.

"It's not my *main* concern," he amended.

I kept staring. "Yes, all right! I'll try to be gentle."

I burst out laughing, then coughed into my napkin.

"Damn it, I nearly choked on my sausage."

"I've got a—"

"No." I pointed at him. "You're a king. Kings don't make sausage jokes."

"This one does," he said with a smirk, then went on to tell me all the ways he'd like to choke me with his sausage . . . gently.

I have to admit, I was impressed.

Chapter Twenty-Two

Four hours into my bed rest, I felt absolutely fine and utterly bored. We had fucked a few times, and Taroc had even managed to be gentle—spooning me while slowly sliding in and out. It had been fantastic, but there are only so many times I can come in one day, and I think I'd used them all up.

Captain Vettan had discovered the violinist's name —Edmund Oliver—but had not located him as promised. According to Edmund's wife, the violinist hadn't come home yet, and she had already been worried about her husband before the palace knights had shown up. Now, she was in a state of panic and, according to Vettan, was running about the city, trying to find him. That made one of them.

The Captain concluded that the violinist had probably been a victim and not the one who hit me. Which meant that he was likely dead and to search for him was a waste of time. He alerted the Talons and would be notified as soon as the man or his body was found. The King was not pleased.

To mollify Taroc, Vettan brought me a map of the palace with the patrol routes noted, a schedule of the soldiers selected for each patrol, and the Palace Guard's log that noted every reported activity. It was all spread out on the bed before me but, from the look of them, there wasn't much I would have done differently last night. The one thing I'd requested that hadn't been done was the posting of stationary guards at strategic points around the palace, including the King's private garden. Captain Vettan admitted that he simply didn't have enough knights to do the double patrols I'd insisted upon *and* guard certain areas. So there hadn't been anyone stationed in *any* of the gardens.

Yes, I was angry, but the Captain had made a judgment call, and I couldn't fault him for it. In the end, this was on me. I was the one tasked with finding the culprit behind these attacks, and I was the one who had left the King in the middle of the night only to get bashed over the head for my stupidity. There was only one course of action left for me to take; I needed to get out of the palace and do some investigating.

I glanced at the bedroom door. Taroc was off doing king stuff and would be for a while. After our last romp, he'd declared that I really did need my rest and that wouldn't happen with him there. So he left. Unwittingly playing into my plans.

All right, I didn't have any plans back when he'd left, but his leaving was now fortunate.

I looked at the balcony doors. If that Argaiv could get in, I could get out. Hopefully. If the Captain hadn't suddenly gotten his shit together and organized proper patrols. But so what if he had? If I were caught trying to leave, Taroc would be livid, but he'd get over it. And I would quick; I just needed to speak with Teng.

I got out of bed and crept down the hall to my room. As I got dressed, it hit me; Taroc had put me in his bed. Granted, I had been injured in his bedroom, but I would have expected him to have me moved to this room to recover. At the very least, he wouldn't want blood on his sheets. And then there were his pants. When he fled the bedroom, he'd been naked, but I woke to him wearing the same pants from the night before. He must have grabbed them off the floor and put them on while the doctor was tending me. But why not take them off afterward? Had he really been that worried about me?

"Huh," I murmured. "Maybe I am important to him."

I looked in the mirror and checked out the new outfit I'd put on—the clothes Taroc had bought for me. Stretching my neck, I turned away. I'd known from the start that I belonged to him, but it was in the way of a prisoner or an indentured servant. Now, I felt kept, claimed in a more intimate way, and I wasn't sure how I felt about that.

I pulled on my assassin vest over my new clothes and headed for the window. It would be easier to escape from that room than the King's bedroom. With my climbing claws, I wouldn't need a rope, and I could leave the window open to sneak in later. I fastened a set of iron claws on my boots, then went to the window. After opening it and checking out the garden, I hooked the hand claws on and shimmied out the window. Once outside, it took only seconds to get down to the garden.

It was aggravatingly easy. After last night's attack, Captain Vettan should have corrected his mistakes and put men on watch as I'd suggested. He hadn't. This stirred mixed feelings in me. On one hand, I was furious. On the other, if he had posted extra guards, I might not have made it off the palace grounds.

"Pompous asshole," I muttered as I strode up the alley I'd landed in, stowing my claws as I went. "Even now, he thinks that he knows better than me. *No, don't listen to the human even though he's been proven right. He's just a human. What could he know?* Asshole."

I hailed a carriage and went to the Shrieking Ghost first. Teng wasn't there so I had the driver take me to the docks next. I found Tengven on the dock before his ship, talking to his first mate. They both nodded at me when I walked up.

"We were just wondering when you would show up," Ry, the First Mate, said. "I thought maybe the Dragon King ate you."

"He did, in a way." I grinned. "And I must have been delicious because he went back for seconds."

Teng looked at my fine clothes and lifted a brow. "Did he? You fuckin' the King now, Lock?"

"Don't act as if the gossip hasn't reached your ears. You know I am."

Tengven chuckled. "We heard that he calls you his assassin. There goes your cover, my friend."

"I know." I grimaced. "If I ever get out of this, I'll have to move."

"You can always sail down the coast with us."

"I appreciate that, and I just might take you up on it. But I'm sorry, I have to be rude and cut off the small talk. I snuck out so I could check in with you."

"You *snuck* out?" Ry asked. "Is he like your daddy now? 'Daddy, may I go out and see my friends?'"

"I'm supposed to be on bed rest. There was another attack last night." I looked around. "Let's take this on board."

The men instantly went serious and preceded me up the plank and onto the ship. Ry came with us into the Captain's cabin, but I didn't mind. Teng would have told him everything anyway.

"Another attack?" Teng asked as he shut the door behind us. "Did you recognize the assassin?"

"No. He was an Argaiv. I managed to stab him, but I must have missed his heart because he flew away."

"Did you get him deep?"

I nodded. "Fairly."

"A deep chest wound will take a bit of time to heal. I'll send someone to ask around, see if any injured Argaivs have been seen."

"He got me in the back," I said. "If it wasn't for one of your kind, I'd still be groaning in the King's bed, and not in a fun way."

"What do you mean?"

"A Neraky doctor patched me up. He used some kind of magic potion with srapa venom in it to speed my healing. That shit is powerful! I'm completely healed."

"What the fuck are you talking about?" Ry asked. "Our doctors don't have magic potions. The only thing magical about us is our ability to go from breathing water to air. And srapa venom is used for numbing, that's all."

"Look for yourself." I turned and lifted my tunic.

Teng pushed it further up, taking my belt with it. "What am I supposed to be looking at?"

"That's where I was stabbed."

"There isn't even a scar, Lock." Teng dropped my tunic. "That's impossible. I think you must have hit your head."

"As a matter of fact, someone did hit me on the head, but that doesn't change the fact that I was stabbed. The doctor came by to check on the wound this morning. Why would he do that if I had just imagined it? Oh, and I was bandaged."

The Nerakians looked at each other, then at me. Their steady stares sent a zing of panic down my spine.

"No. I *know* I was stabbed. I didn't imagine that. It was fucking deep. And I was lucid this morning when the doctor came by."

"Whatever healing potion that doctor gave you, it didn't come from our people," Teng said. "But I'd sure like to get my hands on it. Is there any way you could get me a vial?"

I blinked. "Yeah, sure. I'll sneak into the doctor's room and get you one."

"You mean the hospital?"

"I don't know if there is a hospital at the palace. It's not as if Dragons need a doctor."

"They're not invulnerable," Teng said. "None of the immortal races are. We still need doctors to help us heal."

"True. If Dragons were invulnerable, I wouldn't be in this mess." I shook my head. "But they do heal rapidly. I saw it for myself. The King cut his hands and before I could bind them in bandages, they were healed."

"Fuck, that must be nice," Ry muttered.

"It must be nice to live forever," I shot back.

Ry chuckled. "Yes, it is. Though it can get boring."

"Unless you're a pirate."

"One does what one must to keep oneself entertained."

"What the fuck kind of talk is that?"

"It's classy talk. I figured you'd understand it now that you're rubbing elbows with those rich assholes."

"That sounds kinky," Teng said.

I snorted a laugh, then jerked my chin at Teng. "Back to business. What have you got for me?"

"A lead on the hooded man."

"You found him?"

"I found the place he uses as a changing room."

"Excuse me?"

"The hooded man goes in and then, eventually, he comes out without his hood."

"Then you know who he is!"

"No. You see, that's the problem. The place he uses is the Blue Feather. Most people enter it with a hood pulled low. All our guy has to do is go inside, have a little fun, and leave without his mask on."

"Weren't you able to tell his cloak from the others?"

Teng gave me the look that question deserved.

"Yeah, fine. I'll go speak with Yasima. Maybe she can tell me who he is."

"I tried that; she says she doesn't know."

"She may know for me." I winked at him. Then I went serious, "Thanks for this, Teng. I'll get that potion if I can."

"If you can't figure out which one it is, take them all," he suggested. "I have someone who can analyze such things."

"All right. I'd better go before someone realizes I'm missing. Thanks again."

"Be careful, Lock. Dragons make dangerous lovers."

Chapter Twenty-Three

I crawled back into the guest room's window, shut it, and went into the dressing room. I had just stowed my assassin's gear when Taroc came storming in. He pulled up short when he saw me, his eyes going from narrowed rage to wide relief.

"Ensarena damn you!" the King snarled. "What are you doing out of bed? I thought you..."

"What?" I smirked and sauntered over to him. "You thought I left you?"

"No." He crossed his arms.

"Were you worried?" I slid my hands up his chest and beneath his arms, nudging them open.

With an annoyed look, he wrapped his arms around me. "I thought you had gone investigating again."

Oh, fuck, This guy knew me too well.

"I just got bored lying there. I feel great; I promise." I nipped at his chin. "You want me to prove it?"

A low growl rose from his chest and his hands swept down to cup my ass. He began squeezing and kneading it, pulling my cheeks apart. While he was playing with my ass, I kicked off my boots and undid my belt. I was about to push down my pants when he grabbed the waistband and tore the back right down the middle.

"Holy fuck! These are brand new, Taroc!"

"Take out my cock, Assassin," he shot back. "I'll buy you more pants."

With that, he lifted me, hooking my legs around his waist and splitting my pants further. As I struggled to get his belt undone and his pants open, he walked me out of the bedroom and down the hall to his room. Anyone could have seen us—frankly, there should have been guards in the hallway—but even with my ass hanging out, I didn't care. Not with his hands gripping it possessively.

The King kicked his bedroom door shut behind us and took me to the bed. Or near the bed, rather.

"Get me oiled now, Lock! Now or I will fuck you dry!"

"All right! Keep your pants on." I leaned over and grabbed the bottle, then chuckled as I realized what I'd said. "You probably will keep them on."

"I can't do another gentle fucking. Hurry! I need to claim you now!"

"I'm hurrying!" I rubbed oil over his twitching cock, capped the bottle, and tossed it on the bed.

As soon as he was slick, Taroc lifted me, carrying my weight on one palm as he directed his dick into me with the other hand. We both groaned as I sank onto him, but I only had a few seconds to enjoy that blissful feeling, that wet cock working into me. As soon as the Dragon King had both hands on my ass again, he began lifting me up and down rapidly while he pumped upward with his hips.

All I could do was wrap my arms around his shoulders and hold on. My hair, longer than when I'd arrived since I hadn't bothered to get it cut, flopped in my face while every ounce of fat on me, no matter how little, began to jiggle. I leaned forward, trying to steady myself, and the King growled against my throat. His teeth nipped my neck. My dick, trapped within the remains of my pants, ached to be set free, but I couldn't let go of Taroc's shoulders; I was afraid I might bite my tongue.

"I need to fuck you like a Dragon, not some simpering human." He bared his teeth at me as if it were my fault. "No more gentleness, Lock."

"Whatever you want, Your Majesty."

He slowed. Briefly closed his eyes. "Am I hurting you?"

"Not one bit."

"Good." He went back to his wild fucking. "Then you will come for your king."

"As my king commands." Shocked that I really was going to come on command, I groaned through my release, soaking the pants. I guess I had another orgasm left in me after all.

Seconds later, Taroc jerked me down on himself and threw his head back to roar so loudly that it set my ears to ringing. He filled me with that tingling nectar, hips locking against me over and over, then clasped me close. As he shivered through the little zings of pleasure that followed such a great release, he kissed me. Deeply. Possessively. Powerfully. I groaned into his mouth, slid my fingers through his hair, and kissed him back.

That's when the door flew open and a group of knights came rushing into the room.

"Sire!"

"Your Majesty, are you all right?"

With a movement so fast that I was left dazed, Taroc dropped me on the bed and spun. Claws sprouted from his hands as he snarled at the men.

"Forgive us, Your Majesty!" one of the knights said. "We thought you might be in danger."

Taroc didn't say anything, only let out a rumbling sound that sent a shiver down my spine.

The men fled.

I sat up hesitantly, watching the furious rise and fall of the King's shoulders. "Taroc?"

He turned, and I got to see what had terrified the knights. The Dragon King's face had shifted, bones becoming more prominent and sharper, ridges lifting on his cheeks and brow, and eyes blazing as if a fire burned behind his irises. His nostrils flared, his stare met mine, and his shoulders finally lowered.

"Hey," I said casually. "You want to put the dragon face away? It's not bad, kinda sexy actually, but it's also a little scary."

Taroc took a few breaths and his face transformed back to normal. With a final sigh, he tucked his flaccid cock away, buttoned his pants, and walked out of the room.

Yep, he just left me there in torn, cum-stained pants, gaping at his retreating back.

"Da fuck?"

As if my words had summoned her, Ren ventured out of the dressing room, took a quick look around, then hurried after her master.

"Fucking Dragons and their fucking dogs." I got up and

headed back to my room with my ass hanging out. This time, I wasn't worried about being seen; the King had scared everyone away.

Chapter Twenty-Four

I changed my clothes, put my assassin vest back on, and went to speak with Captain Vettan. We had a brief argument about the lack of stationary guards, during which I pointed out all the weak points on a palace map, areas that I had designated during the weeks I had worked on improving palace security. I had thought those improvements had been made but after my little jaunt earlier, I wasn't so sure. I needed to know if this was just a momentary lapse because the palace guards were still getting reorganized after the attack or if those changes had never been implemented at all.

Captain Vettan was vague in his answers, leaving me to believe that my weeks of work had been for nothing, and he hadn't done more than put up a few lampposts in the gardens. But now that palace security had failed again, he was forced to heed my advice. This time, I stuck around to witness him give the orders to add stationary posts for several guards, including four lookouts to be set in towers. He also ordered the locks changed to the type I recommended, and the spikes removed from the outer walls, then replaced with smooth, rounded caps. I knew I may have been making things harder on myself, but Taroc had to let me out of the palace sometime and after this new attack, I had the perfect reason to leave.

I just had to find him to make that argument.

By the time I did locate the King—in a meeting with

some visiting silk merchants—I was getting really annoyed. He didn't want me to leave the palace because he said he needed me to guard him, but then he went off without me. He had Ren with him, so I wasn't worried, but that was *my* point. And I suppose he'd just proved it.

I slipped into the room and stood along the wall, watching the well-dressed men the King was speaking to. Three were Neraky and one was human. All four of them cast me curious looks, but the King didn't offer an explanation for my presence, and they weren't stupid enough to ask.

"Enjoy the city," Taroc said as he stood.

The merchants hastily got to their feet as well and bowed to the King as he left the room, Ren and me trailing after him. I didn't say anything to Taroc, his mood was too strange, I just followed where he led. Then he turned down a hallway that had an unknown Dragon in it. The Dragon was dressed too finely to be a newly hired knight, and he wasn't one of the visitors who had come to the city for the rite. Not that I could recall every Dragon I'd seen the day before, but this guy had a face I would have remembered.

Striking, stunning even. He had golden-blond hair, but it was an old gold, one that could use a good polish. His skin was fair, though in Dragons, that didn't necessarily mean that he hid indoors; their rapid healing included sun damage. Which meant that Dragons with tan skin had either been born that way or spent so much time outside that their healing couldn't keep up. The Dragon was too far away for me to see the color of his eyes, but I could tell they were focused on the King. He started for Taroc aggressively, shoulders hunched and expression determined. The King went still while Ren stepped in front of him and growled. The other Dragon didn't even glance at the dog, just kept coming.

I stepped in front of Ren, "Stop and declare yourself!

Who are you?"

"Get the fuck out of my way, human," the man growled.

"Stop right there! I'm warning you." I withdrew a lightning glove, pulled it on, and rubbed it down my pants to charge it.

"*You're* warning *me*? Oh, you've just said the wrong thing to me on the wrong day." The Dragon put on speed but now he was focused on me.

Just as I'd done with the palace knights, I charged him.

"Lock!" Taroc shouted and reached for me, but he was too late.

I dove for the man's stomach, intending to flat palm him there. Instead, he smacked my arm aside with a blow to my forearm, grabbed my waist, and tossed me upward. Taroc started cursing as Ren leapt to help me. My momentum carried me in an arch that I assume the Dragon had intended to use to fling me down the corridor, but he suddenly had a metal-toothed vanrussa flying at him. He had to abruptly let go of me to defend himself, and I fell straight down behind him. His forearm bashed into Ren's head as he flat-palmed her stomach, sending her into the wall, but she rebounded instantly.

As I fell, I slapped the man's ass and shouted, "Heel!"

The Dragon probably thought I was talking to him, but it was Ren who pulled up short at the command and went running back to her master, just as I'd intended. Meanwhile, lightning jolted through the Dragon, sending him to his knees. As I jumped to my feet, the Dragon turned to look at me with wide eyes. He bent forward and went into spasm . . . but stayed conscious.

"Oh, fuck," I whispered as the Dragon staggered back

to his feet. His eyes—they were a beautiful shade of green—narrowed at me.

"Cease!" Taroc roared.

The other Dragon spun to glare at Taroc. "What the fuck kind of welcome is this?"

"This is my assassin, Locrian, and he did warn you," Taroc said smoothly.

"You know him?" I asked as I got to my feet.

"This is Prince Racmar of the Zaru Kingdom," Taroc said to me. "I'm impressed you were able to send him to his knees; that's more than most men can do."

"It's because that damn dog helped him." The Prince waved at Ren. "When did you get a dog?"

"Recently. I was told that I needed protection."

"Your assassin isn't enough?"

"It was his suggestion since he wasn't *my* assassin at first." Taroc stared at him meaningfully.

Racmar blinked. "Fuck." Then he looked at me. Back at Taroc. "Why the fuck is he still alive?" Then he sniffed, turned back to me, and sniffed more. "Oh. I see." He swung to face Taroc once more. "Are you fucking out of your mind?"

"Do not presume to speak to me about intimacies, Racmar."

The Prince grimaced, glanced at me, the dog, and then said, "We need to talk."

"I assumed so. This way." The King turned and headed back the way we'd come.

Before I could follow, the Prince grabbed my forearm and lifted my arm to look at the glove. "What did you hit me with?"

"A lightning glove."

Prince Racmar grunted and dropped my arm as if it disgusted him. "You're lucky it was Tarocvar you tried to kill. If it had been me, you'd be dead."

"And you're lucky I hit you with my glove instead of letting Ren have you." I followed my king. Over my shoulder, I said, "If it was her, you'd be dead."

No, that wasn't in the least bit true, but it was sure fun to see the Prince's furious reaction.

Chapter Twenty-Five

The King led us back to the meeting room he'd been using with the merchants. I took up a position near the door, arms loose at my sides, and Ren sat on the floor beside her master's chair.

"So, what has brought you here, Rac?" Taroc asked.

"We've got a problem."

"Which we is that; you and me or you and your brother?"

"All of us if you don't help me and my brother."

"Go on. What's the problem?"

"It's the dead."

"The dead?"

"Yes, the dead."

"What's wrong with the dead?"

"They're not staying dead."

"The dead are coming back to life?"

"Not exactly. For the last two weeks, everyone who dies, revives after a few hours. But they're not themselves. They are confused and aggressive. We've had to quarantine them."

Taroc slid his stare to me.

"Don't look at me." I held up my hands. "The people I kill stay dead. I've never had any complaints from my customers."

"Yes, but you know a lot of people who I don't. People who might know something about the dead awakening."

"You mean necromancers."

"We hired one of those," Prince Racmar said. "She didn't do shit."

"Perhaps she was the one creating your problem," Taroc said.

"Could be, but since she's currently locked in His Majesty's dungeon, we'll know soon enough."

"You tossed her in a dungeon for failing?" I asked.

"You're going to allow him to join this conversation?" Prince Racmar asked the King instead of answering me.

"Since I invited him into it, yes. And I'm wondering the same thing. Why did your brother imprison the necromancer?"

"Because he had the same suspicions you just voiced. He's keeping her there until he's sure she isn't involved."

The King grunted. "It must be a necromancer's spell. In which case, only another necromancer will know how to stop it."

"I don't know. The necromancer we hired said the land felt unsettled to her. She wasn't sure if someone was deliberately bringing back the dead or if it were a side effect of another spell."

"The land? Did you try not burying the dead?"

"Yes. That didn't work either."

"Pardon me for speaking and existing, Your Highness, but I have a question," I said to the Prince.

Taroc snorted a laugh at Prince Racmar's rolling eyes.

"What is it, Assassin?" the Prince demanded.

"What race is your necromancer?"

"I don't see why that matters, but she's an Eljaffna."

"Necromancers use specific techniques unique to their cultures. Additionally, every necromancer's magic is unique to them. They can bring about similar results, but the way they get those results differs, and in a situation like this, that may matter. I don't know much about the Eljaffna, we don't see a lot of them here, but I do know they consume blood, and I assume blood is a part of their process. Whereas, a Raltven necro would not resort to such measures."

"A Raltven?" the Prince growled. "You can't trust Raltven."

"It depends on the Raltven. From my experience, their loyalty is hard won but once given, it's unshakable. That, however, is moot. You don't have to trust Raltven to hire one."

"Lock used to work with Raltven," Taroc said to the Prince. He looked back at me to ask, "Do you have someone in mind?"

"I do. And I'll tell you this, Prince Racmar, there are no better necromancers than a Raltven necro. They are born with one foot in the spirit realm. Death walks beside them."

"Yes, I expect it does. Just as it does with you." The Prince didn't look happy. "The situation is dire enough that I'm willing to try anything."

"Fetch your necromancer, Lock," the King said.

I blinked. "You mean . . ."

"Yes, go and fetch the Raltven. You have two hours."

"Your Majesty, it may take more time than that. I don't know where he is."

Taroc grimaced. "Very well. You may have five hours. That is all, Assassin."

"Yes, Your Majesty." I bowed and hurried from the room before he changed his mind.

And before he realized that I wouldn't just be looking for the Raltven necromancer.

Chapter Twenty-Six

The Blue Feather was across the Vevaren River from the palace, in a well-to-do shopping district. Why would those snobs want a brothel in the middle of their fine stores and restaurants? Two reasons; Yasima, the owner, was discrete. Nothing outside the Blue Feather announced that it was anything other than a fancy gentleman's club. And second, the real entrance, the one the whores and their customers used, was at the back of the club. You had to go down an alley and along the city wall to reach it. The back entrances of homes and shops were for servants and employees, so no one of means would be venturing down those alleys. Unless, of course, they were cloaked and heading to the Feather.

I, not being a man of means, shouldn't have to bother to cloak myself. However, I wanted to look like a rich man, and I had the wardrobe for it now. Plus, why not? This sort of investigation was best done undercover. So, I got out of the carriage with my hood up, pulled my cloak in around myself, and hurried into the alley as furtively as every other patron of the Blue Feather.

A Ricarri guarded the back entrance, his beefy arms crossed. I nodded to him as if I knew him, and he opened the door for me without a word. Yet another reason to wear the cloak. It was fine enough that he didn't bother to inspect who it hid. I mean, a wealthy man would take offense to that, wouldn't he?

A few steps down a dark passage led me into the luxurious main salon. Feathers featured predominantly in the décor. There were massive urns full of great big ones, boas strewn over elaborate furniture and people, and even the curtains were trimmed in them. And they were all blue. A fucking sea of feathers. I stood in the center of the salon and scanned the prostitutes on duty. Yasima prided herself on offering a variety of options to her clients so there were members of every race native to Racul and both genders in the room. The customers were still cloaked but none were additionally masked. They just tended to keep their heads down as they made their selection.

I watched an Argaiv, her wings out on display, their opalescent membranes painted with flowers that matched her, uh, I suppose you could call that collection of chiffon and blossoms an outfit. She was full-figured and stunning, but all she did for me was remind me of the assassin I had stabbed.

"See anything you like, sweetheart?" a Neraky woman drawled as she glided up to me.

Her pale skin glistened pink, nearly the same shade as the Argaiv's wings. That pink wasn't a flush but came from the scales covering the wealth of skin she had on display. Out of the water, a Neraky's scales withdrew into their skin, leaving only a few on their hands and feet, so she must have been fresh from a swim. This didn't surprise me. Not only did Yasima like to offer a variety of partners but also a variety of options for their use. She probably had a pool on the premises.

"I need to speak to Yasima," I said.

The woman's demeanor changed instantly, her spine straightening and her expression going shrewd. "Is there a problem?" She pulled her transparent robe in.

As if that chiffon could cover anything.

"No problem. Just tell her that Lock is here."

"Very well." She spun and clicked away on a pair of high-heeled shoes adorned with seashells.

I moved to lean against the wall, lowered my head, and surreptitiously watched the customers from the shadows of my hood. One of them was fondling the balls of a couple of human males, going back and forth between them as if he couldn't decide which pair were more worth his coin, all while they patiently waited, polite smiles on their faces. There was only so much of that the club guards would allow before they'd insist on a selection. One of them was already frowning at the man. I'd say he had about three more seconds of free fondling.

Most of the customers kept their hands to themselves and visually inspected the merchandise, like the man who had a Shanba woman leaning back in a chair with her legs spread, exposing everything for him while he crouched to get a good look. Yet another client watched two Raltven women rub each other, their hands fading in and out of solidity. They reminded me that this wasn't my only mission. I had to be quick.

The Neraky woman returned and waved me toward a narrow staircase set along the east wall of the room "Yasima will see you now."

"Thank you."

She escorted me to the bottom of the stairs and nodded at the Ricarri guarding them. He stepped aside for me to go up, but eyed me suspiciously as I passed. At the top, an unadorned hallway led me to Yasima's office. Not even a painting hung on the paneled walls. Before I reached the door, I heard moaning and rolled my eyes.

"I guess this is what I get for showing up without an appointment," I muttered, then knocked.

"Come!" a woman called.

I hesitated, wondering if she was talking to me.

As if she'd read my mind, she added, "You, Lock. Come in."

I opened the door, grimaced at the scene before me, and shut it. "Hello, Yas."

"One second, Lock. Sorry, I'm just finishing up two interviews."

"I could have waited downstairs."

"No, it's fine. None of us care."

"I care a little."

She glanced over her shoulder at me as she continued to thrust into the woman bent over her desk. "Oh, you're adorable. Have a seat." She waved at a chaise lounge near the door. Then, to the woman, she said, "You have to do better than that. Here, listen to Carik again."

She pulled her massive cock out of the woman and slid it into the man who was bent over beside her. As Yasima started to pump deep, the man moaned, slowly increasing his response until he was writhing and crying out dirty things.

"There! You see? You don't just dump your load all at once. You have to build up to an apex or it isn't believable." She pulled out, slapped the man's ass for a job well done, then waved them away. "You're both hired. Go downstairs and wait for me in the entry hall; I'll be with the two of you momentarily, and then we can find something for you to wear."

As the woman and man gathered their clothes, Yasima turned to me, cock out. I think she did it on purpose, just to get a reaction from me. Unfortunately, the massive tits defying gravity above that cock and her very feminine face ruined it for me. I need more than a dick to get aroused. Oh, and then there was the fact that just below her shaved balls, a pussy lurked.

I tried not to shiver in distaste.

Yasima laughed when she saw my expression and tucked herself back into her pants. "So, what can I do for you, baby? The Wraiths need something?"

"I haven't run with the Raltven in a long time, Yas. You know that."

"Oh." She frowned, then nodded. "Yes, I recall that now."

"You don't have to pretend that you forget details about me. You don't know enough to threaten me."

"Or do I?" She waggled her brows.

I waited until her employees had left and their footsteps fading before I said, "I'm here on behalf of the King."

Yasima burst out laughing.

I stared at her.

She laughed harder.

I stared harder.

She stopped laughing. "Which king?"

"The Dragon."

"No fucking way. You can't be. The Dragon King would never associate with you. And he certainly wouldn't send you to speak to me on his behalf."

"It's more of a forced servitude situation."

"Forced servitude?" She licked her lips and adjusted the bulge in her pants. "Sounds kinky."

"Let's just say that I'm fulfilling an obligation, and move on."

"Fine. You're no fun." She plopped down on a settee next to me, her dark, sausage curls bouncing. Under the low lights, her Ricarri skin gleamed like polished silver. "So, what does the King want from me?"

"There's a man who comes here wearing a hooded cloak and a mask."

"Many cloaked men patronize my establishment." She lifted her chin and slid her steel gaze away. "And even some women."

"As I said, he also wears a mask. Don't fuck with me, Yas. I can already tell that you know who I'm talking about. This directly concerns the King. That man arranged an assassination attempt with His Majesty as the target."

"An assassination attempt?" She went still. "And now you're working for the King. Interesting."

"Yes, all right, you've heard the rumors," I grumbled. "They're true; I'm his assassin. I tried to kill the King and failed. Now, I'm his. But I am not the assassin who tried to kill him last night. That man was an Argaiv."

"An Argaiv? So there have been two attempts on the King's life?"

"Yasima, listen to me; you don't want to get any deeper into this. King Tarocvar has given me free rein to conduct this investigation as I please. As his *assassin*."

I let that sink in.

Yasima drew herself up. "Are you threatening me?"

"I'm warning you. The masked man was my broker, and I already have proof that he came here after meeting with the Argaiv assassin. He slips in, takes off his mask, and leaves without it. Do you understand what position that puts you in? You are his accomplice."

"I damn well am not!" She slapped the cushions.

"You know that he uses the Blue Feather as his changing room. I'm betting that you charge him extra for that. Now, I'm willing to tell the King that you had no idea why he needed to resort to such measures, even though I know you would never let anyone use your business like that without knowing the full situation."

"And in exchange, I must give him up?"

"We're not after him either, Yas. We want the person who hired him."

"If I give you his name, I will lose the respect and trust of many of my associates."

"Your associates are not who you should be worried about. Yas, you can either be a hero to your kingdom or a traitor. That is your choice."

"Fuck, Lock! When did you become such a prick?"

"I've always been a prick. But now my life is on the line and that makes me an even bigger prick. Bigger even than the monster in your pants."

She inhaled deeply, then let it out slowly, watching me. "His name is Yuref Lancarester."

"Lord Yuref? He's on the Human Council, isn't he?"

"That's the one. And I've enjoyed being the brothel of choice for him and his fellow council members. If possible, do not ruin that for me, Lock. I will consider it a favor."

I nodded. "I won't mention your name to Yuref. I give you my word."

"Thank you." She grinned. "Now, get the fuck out of here before I do something naughty to you."

I chuckled as I stood. "Always a pleasure, Yasima."

"Not as much as it could be, Lock."

Chapter Twenty-Seven

I took another carriage across the city to the Shrieking Ghost. Or rather, to Bracken Road, where the driver refused to go any further since it was after dark. Then I walked to the Ghost.

In the back of the Ghost's main room, partially hidden by one of the privacy curtains, a Raltven sat with his back against the wall. He was solid, his sharp, brown eyes tracking me as I made my way to him. He smirked when I sat down.

"Locrian Mahvis, what has brought you to my table?"

"The Dragon King."

Fahar grunted. "I heard about your new . . . position."

"Prince Racmar of Zaru is here." I ignored his insinuation. Mainly because it was true. "There's a problem with the dead in his kingdom."

"All right, I'll bite, even though this feels like the set up of a joke. What's wrong with the dead?"

I took great pleasure in using the Prince's line, "They won't stay dead."

"Ah. That *is* a problem."

"They've tried an Eljaffna necromancer with no success."

He snorted. "An Eljaffna? Of course, they failed. Eljaffna necros have no finesse; they rely too heavily on blood."

"I thought this would be a good opportunity for Daha. No sense in having the King's ear if I can't use it to help out my old friends."

Fahar grinned. "And look good in the process."

"Of course." I grinned back. "What do you think? Can Daha do it?"

"Daha can find out what's raising the dead; that's a certainty. Whether he can lay them all to rest and stop more from rising, I can't answer. It depends on what he has to work with and what's animating those bodies."

"Fair enough. Think about it. Talk to him. When you decide, send word to me at the palace."

"Shall I address it to the King's Assassin?"

"Yes."

He burst out laughing. "An assassin whose identity is known is fucked."

He was right, but I couldn't help arguing, "Not necessarily. I just can't take credit for my kills."

"And what's the point of killing, if you can't take credit?"

"The point is, I get to live." I turned, waved at one of the barmaids, then asked him, "Another drink?"

"No, thank you." He stood up and shot the rest of his drink. "Daha is here. I'll have an answer for you in a few minutes."

With that, Fahar slipped around the hanging partition and disappeared.

I ordered a drink for myself and sipped it as I waited. I was halfway through when Fahar returned with Daha. The Raltven necromancer was slender to the point of delicacy and his features refined. Yasima would have been thrilled if he applied for a job with her. He was the kind of man who attracted the attention of other men, even those who aren't aroused by men, and I'd envied him for it once. The way he moved so gracefully, how his shoulder-length hair fell in thick swaths just where it should, and how his lips constantly looked ready to suck cock. But then I learned that envy is useless and so is mimicry. It's always better to be exactly who you are.

"Lock," Daha said in greeting as he took the seat beside mine.

Even the sound of his voice was perfect, not too deep but not feminine either. He had the dark hair and pale skin of his people—the Raltven were not sun-worshipers—but his eyes were a strange, silvery gray, as if his ability to work with the dead had marked him. Those eyes startled many people but the only time I found them unsettling was when he was raising the dead.

"Hello, Daha. How are you?"

"I'm well. Fahar says that you've brought me a job. Thank you for thinking of me. Especially since the customer is a prince. Fahar and I agree that this would be beneficial to the Wraiths in many ways. Perhaps even the Raltven race as a whole."

"You're welcome. So, is that a yes?"

"Yes. Is the client ready to meet me?"

"More than ready. Are you able to come with me now?"

"I am."

"Excellent!" I downed the rest of my drink and shook Fahar's hand. "Good to see you, boss."

"You too, Lock. Take care of my necro. I want him back in one piece."

"I'm only escorting him to the Prince. What happens after that, I take no responsibility for."

Fahar laughed. "Fair enough. And we won't forget your loyalty."

"Thank you." I went serious to add, "I've never forgotten yours. You were my family when I needed one."

Fahar's smile softened.

"Fahar." Daha stood and bowed to his boss.

"No matter where you are, you are not alone, brother. There are Raltven in the shadows of every city. Call upon your kin if you need them."

"Thank you. I will do my best to represent our people well."

I left the Shrieking Ghost with a Raltven necromancer, feeling pretty damn smug.

Chapter Twenty-Eight

That feeling of accomplishment vanished a few minutes later when arrows came whizzing at Daha and me as we walked to Bracken Road.

"Son of a bitch!" I ran for the cover of an alley as Daha went see-through.

Since it was going on midnight, that worked well for him. He paused, taking the time to get a look at our attacker. Although the arrows would go straight through him in his transparent form, his clothing remained solid, and Daha took great pride in his clothes. So, after getting that look, he hurried to join me.

"It's an Agraiv in a mask, flying about the road," Daha said as he removed a pocket crossbow from his cloak.

"That fucker is already hunting me?" I peered around the corner, then pulled back when an arrow pinged off the wall near my face.

"You know him?" Daha, standing in the middle of the alley's mouth, aimed and pulled the trigger. "Correction, you *knew* him?"

"You got him already?" I ducked my head around the corner again. Sure enough, there was now a body in the middle of the road.

"I did." Daha strolled over to the Argaiv, put another arrow in the assassin's heart (you can never be too careful), then pulled both shafts out of the corpse. He flung bits of blood and flesh off them, as I stepped up beside him.

"Damn. I would have liked to have questioned him."

"My apologies," Daha said.

"No, that wasn't a reprimand. I appreciate your help. This man tried to assassinate the King last night." After a quick scan of the dark street, I crouched to remove the assassin's mask. "I don't recognize him. You?"

"No."

I searched the Argaiv's pockets, especially the deep ones in his cloak. He was pro; the only things on him were the tools of his trade. I divested him of those tools (it's always nice to have backups), slid them into my vest, then stood. "Shit. I don't think a carriage will pick us up if we're carting around a body, not even outside the Broken."

"It doesn't have to be a body."

"Doesn't it take time to raise the dead?"

"Not when they're this fresh. But I warn you, he will nearly be the same man that he was. Death has not had the time to wipe the slate clean."

"You mean, he'll try to kill us again."

"I'm inclined to think that you were his main target, but yes."

I pulled a length of cord out of the assassin's cloak and bound his hands behind his back. Then I broke his wings. Vicious, yes, but I couldn't have him flying away. "All right. Do it."

Daha nodded in approval. "Step aside."

I moved aside, casting a quick look around. No one was on the streets. In the Broken, people know when to run or at least hide. There were probably many eyes watching us, but most would know exactly what Daha was doing, and so, watching would be the most they'd do.

Daha's hair and cloak undulated in the breeze of another realm as he spoke ancient words, and his eyes began to glow. Not brightly, just a dull, gray light, as if wherever that light came from, it was too dark to shine brilliantly.

Suddenly, Daha surged downward and slammed his palm onto the chest of the Argaiv.

The man came gasping back to life, coughing and jerking against his bonds as his stare shot around the street. It landed on me, and he tried to stand. His bound hands made this difficult and his broken wings probably made it painful, but he kept at it. As he struggled, I strode forward and slapped him across the face.

The Argaiv shook his head as if clearing it, blinked, then screamed, "My wings!"

"You are charged with the attempted assassination of King Tarocvar Verres. As you're dead, that doesn't really matter anymore, but if you refuse to come with us quietly, I'll break a lot more than your wings."

"I'm dead?"

"Yep."

"I don't feel dead."

"That's because you're freshly dead," Daha said. "I reanimated you mere minutes after I killed you."

"*You* killed me?!" He lunged toward the necro.

I slapped him again. "Yes, he killed you, and he's the one who will either release your soul or tether it to your rotting corpse. So you may want to be respectful to him." I turned to Daha and asked, "I thought you could control the dead you raised?"

"Now, that would have taken a lot more time."

"Ah. All right then." I looked back at the not-corpse. "What's it gonna be?"

"I'll go with you."

"Good decision." I helped him up, and we started walking.

Luckily, we weren't too far from Bracken Road and as soon as we crossed it, we spotted a few carriages parked on the Bracken side of the road, waiting for customers. Although the drivers refused to enter the Broken at night, they knew there would be people emerging from it, people who needed rapid transportation.

"Where to?" the driver asked us as we stepped up to his carriage.

"The Royal Palace," I said as I opened the door.

The Argaiv drew back.

Daha said, "The only thing you have to fear now, is me."

The Argaiv got in the carriage.

Chapter Twenty-Nine

I realized a little belatedly that all three of us were cloaked and hooded. The palace guards at the gate let us past because they recognized me, but they gave us some strange looks, especially when they noticed the broken wings dragging behind the Argaiv. As for him, he didn't say a word, not even to complain about his wings. He strode after us stoically, looking less fresh by the minute. A necromancer could bring a soul back into a body, but they couldn't keep the body from deteriorating. That would be something completely different.

The guards outside the palace's main doors were less obliging. They took great pleasure in making us wait while they fetched the Captain. One of them stared me down as his friend sauntered away.

"You do realize that you're keeping the King waiting, not me," I said in a tone as smug as his expression.

The soldier glanced over his shoulder.

"And you know I'm fucking him, right? He's claimed me publicly. How many lovers has he done that with?"

The man went still.

"Do you really want to mess with me?"

Daha lifted a brow at me, but I kept my stare on the guard.

"Fuck," the Dragon muttered. "Yes, I know who you are to him, human. We all do. Just go in already."

"Thank you."

"And your friend stinks."

"That's because he's dead. What's your excuse?"

"What?"

"Bye now. I recommend using soap when you shower."

As the Dragon snarled after us, Daha snickered.

"I've missed you, Lock," Daha said.

"You have? I didn't think you knew I existed."

He shot me a surprised look. "You were the only human in the Wraiths. All of us knew you existed."

"Fair enough. I didn't know you *cared* that I existed."

"I do," he said softly.

I swung a look at him. "Thanks."

"Ain't this fucking sweet," the Argaiv muttered.

"Hey, what's your name?"

"Me?" The Argaiv blinked.

"Yes, you."

"Uso."

"Uso, you stink even more when you speak. Maybe you should shut the fuck up until someone asks you a question."

Uso made a face at me.

"That's not decomp," Daha said.

"What?" I looked at him.

"It takes a bit for a body to decompose. He doesn't stink because he's dead."

"Then why?"

"My guess is bad dental hygiene. Thus, the smell when he speaks."

Uso's face twitched and twisted as he fought the urge to tell Daha to fuck off.

"Gross, Uso," I said. Then, before he could reply, "This way." I took them to the meeting room, but the King and Prince weren't there. "All right. Maybe not."

"They're in the King's private dining room," Captain Vettan drawled from the doorway. "Having a late supper."

"Really late," I muttered.

"They finished eating, then started drinking."

"All right. Thank you for the detailed update." I went to step past him, and he grabbed my arm.

"You don't get to bring your friends into the royal suite for a tour."

"This man is a necromancer who was requested by Prince Racmar." I waved at Daha. Then I motioned toward Uso. "And this is a corpse that the necromancer has reanimated. He is also the assassin who tried to kill the King last night."

"What?"

"Why are people not understanding me tonight?" I asked Daha. "I feel as if I'm speaking another language."

Daha shrugged and shook his head. "Happens to me all

the time."

"Excuse us, Captain. We don't have time to explain the meaning of words to you." I pushed past him, and my entourage followed.

The guards outside the royal suite didn't try to stop us, only opened the doors. Either the King had warned them to let us pass, or they were smarter than their comrades. I nodded to them and took my guests down the corridor to the dining room. I heard the King and Prince talking as we approached, and their words slowed my steps.

"When are you going to tell him?" Racmar asked.

"That is not your concern."

A snort. "Even a human has the right to know that—"

"Enough! You may be a prince but you are not a king, and even a king knows to respect another monarch's personal decisions."

"He means that much to you, eh?"

"Are we going in or what?" Uso asked.

I punched him in the face.

"What the fuck!" Uso clutched at his face.

"Who's there?" the King demanded.

I stepped into the room. "I found the necromancer, Your Majesty."

"And he has a foul mouth," the Prince said.

"That was not my foulness, Your Highness," Daha drawled as he entered the room. "It came from the corpse I raised. And, forgive me, but that is to be expected. Being raised from the dead tends to make people touchy."

Racmar slid his stare to the Raltven, his mouth opening as if to speak, but when he met Daha's gaze, he remained silent—open-mouthed but silent.

"Did you say corpse?" Tarocvar asked.

Ren, who was already standing, hackles raised, started to growl.

"Quiet, Ren," Taroc said, and she sat down.

"We found the Argaiv assassin on the way back, Your Majesty," I said, waving Uso into the room. "Or, rather, he found us. He attacked us, and Daha killed him." I pulled Uso's cloak open so they could see the wounds in his chest. "I wanted to bring him in for questioning, so Daha reanimated him."

"This is *your* work?" Prince Racmar had found his voice at last. He stood up and inspected the corpse, but came to a stop beside Daha.

"Yes. The corpse was fresh; it was an easy enough task."

Prince Racmar's stare slid to the necromancer and glided over him. "Did Locrian explain the situation to you?"

"Yes."

"And? Can you help us?"

"I'm nearly certain that I can determine why the dead are rising, but until I've done that, I won't know if I can stop it. The most I can promise is that if I can't, I will at least be able to advise you on what or who can."

The Prince grunted. "And you know I'm from Zaru? That you will have to leave the kingdom with me?"

"Yes. I'll need to pack, but I can be ready by dawn."

The Prince looked over the necromancer once more. As he did, Daha flung open his cloak and turned in a circle.

"What are you doing?" the Prince asked.

"Making it easier for you to find whatever it is you're looking for," Daha said.

Taroc laughed boisterously. "I can tell he's a friend of yours."

"Yes, your Lock and I go way back, Your Majesty," Daha said.

The King's smile faded.

Fuck. I knew exactly how the King had interpreted that statement. I shook my head at him to try to tell him it wasn't what he thought, but he only glared at me. *Fuck, shit, damn!*

"I admit that I'm not comfortable with your race," the Prince said to Daha. "But I'm willing to give you a chance."

"I will need a little more than that, Your Highness."

"What does that mean?"

"If I'm to go with you to another kingdom, far from my home and clan, I need to know that I have at least one person on my side."

"Are you asking me to be your friend or bodyguard?" Prince Racmar smirked.

"Neither. I don't need your friendship or physical protection. I can kill if I have to." He waved a hand at the Argaiv. "But you're not hiring me to kill. You want my skills with the already-dead, and for that, I expect to be well compensated and welcomed. To be given all the access I request and any help I should need. I will not suffer scorn from you or your people, not even your king. I want your vow that I will be treated with respect and that if I'm not, you will rectify the mistake personally."

"Understood. And you have my word," the Prince said. "I will personally see to it that no one disrespects you without consequences, not even the King himself. And, believe me, we will do everything we can to assist you. Whatever you need, you will have it. Is that acceptable?"

"It is, Your Highness. When would you like to leave?"

"You said you can be ready by morning; we will leave then."

"I will meet you at the palace gates at 8 a.m." Daha waved Uso forward. "Now, Your Majesty, please ask your questions so I may put this man's spirit to rest."

"Who hired you?" the King got right to it.

"I don't know," Uso said.

"This again," Taroc snarled.

"Dead men tell no lies," Daha said. "They are still themselves, but they are beyond the need for deception. You can be assured that everything he says is the truth, Your Majesty."

"Fascinating," Racmar murmured.

"How much were you paid?" I asked.

"Ten gold to prepare, with the promise of ten more when the kill was confirmed."

"It was the same for me," I said to Taroc.

"And how did you get into the palace the night you attempted to kill me?" Taroc asked Uso.

"I bribed one of the footmen for Lord Greshmen's carriage and took his place."

"Is Lord Greshmen a part of this?"

"No."

"And how did you get into my bedchambers?"

"Once I was in the courtyard, I slipped away, hid in one of the rooms on the upper floor, and waited until the palace was quiet. I then exited through a window and flew to your balcony."

"How did you know it was my balcony?"

"It is easy enough to get a map of the palace."

I grimaced, annoyed that Vettan had been right. "It's a good thing we've secured the windows on the upper floors as well as the lower. That is, if the Captain listened to me this time."

"He has," Taroc said. "Can you think of anything else to ask this man?"

"No, Sire."

"You could ask who arranged the job," Daha suggested.

"I already have that information."

Daha and Taroc both looked at me in surprise.

"Why didn't you tell me this sooner?" the King demanded.

"I discovered the man's identity while I was out fetching Daha. I thought we'd see to Uso before I brought it up."

"Who the fuck is Uso?"

"I am," Uso said.

"Release Uso's spirit, Daha," the King said. "If we have the identity of the intermediary, we have no further use for him."

"Yes, Your Majesty." Daha went to Uso and laid a hand on his forehead.

The Argaiv dropped to the ground instantly.

"You make that look easy," the Prince said.

"Thank you. It is not." Daha looked around the room, his stare catching on Ren for a second, then said, "If that is all, I will take my leave so I may pack."

"You may go," Taroc said. "And thank you for your service this night, Daha. I will not forget it."

Daha bowed to the King, then the Prince, and finally, shook my hand.

"May your path be wreathed in shadows, Daha," I offered him the traditional traveling blessing.

"Thank you, Locrian. May darkness embrace you."

Before Daha made it to the doorway, Captain Vettan came through it.

"Sire, we've found the violinist," Vettan said, his expression grim. "The Talons pulled him out of the river. His throat has been cut."

"Damn!" Taroc hissed, then he looked at Daha.

Daha was already shaking his head. "If the vocal cords are severed, he won't be able to speak."

"Could he write?"

"How dead is he?" Daha looked at the Captain.

"A couple of days, but those days have been spent in the river." Vettan grimaced. "He's not pretty; the river creatures have been at him and it looks as if he may have been smashed about by a few ships. His wife had to use a birthmark to identify him."

"I'm sorry, Your Majesty, a body like that would take at least a day to raise and it would probably be senseless. Cold water can slow down the putrefaction process, but the Vevaren isn't cold enough for that and it's full of bacteria that will—"

"Just a conclusion, please," Taroc cut him off. "Save us the specifics."

"My apologies, Your Majesty. I've been asked to raise many bodies pulled from the river," Daha said. "My conclusion is that once out of the water, the body will rapidly rot, and when the brain starts to rot, the spirit can't use it."

"Does a spirit need a brain?"

"It does if you want it to perform fine motor skills such as writing. If you had a selection of possible killers we could stand before it, it might be able to shamble toward one or maybe lift an arm to point, but that would be all."

"This body is not going to shamble," Vettan said, his nose wrinkling. "He's barely in—"

"Yes, thank you," Taroc said crisply.

"What happened to that whole, Dragons are killers thing?" I whispered to Taroc.

"Killing and listening to descriptions of rotting corpses are two different things."

"Good point."

"Thank you, Daha, you're excused."

"Your Majesty." Daha bowed to the King again and left.

"You are excused as well, Captain. But take the corpse with you." Taroc waved at Uso.

"The corpse?" Vettan looked at the body. "Where shall I take him?"

"I'm not telling you to keep him somewhere. Put him wherever it is you put random corpses, Captain. I don't care where that is. I just want him out of my fucking dining room!"

"Yes, Your Majesty!" The Captain rushed over to the body as I desperately tried not to snicker.

Chapter Thirty

Once Uso's body was gone, the King turned to me. "Now who is the intermediary?"

"His name is Lord Yuref Lancarester. He's on the Human Council."

"A councilman has plotted against me?"

"Technically, he only served as the middle man."

Taroc lifted a brow at me.

"Are you truly surprised?"

"A little. Council members are the only people I didn't suspect." He looked at the Prince. "Excuse us, Prince Racmar, but this matter can't wait."

"Of course." Prince Racmar bowed to the King. "I must prepare for my departure anyway. Thank you for your help, Your Majesty."

"You're welcome. I shall bid you goodbye now, so you will not have to seek me out in the morning."

"Thank you again, Sire." The Prince bowed. "Goodbye."

"Goodbye, Prince Racmar. Safe travels and give my best to your brother."

"I will." The Prince nodded to me. "Thank you for your

help as well, Locrian."

"My pleasure, Your Highness. And, for what it's worth, Daha is a good man. Even if he wasn't, you have made a vow to protect his honor. For a Raltven, that means that a sacred pact has been forged between you, one that he must honor as well. As long as you keep your promises, he will do his best for you."

"That's worth quite a lot, human." The Prince laid his hand on my shoulder. "Don't worry, I'll look after him physically too."

I bit my tongue before I could say that I was sure he would. Daha would have some fun in Zaru, maybe even before he got there.

As the Prince left, the King went to the door and called for the Captain again.

"What are you going to do?" I asked him.

"I'm sending some knights to arrest Yuref."

"I would advise against that. If the royal knights show up at Yuref's house and arrest him, the man who hired him may learn of it. Your enemy is wealthy, whoever they are, and a council member being arrested in the middle of the night is gossip that will doubtless reach them. I suspect that they already know that Yuref is the broker, since a wealthy client would be less inclined to work with someone unknown. Even if they don't know his identity, they might figure it out merely from your treatment of him, and if they think you're about to learn of *their* identity, they could decide to run."

"Then what do you recommend?"

"Send Vettan alone, dressed as a courtier. Have him summon Yuref to speak with you. And maybe wait until after dawn to send him."

"And what shall I tell Yuref this meeting is about?"

"Don't. You're the King, you don't have to explain yourself to him. Just summon him. If your enemy is having Yuref watched, he may be concerned about a visit to the royal palace, but I doubt he'd run prematurely. He'd want to be sure you were onto him before he gave up and fled. If for no other reason than he'll still want to see you dead."

"You make a fine argument."

"Your Majesty?" Captain Vettan was back.

The King looked from me to the Captain. "Tomorrow morning at first light, I need you to dress like a civilian, go to the home of Lord Yusef Lancarester, and bring him to me."

The Captain scowled. "As a civilian, Your Majesty?"

"Yes. Be as discrete as possible; he is the man we've been seeking. The intermediary. Tell him I wish to speak to him but don't say why."

"If he is the broker, shouldn't I go now, Sire?"

"No. We don't want to alert the one who hired him. Dawn is soon enough."

"Yes, Your Majesty."

As soon as Vettan was gone, Taroc took my hand and led me to his bedchambers. After Ren came in behind us, he shut the door and turned to me.

"He was not my lover," I said before he could speak.

Taroc lifted his brows. "Who?"

"Daha. We weren't even friends."

"Then what did he mean by that comment?"

"He's a member of the Raltven clan I worked for—the Wraiths."

"The Wraiths?" He rolled his eyes. "How creative."

"We've known each other a long time but never intimately."

"I'm not sure why you feel the need to clarify this for me."

"You're not sure?" I snorted. "Your expression soured after he said we were close and then you glared at me. *That's* why I felt the need to clarify."

I wanted to ask Taroc what he hadn't told me, what was it that Racmar thought I had the right to know, but I wasn't that stupid. All he'd have to do is deny it was me who they were speaking of, then he could chide me for eavesdropping. So I only held his stare and silently willed him to answer the question I hadn't asked.

That didn't work.

"I don't believe I gave you permission to conduct your investigations today. You were supposed to fetch the necromancer and return to me. That is all."

"I needed to speak to my contact, and I had the chance to, so I took it. If I hadn't, we wouldn't know who Yusef was."

"Still, let that be the last time you disobey me, Assassin."

"I can't guarantee that."

"What did you just say?" His expression shifted from teasing affection to horrified rage.

"I did what I knew was best, and it got us the information we were after. You have my loyalty as my king and lover, but not my blind obedience. If that's what you want, then stop fucking me."

"That is not how this works." He closed in on me and bent his head to mine. "In case you've forgotten, you tried to kill me, and I spared your life. *That's* why I demand blind obedience from you—because you belong to me. Your life is mine. Every fucking breath you take is a gift from me. Every day you wake up is because of my benevolence. So do not, for one second, think that bending over for me grants you any kind of special treatment. Your ass belongs to me; if I want to fuck it, I don't need your permission."

"Yes, you do."

Taroc bared his teeth and snarled.

"Go ahead and growl, Taroc, but I know you now. You would never force anyone into bed with you. The thought of someone lying beneath you, allowing you to fuck them because of some kind of debt, is repugnant to you, isn't it? It's why you have such a hard time fucking your courtiers. There's a part of you that wonders if they really want to be there."

Taroc's face twitched and trembled. "Every person I've taken to my bed has wanted to be there!"

"Yes, they sure seem to, and that's why you can do it. But you don't kiss them, do you? You don't take anything more than what you need to get off. Because you're not completely sure."

"Watch your words, Assassin."

I didn't heed his warning. Instead, I pushed harder. I had to make my point after all. "If I said no to you, that I felt no desire for you, that if you wanted to fuck me, you'd have to order me to do it, force me, *rape* me, I doubt you could even get it up."

"I'm not a rapist," Taroc snarled as he spun away from me. "Regardless, you are mine, and you *will* obey me."

"I will obey you."

He glanced back at me and started to look mollified.

Then I added, "Unless I feel strongly that it isn't the right thing to do."

Taroc roared and came at me. I stood my ground, even when he wrapped his hand around my throat. He stared me down. I stared him . . . up. He flat-palmed me in the chest as he released my throat, sending me flying onto the bed.

"Oh, are we going end this with a fuck and then pretend that nothing was said?" I asked as I rose onto my elbows.

"Get the fuck out!"

I got off the bed, bowed to him a bit mockingly, and left. As I shut the door behind me, I heard something shatter against the door.

Chapter Thirty-One

It was late, and I was exhausted, so I went to the bedroom I'd never slept in and got ready for bed. I felt comfortable leaving the King alone for the night since half of it was gone, he had Ren with him, and the knights were finally following my instructions. Still, I kept a knife beside the bed and slept with my pants on.

So, when someone stormed into my room the next morning, I was prepared. Even tired as I was, I was used to coming awake quickly and jumped up as soon as I heard the door open, my hand automatically going to the knife. Then the lights came on, and I realized it was Vettan.

"What the fuck do you want?" I growled.

"Your presence has been requested by His Majesty," Vettan said.

Something about him was wrong, and it wasn't his scathing tone or the way he lifted his chin to stare down his nose at me. All that was pretty standard for Vettan. It took me a second to figure out what *new* aspect of his appearance bothered me.

"Is that blood?"

"It's not mine." He turned and left the room.

"Fuck!" I tossed the knife aside, yanked on a tunic,

shoved my feet in my boots, and grabbed my assassin's vest. I was still fastening it when I entered the King's dining room, seconds after Vettan. "What's happened?"

Taroc stood near the table and a half-eaten meal. He was speaking with some of his knights and didn't pause to answer me. I waited, listening in on their conversation.

"No one enters that house unless they're one of ours," the King said. "Not even the Talons."

"Yes, Sire."

"And block the street as well."

"Yes, Sire."

Taroc headed out of the room, the rest of us following in his wake. Ren was the only one who kept pace with him, even I held back.

That is until he snapped his fingers and said, "Assassin!"

I ran up beside him, glancing at his strained expression before setting my stare forward. "Your Majesty?"

"Captain Vettan found Lord Yusef dead in his home this morning. You will help me investigate his murder."

"Fuck!"

"Yes," he said with a grimace my way. "It is unfortunate."

"Motherfucker! I shouldn't have suggested we wait until morning."

"It was my decision, and I agreed with your recommendation. He should have been safe until morning."

"Yes, he should have been," I murmured, my anger simmering into something more pensive. "So why wasn't he?"

"Who else knew his identity?" the King asked as he led me through the hallways, toward the palace's main doors.

"No one who would share it. I had to threaten my source to get it out of them."

"And who was that?"

"I will answer you when we are alone, Your Majesty. I promised to keep their name out of this."

He grunted.

The palace doors were opened for us, and we went out into the pallid morning, a crisp breeze greeting us. A carriage waited at the bottom of the steps along with saddled horses for the knights. The King got in the carriage, Ren went next, and I climbed in to close the door after us. I had barely sat down when the carriage lurched forward.

"I'm sure you realize that you shouldn't be leaving the palace," I said. "So I won't say it."

"You just did. Now, who is your source?"

"Yasima, the owner of the Blue Feather."

"The hermaphrodite?" He lifted his brows.

"Yes. Yusef was using her establishment as a changing room. He'd meet with a client, then go to the Blue Feather where most patrons arrive cloaked. Once inside, he could remove his mask and then leave looking like everyone else."

"Smart."

"Yes, but Yas knows everything that goes on in her place. He made a deal with her, that he would encourage his fellow council members to patronize the Blue Feather in exchange for her discretion."

"So she has no way of knowing who hired him and therefore is incapable of warning them that we were onto him."

"Yes, Your Majesty. She didn't even know what his business was."

Taroc suddenly narrowed his eyes at me. "That was a lie."

I blanched and whispered, "How the fuck did you know that?"

"I know you too, Lock. Just as well as you know me. Now, why did you lie to me about Yasima?"

I heaved a sigh. "I promised Yas that I would protect her. It was the only way she'd betray Yusef."

Taroc grunted, stared at me a bit, then nodded. "I suppose you were trying to be honorable, but do not lie to me again. Not even for honor's sake."

"I won't, Your Majesty."

After a brief, awkward pause, he asked, "So, if not Yasima, who warned them? Someone must have. I can't believe this is a coincidence and Yusef was murdered for a completely different reason."

"Neither can I. The timing is too perfect. Someone found out that I discovered Yusef's identity, and they passed that information on to the person who hired me. Either that or the one who hired me already knew who Yusef was and was watching him."

"No, that can't be it; we didn't approach Yusef until this morning."

"Perhaps they followed Yusef to the Blue Feather and

have been watching it. They could have been there when I showed up, and . . ." I trailed off and shook my head. "No, that doesn't make sense either. I went in cloaked and even if they had seen me and recognized me, all they'd be able to do is follow me back to the palace."

"Then it's unlikely that they were watching the brothel. How else could they have learned that we discovered Yusef's secret?"

"I don't know."

"Who told you about Yasima?"

"A friend," I said fiercely. "The only man I trust. So, no, it's not him, and no, you can't have his name."

Taroc leaned back, his stare locking on mine. "You only trust one person?"

"Only one implicitly."

"I see." The skin around his eyes tightened. "You won't give me obedience or trust."

I blinked. "I . . . you expected me to trust you already?"

"You expected it of me."

I went still. "No, I expected you to not treat me like a slave when we've clearly established an intimate relationship."

"Intimate but not trusting?"

"I trust you to a certain extent."

"But not implicitly?"

"Can you ever trust a lover implicitly?"

"Dragons can."

"You're talking about mates, aren't you?" I shook my head. "I don't profess to know all the cultural details about your people, but I do know that taking a mate isn't just about sex for you. It's like a marriage."

"A marriage is nothing compared to a Dragon mating."

"Right. Because there's a magical bond that forms between the two mated Dragons. Magic changes things."

"So, you would trust a lover if they were magically bound to you?"

"I wouldn't have a reason to. But that isn't an option for us lowly mortals."

"Humans have magic practitioners."

"Sure, and maybe one of them could cast a love spell for me, but now we're talking about magical force. I would never do that to anyone, especially not someone I cared about. Besides, I heard that shit wears off. So what's the point?"

"True. A Dragon mating bond is eternal."

"And, again, it's not an option for me."

"It is if you mate a Dragon."

"What did you say?" I whispered.

"A Dragon can take a mate from any race."

"But why would they choose a human when a human will eventually die?"

"If a Dragon's mate is mortal, the bond will share his or her immortality with their mate."

"Holy fuck! Are you saying that Dragons can make humans immortal?"

"If they take one as their mate, yes."

"Whoa."

"But the human would have to accept the Dragon as their eternal lover, and humans are infamously fickle when it comes to love."

"Some of us can be. But others want to find one person who they can spend their life with, all of their life, no matter how short or long it is."

"And which are you?"

"Let's just say that I expect fickleness from my lovers but hope for more."

"And could you handle eternity—living forever?"

"I . . . what are you asking me, Taroc?" *Holy fuck balls! Was this what he'd been talking about with Racmar? Did he want to take me as his mate?*

"I'm just curious. Could you handle eternity, Lock? Or does the thought of living forever scare you?"

"To be completely honest, I don't know what I can handle until I'm handling it. But forever doesn't scare me; it excites me."

"What a shame you don't trust me." He smirked.

I made a choking, annoyed sound, then shouted, "You asshole! You had me thinking that you were about to offer to mate me. What the fuck, Taroc? Do you get off on giving people hope only to dash it away?"

Taroc's stare immediately went intense. "Why would that give you hope? You say that I treat you like a slave and you can't trust me. So why would you want to be with me forever?"

"I don't know if I do, but I'd like to have the option. No one ever knows where a relationship will go when it begins, but beginning one while knowing that at some point, inevitably, it will end, is disheartening, to say the least. If you know it's not going to last, you can't possibly give your all to it. But if there is a chance for more, you can be vulnerable."

"Vulnerable?"

"Emotionally, Taroc. And stop giving me shit for not trusting you when our relationship has just begun. It's perfectly normal for trust to take time to develop. Just because we're fucking, it doesn't make you automatically trustworthy."

"According to you, it makes me the opposite."

"All right, now you're being deliberately obtuse. Fine, Taroc. I understand now that I can't expect anything real or lasting from you, even if it might be an option."

The King opened his mouth to speak, but the carriage stopped, and I was too angry to listen. I jumped out and held the door open for him. He shot me a heavy look as he passed, but I ignored it along with the ache in my chest.

Chapter Thirty-Two

The only people awake in Yusef's neighborhood at that hour were the servants and us. Those servants paused to gawk at the barricades the royal knights were putting up and at the King himself as he exited his carriage. After shutting the carriage door, I followed His Majesty up a set of stone steps and through an open doorway. Knights were already posted at the door and throughout the home, something that made me respect Vettan a little more. At least he'd thought to guard the scene while he reported to the King. Not that Yusef could get any more dead, but there might be crucial information hidden somewhere in his home.

Yusef's servants were gathered in one of the sitting rooms, watched over by a knight. As Captain Vettan joined us, Taroc paused and looked in at the household staff.

"Where were these people when you arrived?" the King asked Captain Vettan.

"The housekeeper answered my knock. The cook was making breakfast, several maids were cleaning, and a manservant was sent to fetch Lord Yusef. It was he who discovered the body."

"Have you questioned him?"

"Yes, but I responded rapidly to his shouts. He couldn't have been alone with the body for more than a couple of minutes."

"Anyone who saw anything would have fled," I said. "They'd be too scared to stick around."

"Nonetheless, question them, Captain." The King waved toward the servants.

"Yes, Sire." Vettan headed into the room.

"Where is the body?" Taroc asked another knight.

"This way, Your Majesty." The knight led us up a creaking staircase, past paintings of sour-faced people and musty tapestries of far-off lands, to the master's bedroom. He waved us toward the doorway, then headed back to his post.

The room was spacious but crowded with heavy furniture—the sort people buy to pass down to future generations—and yet, Lord Yusef was unmarried. The drapes were open and light poured in through twelve-foot high windows but in addition to the sunshine, several ceiling lights were on. There was no way to miss the dead body. Especially since it lay in the middle of a massive bloodstain.

I suppose it would have been a pool of blood if the bedding and mattress hadn't absorbed it, leaving the pale body lying on a red splotch. The man's nightshirt—who wore a fucking nightshirt anymore? It was the year 6596, for fuck's sake—was soaked as well. Not so surprising since his throat was cut.

"Just like the violinist," I whispered.

Yusef stared at something above him with wide, startled, dead eyes, his arms and legs akimbo as if they'd fallen into the position after a struggle. But he wouldn't have struggled long and he couldn't have cried out, not with his vocal cords severed. It was well done, a quick death, but not a professional one. An assassin wouldn't have given Yusef a chance to struggle; he would have been dead before he knew he was in danger. And no assassin would leave a mess like this unless they'd been specifically asked to by their employer.

"Do you recognize the work?" Taroc asked me.

"Recognize the work?" I made a face at him. "What the fuck is that supposed to mean?"

"Don't assassins have weapons they prefer? Or styles of killing?"

"All right, yes, most do, and some even leave a mark on the body so people know it's their work. But this is not the work of an assassin."

"Why do you say that?"

"It's too fucking sloppy. This is someone who knows how to kill and has no problem with killing, but they don't have the skill or refinement of an assassin. I think your enemy finally got his hands dirty."

"Then he probably killed the musician as well."

I nodded. "He was at the party, just as I'd thought. But how did he know the violinist was meeting me?"

"Maybe he overheard you."

"Maybe." I tried to remember who was around when I was speaking to the musicians, but the only ones I could think of were the carpenters and a few soldiers.

Taroc inhaled deeply as he walked slowly around the room. "The only familiar scents in this room are yours and Vettan's."

"You'd still smell them if it had been hours since they'd

been here?"

"Absolutely. And if this person was at the celebration and is someone I know well enough to have angered, I should recognize their scent."

"Well, fuck, maybe they didn't do this themselves."

"There is always someone willing to kill for the right amount of coin."

"True. He must have hired a thug." Something gleamed on the bed, catching my attention, and I went over to pick it up. "A button." I held it out to Taroc. "A gold button. There aren't any on Yusef's nightshirt."

Taroc took it from me, sniffed it, made an annoyed face, and shouted, "Captain Vettan!"

I winced. "You do know that the maximum volume of your voice is considerably higher than that of a human?"

"And?"

"And it hurts my ears."

"Aw, my poor, delicate assassin. Did I hurt your sweet, little, human ears?"

I snorted a laugh. "I like this side of you."

Taroc lifted a brow.

"Playful."

"Playful, eh? And you like that?"

Then I remembered that I was angry at him.

"Yeah. It's better than your 'I'm the King, obey me' bullshit."

"Lock, I—"

"Your Majesty?" Captain Vettan and his amazing timing stood in the doorway.

Taroc cleared his throat and held up the button. "Missing something, Captain?"

Vettan blinked, frowned, then stepped forward and peered at the button. "I don't think so, Sire." His hand swept down the front of his immaculate uniform, gliding over the gold buttons of his coat.

"Is this what you were wearing when you came to fetch Yusef?" The King indicated Vettan's uniform.

"No, Your Majesty. I wore my finest civilian clothes as you ordered."

"You changed before you reported the death?" I asked.

Vettan shifted his shoulders. "I had to fetch my weapons anyway, and I was uncomfortable in the other clothes."

"Vettan, this button is drenched in your scent." Taroc put it in the Captain's hand. "I think you'll find that your civilian coat is missing one."

"Oh." His hand closed around the button. "It must have fallen off when I was checking the body. It's an old coat, Sire. I don't have much cause to wear it these days."

"Great," I huffed. "Did you leave anything else lying around the house of the murdered man, Captain?"

"I was in a rush to confirm his death and return to the palace!"

"Maybe you should return to the palace now before you drop another button on the body."

"I am in the middle of interviewing the servants!"

Taroc stopped us before it went further. "Vettan, finish the interviews, then return to the palace, and send Balahar, Mikbal, and Sha to me."

"Sire?" Vettan looked as if he'd been slapped.

"Locrian is right; you've compromised our investigation. Now, do as I say."

"Yes, Your Majesty." Vettan left, casting a glare my way.

"We need to search everywhere," I said as I started opening drawers. "Yusef must have kept notes on his customers. A record. Something. And he'd hide it well. Look for hidden panels in the walls and loose floorboards. Check behind and beneath everything."

Taroc stood there, silently watching me awhile. I felt his stare on me but didn't look at him. This wasn't the place to get into what was fucked up about our relationship. He finally started to help, going into the man's dressing room to search there. I was grateful for the space.

First, Taroc gets mad at me for wanting him to treat me with more respect, then he throws a fit over me not trusting him. What the fuck? And what was all that shit about a Dragon making a human immortal? Why say that to me? Was he just being a dick? Or was it meant to inspire me? Make me fall in line. Dangling immortality before me like a carrot. Be a good boy, and I might make you immortal.

I snorted. "Sure. As if the King of Racul would ever take a human assassin for a mate."

It was an old trick. Offer the possibility of a reward without ever committing to anything. He could use that against me for years before I finally got fed up. Except for one thing; I'm smarter than that. I knew who I was and what I could expect from life. Kings don't marry assassins. Not gonna happen. No matter how good the sex was.

And damn that motherfucker for putting the idea in my head. I had been perfectly content to be his lover. I would have stayed as long as he wanted me and treated me well. That's all I'd wanted, just to be treated like a lover instead of a pet. I didn't ask for eternity. But now I was thinking about it.

"Fuck," I muttered under my breath. "He couldn't just leave it alone."

"Lock!" the King called, startling me.

I ran into the dressing room to find Taroc standing before a safe. It was an expensive model of Ricarri design and was built into the wall. A wood panel sat on the floor and Yusef's fine tunics had been pushed to either side of the rack above.

"How did you find this?" I asked.

"I inspected the wall as you suggested. There were strange junctures in the wood paneling. When I pushed against one, this piece popped out."

"Well done, Your Majesty," I said as I leaned in to inspect the lock.

"Can you open it?"

"Well, safes aren't my specialty."

"Your name is Lock, for fuck's sake."

I snorted a laugh. "I said they're not my specialty, but that doesn't mean I haven't opened a few." I knelt before the safe, pressed my ear against the metal door, and gripped the knob. "This isn't a key lock, it's a combination. Within this door is a mechanism with discs that turn. Each one has a notch to hold a bar. The door will open if all the notches line up and the bar falls into position. I may be able to hear the bar click into place if we're very quiet."

"Did you just tell me to shut up?"

"I believe I did."

The King snorted. "Very well. Listen for your clicks, Assassin."

It looked as if that summer Fahar had partnered me with Rasmur—the best safe-cracker in the Wraiths—was going to come in handy at last. I'd get to see how much of his training I'd retained. With the King standing over me. Watching my every move. No problem; I was good under pressure.

Click. I grinned and turned the knob in the other direction. Click. Two more to go. Turn, feel the tapping through the metal door as the bar coasted over the discs. Click. One more time. Turn.

"Can you do it or not?"

"Taroc!"

"Sorry."

I centered myself and pressed my ear back against the cold metal. Turn. Click. "Yes!" I shoved the lever down and pulled the heavy door open.

"Sweet Ensarena, you actually did it," Taroc whispered.

"Thanks for having faith in me," I muttered as I removed a wooden box from the safe. When I opened it, I found several rows of gold coins, set on their sides in specially made channels. "Holy shit! Fucking rich people have fancy boxes just for their money." I closed it and slipped it into my jacket.

"Lock," the King growled.

"I'm owed this for the work I did for him."

He narrowed his eyes at me.

"Fine." I opened the box and took half a row of coins. "I'm owed this."

"Very well."

Holy fuck, those coins were three times the amount I'd been promised! Enough to start a new life with.

I pocketed them with a shaking hand but a straight face.

Taroc held out his hand and made a gimme gesture. As I lifted the box, blocking Taroc's view of the safe, I grabbed a velvet pouch that had sat beside it and slipped it into my pocket with the gold coins. Technically, I wasn't owed anything since I didn't kill the King, but you never know what you can get away with until you try. And it wasn't as if His Majesty needed the money.

Of course, that didn't stop him from taking it.

The King clicked the latch on the money box, slipped it into his coat, then nodded toward the safe. "What else is in there?"

"Uh, some jewelry." I handed him a jewelry case. "And, hopefully, one of these is a record of his clients." I pulled out a stack of books.

"Bring them here." He turned and set the jewelry on the dresser that ran down the center of the room.

I brought him the stack of books, took one, and passed him the rest. Within a few pages, two things became evident; these were indeed Yusef's records of assassinations, and he wasn't just careful about *his* identity. Every entry used initials only. All I could determine was that the assassins he hired had an A before their initial.

"These are useless," the King said.

"I think this is the most recent book." I tapped a page that was only half full. "And the last entry is 'AU hired to complete unfinished HMK.' AU must be Assassin Uso and HMK is you, His Majesty the King."

"You're assuming a lot, Lock."

"No, look." I pointed at the previous entry. "AL hired for HMK by CV. I am Assassin Locrian, hired to kill you, His Majesty the King, by CV."

"So who is CV?"

"I don't fucking know. Go through your long list of people you've pissed off and see if any of them have those initials."

"That may take a while."

"Well, it's still the best lead we've had in—"

"Your Majesty," Vettan was back.

"I told you to fetch my advisers!"

"I know, Sire, but one of the maids told me that Yusef keeps all his important paperwork in his desk. I broke into the top drawer and found this." He handed the King a folded letter.

Taroc took it with a scowl, unfolded it, and read. As he read, his expression went slack.

"What is it?" I asked.

Taroc looked up at me and grinned. "It's CV." He handed

me the letter. "Crushei Venlebar."

"Lord Crushei? Holy fuck, I was right?!" I scanned the letter, more of a note, really, there wasn't even a greeting. Then I read the best bit aloud, "I need your help with the King. I'll pay triple your usual rate." I shook my head and handed him back the note. "Who the fuck signs a letter like that with their full name and title?"

"Pompous assholes like Crushei." Taroc turned to the Captain. "Arrest Lord Crushei Venlebar and bring him to me."

"Yes, Sire." He rushed out of the room.

"Bring the books, Assassin."

"Yes, Your Majesty." I grabbed the books and the jewelry case, then turned to follow him out of the dressing room.

He grimaced and held out his hand.

Pouting, I handed over the jewelry.

Chapter Thirty-Three

Lord Crushei was dragged into the throne room by two guards under the watchful eyes of Captain Vettan, who brought up the rear. The Shanba lord struggled against the chains that bound his wrists and the grip of the knights, but he did so in a way that expressed affront, not fear. Even after they halted him before the throne to be glared at by the King, he retained his indignation.

I stood behind Taroc on the dais, to the left of his throne, while Ren sat beside him on the right. My view was almost as good as the King's, so I saw every nuance of emotion that ran across Crushei's face. None of them was fear.

"This is an insult against my people, Your Majesty, and it will not go unanswered. You have no right to treat me like a criminal merely because I made up some story about your assassin flirting with me."

Oh, vindication. How lovely.

"You are not here because of my assassin," the King said. Then he paused and added, "Well, you are, but not because of that."

"What then?" Crushei looked from the King to me. "What lies have you told about me, human?!"

"Do not speak to him," Taroc said in an even tone. "He has accused you of nothing more than the lie that you've just admitted to."

"What the fuck is going on here?"

"We have discovered your treachery, Crushei. You may have murdered the only witness to your crime, but he left proof for us to find."

"Don't forget the violinist, Your Majesty," I said.

"Oh, yes. Two murders and one attempted assassination."

"Murders? Assassination?" Crushei finally showed some fear. "What in Tareth's name are you talking about?"

"I'm talking about the assassins you hired to kill me and the people you killed to cover it up." Taroc withdrew the note and held it up for Crushei to see. "It wasn't wise of you to sign the evidence."

"What is that?" Crushei leaned forward to peer at the letter.

"Show it to him, Captain."

Captain Vettan came up the steps, took the letter back down with him, and held it in front of Crushei for him to read. He stared at the Shanba as if he were seconds away from dismembering the man . . . while he was still alive.

Crushei's frown returned. "Yes, and?"

Taroc drew back, one hand flopping to his lap. "*And?* This letter proves that you hired Lord Yusef to procure an assassin to kill me."

"What the fuck are you talking about!" Crushei shouted. "That is a letter I wrote to your steward, requesting an audience with you."

"Excuse me?"

"I sent that note to your steward, Lord Paslan, to request his assistance in arranging an audience with you. I knew you would be reluctant to see me after the incident with your assassin, and Paslan has intervened on my behalf before, gaining me audiences with you or pushing up the time for those I had scheduled. Why in Tareth's name do you think this is a request for an assassin?"

"This note was found in the desk of Lord Yusef Lancarester this morning, just hours after he was discovered to be an intermediary between the wealthy residents of Mhavenna and assassins. He brokered death, Lord Crushei, so it is rather hard for me to believe that you were requesting anything other than that."

"I have no idea how my note wound up in someone's desk other than Lord Paslan's, and I do not even know who this Yusef is."

"The note is not the only evidence. Yusef recorded the initials of every assassin, target, and client in his log books. CV was found beside an assassin's initials and mine."

Crushei started to tremble. "I'm being set up. Someone is making it look as if I am guilty, but I swear to you, I am not. I've never even contemplated your death, much less hired someone to kill you. We argue, Your Majesty, yes, but you have done wonderful things for this city and my people. I would never want to jeopardize that by having you murdered. How would I know that the next king wouldn't be a tyrant?"

I couldn't see Taroc's face, but his silence was enough to tell me that Crushei had planted a seed of doubt. Fuck, I was starting to doubt his guilt myself.

"Perhaps we should summon Lord Paslan to clear this

up, Your Majesty?" Vettan suggested. "He can verify Lord Crushei's claims."

"Yes, I agree. Fetch him, Captain."

"Yes, Sire."

We spent the next few minutes in a tense silence while we waited for the Captain to return. Crushei was at least wise enough to hold his tongue, though he did stare balefully at the King. As much as I disliked the man, I had to admit it was strange that the note did not address Yusef, or anyone, for that matter, and yet Crushei had signed his full name with his title. That's just not the way I would write a note to a man orchestrating the killing of a king. But then again, I wouldn't have written anything at all; I would have conducted that kind of business in person. Perhaps he thought the vagueness of the letter would protect him.

The Captain returned with a broad-shoulder Argaiv dressed in robes finer than what the King had on. His dark hair was braided back and held in place with a silk ribbon that matched the color of his boots. On his chest, a seal of his station hung off a thick gold chain.

The Steward bowed to the King. "How may I be of service to you, Your Majesty?"

"Captain, the note." Taroc waved toward Lord Paslan.

Captain Vettan passed the letter to the Steward, who looked it over.

"Do you recognize this note, Lord Pascal?" the King asked.

Pascal frowned. "Uh, no, Your Majesty."

"You fucking liar!" Crushei shouted. "My life hangs in the balance, Pascal. Tell him the truth!"

"Have you accepted bribes from Lord Crushei before, Lord Pascal?"

"Never, Your Majesty."

"He will execute me, Pascal! Are you seriously going to deny this because you don't want him to find out about some bribes?"

The King stood up and went to stand before Lord Pascal. "I don't care if you've taken bribes, Pascal. Someone has hired two assassins to kill me and this note is evidence that it was Lord Crushei. He pleads innocence and swears that he wrote this note to you, not to the man who hired the assassins. Now, I need you to answer truthfully because if I execute Lord Crushei and then there is another attempt on my life, I will hold *you* accountable."

Lord Pascal paled and his wings shivered, making a rustling sound. "All right! Yes, I take bribes, and I have taken them many times from Lord Crushei."

"Thank you," Crushei said in relief.

"But I swear to you, Your Majesty, I did not receive *this* particular note."

"What?!" Crushei straightened, then lurched toward the Steward. "You son of a pig!"

"I'm sorry, Lord Crushei, but that's the truth. I've never seen this note before."

Taroc rubbed a hand over his face and glanced at me. I shrugged.

"Take Lord Crushei to a cell in the dungeon," Taroc said to the knights. "I need to think more on this."

"Your Majesty, please!" Crushei shrieked. "I did not do

this!"

"I am not convicting you, Lord Crushei. But you will remain imprisoned until I can prove either your guilt or innocence."

Crushei hung his head, his antlers—no longer gilded—nearly hitting the knights. They angled themselves out of the way and carried him from the room.

Chapter Thirty-Four

"Sire, I—" Paslan started.

"I don't care, Paslan," Taroc cut him off. "Just stop doing it. Now, leave me."

"Yes, Your Majesty." He bowed and scurried away.

"Shall I search Lord Crushei's home, Your Majesty?" Captain Vettan asked.

"Yes, immediately."

"Yes, Sire." He left as well.

The King turned to face me. "Any thoughts, Assassin?"

"Only that if Lord Crushei is lying, he's a phenomenal actor."

"Yes, I agree. I saw nothing but anger in him until I accused him of murder. If he were behind this, he would have been nervous as soon as he was arrested."

"Yes, precisely." I looked at Ren. "What do you think?"

Ren barked.

"So how did that note get into Yusef's desk?" I asked.

"The only explanation—if Crushei is innocent—is that it was placed there by the real villain."

"A villain who had access to Pascal's correspondence."

"Yes." Taroc looked around the room as if his enemy might be lurking in the shadows.

"I assumed it wasn't a Dragon," I said.

"Why is that?"

"During the Rite of Ensarena, when your,"—I waved a hand at him—"fire sacrifice was accepted, the light became so blinding that I had to close my eyes. It was the perfect opportunity for a kill, but no one took it."

"That doesn't mean anything. No Dragon would defile that rite with death. And even if they'd been willing to shit on our goddess, they'd know that they'd immediately become a suspect. It would be far wiser to wait."

"Yeah, I'm seeing that now. And a whole kingdom's worth of Dragons was in this palace the night the violinist was killed."

"I would be shocked if it was a Dragon."

"You just said—"

"I was talking about the rite. Now I'm talking about Dragons. A Dragon wouldn't hire an assassin to kill for them. They'd do it themselves."

"But you've got people around you all the time and knights watching over you. Killing a king is tricky. Maybe they weren't up to the task."

"If they thought themselves incapable, they certainly wouldn't think a human could pull it off."

"Yeah, all right, no need to get nasty."

"I'm not trying to be nasty." He took my hand. "Lock,

what I said in the carriage, I wasn't trying to . . ."

"Be a dick?"

He nodded. "I want you to trust me." He pulled me into an embrace. "I *need* you to trust me. It's important."

"Then show me you're trustworthy."

"How do I do that?"

"Honestly, I don't fucking know. I think it just comes with time. Look, I want to be here—*with you*. All I need is for you to treat me like you want me here too."

"I thought I was doing that."

"Sure, but in a very prison guard sort of way. I want you to treat me as if you want me here but it's my choice to stay."

"It's not your choice." Taroc's voice dropped into a growl and his grip tightened.

"Fuck!" I pushed free of him. "This is exactly what I'm talking about. You act as if you're my master, then expect me to trust you."

"I act as if I'm your king because that is who I am! And you, Locrian, are paying a debt to me. That's why it's not your choice to be here."

"And when will that debt be paid, *Your Majesty*?"

Taroc drew back. "What?"

"If I'm paying a debt, it suggests that it is finite. So when is my debt paid? When do I stop being your dog and start being your man?"

Ren whined.

"Sorry, girl. No offense."

"She can't understand you!" Taroc shouted.

Ren ran to hide behind the throne.

"Great, take it out on the real dog. That's wonderful, Taroc. Real nice. And she can understand more than you think. So can I, for that matter." I started for the door. "It's all very clear to me now."

"Don't you fucking walk away from me!"

I stopped walking.

"Get back here, Lock."

I turned and went to stand before him. "Well? Now what? Do I shake hands? Beg? What's your next command, master?"

For a second, I thought Taroc was going to hit me, but then he closed his eyes, breathed deeply, and shook his head. When he opened his eyes again, he was calm, but his voice was weary, "Do you think it's easy being the King? You have one friend who you trust implicitly, and you think I pity you for it. I don't. I envy you. It is one more than I have."

I blinked.

"I'm surrounded by sycophants and swindlers. People who want to seduce me for their own gains and people who want to kill me. No one wants *me*. They can't because they don't know who I am without the crown. The man within the king. I'm sorry if I get worried that you won't like that man. That if I showed him to you, then released you, you'd leave. I do want you here, and I want you to want to be here. I want you to be the man who knows me, and I want to be the man you trust above all others."

"Well, fuck," I whispered as I slid back into his arms. "Now, you've got me good."

I lifted my face to the King's, and he met me halfway, covering my mouth in a tender kiss that had me clutching at his shoulders and grinding myself against him. His hands slid up and down my back carefully, as if seeking an answer. I replied by drawing back, out of the kiss, and taking his hand to lead him back to the royal dais.

"What are you doing?" Taroc asked as I positioned him in front of his throne.

"Showing you how much I want to stay." I undid his pants and pushed them down.

"Anyone could walk in."

"That's the point." I grinned as I pushed him back. "I don't care."

Taroc sat down with his pants around his ankles and his cock standing at attention just below the hem of his tunic. "Are you sure?"

I got to my knees, took him in hand, and, holding his stare, licked his tip. The taste of him burst across my tongue, and I moaned along with him. The King's hands went to my head, pushing back my hair so he could watch me without impediment. And I gave him a show, sticking out my tongue to lave him before sucking as much of him into my mouth as I could. When he hit the back of my throat, I loosened it and pushed him further in.

"Oh, fuck," Taroc whispered. "Your lips are so strong."

I tightened them even more and felt a thrill go down my spine when he cried out and clenched his hands in my hair. Moaning and sighing, I began to move over him, faster and faster. His cock was dripping wet and the sounds of my mouth on him were so fucking erotic that my dick strained at my pants.

"No, don't make me come." He stopped me. "I want you to ride me."

I sucked my way off him and looked up. "Here?"

"You wanted to make this special. Get up here and show me what you can do."

"Yes, Your Majesty!" I kicked off my boots, then eagerly got out of my pants, tossing them aside before straddling his lap.

"Here." He drew his legs in together tightly. "Get on the seat."

Grinning devilishly, I climbed up on the throne, standing for a second to get my footing. This just so happened to put my raging hard-on in the King's face. Just as I'd hoped, he couldn't resist the invitation and licked my dick. But that wasn't enough. After that first taste, he groaned and went back for another, sucking my entire member into his mouth.

I gripped the back of the throne to keep from falling and tried my best to not face-fuck the Dragon King. But he grabbed my ass and pulled me to him, his greedy mouth sucking me down.

"Stop. Taroc, I'm gonna come," I panted.

He slipped a finger in my ass.

"Taroc!" I shouted as I emptied into his mouth.

And the King drank down every drop.

After he sucked me dry, he eased me down onto his lap, taking my trembling weight in his palms and setting his cock at my hole. Limply, I reached back and helped him gain entry, then groaned as he slipped inside, my dick surging back to life instantly. I'd never had such a rapid recovery before.

"Can you still perform or are you done in by one orgasm, Assassin?" the King drawled, then licked his lips. "I need a lover who can last."

"A challenge, is it?" I smirked as I grabbed the back of the throne again. "As you can see, I've risen to it."

I began to bounce, slowly at first, grinding on his lap until those sexy, glistening lips parted and his head rolled against the throne. Then I sped up. Ecstasy shot through me like an arrow but branched out at its zenith, zinging through my veins and tightening the muscles of my chest and throat. My hands clenched on the throne. The wood groaned along with the King. I pumped faster. Faster.

"Great fuck!" Taroc roared as he lost control and started lifting his hips to meet me mid-drop.

My panting breaths went ragged, the muscles in my thighs began to burn, and still, I bounced on the Dragon King's cock, slamming my ass flat on his thighs to take all of him. The pain in my legs met the pleasure in my channel and bloomed to burst out of my dick, exploding all over His Majesty's fine tunic.

"Don't you dare fucking stop!" he growled as he gripped my ass and took some of my weight.

Whimpering and weak from another climax, I pushed on. In my mind, I begged all the Gods of Serai to make this fucker come. And then, at last, my prayers were answered. The King lurched up, out of his throne, the motion becoming a thrust that speared his cock deep. Standing, clutching me close, he emptied into me over and over, his great body locking up with every hot stream of cum.

I'd never been able to feel my lover's ejaculation before. I'd felt the fullness, but nothing like this. Every nuance of

Taroc's climax rippled through me. His pulsing cock, the twitches of each surge, the heat of his cum, and, of course, that crazy tingling as it absorbed into me. My whole body went into spasm with his release, my dick hardening once more but going straight into orgasm, balls pulled up tight. As he slipped out of me, his cock brushed the skin of my sacs, and the residue of cum on his shaft set my balls to zinging as well.

The Dragon King growled, but it was a low, passionate sound, one of supreme satiation. "Well done, Assassin."

"I swear to your goddess, Taroc, if you pat me on the head like you do Ren, I will smack you."

He chuckled. "It was the furthest thing from my mind." Then he set me down. "Put your pants on."

"Oh? Are you done in by one orgasm, Your Majesty?"

"No. But I want you in my bed next. That fucking throne is uncomfortable."

Chapter Thirty-Five

In the morning, I woke up early and crept into the bedroom I'd been using, carrying my clothes from the night before. From a secret pocket within my vest, I removed the coins and the velvet pouch I'd taken. As I mentioned, the coins were enough to start a new life with, I could even buy a place nicer than Yusef's. But what was in that pouch was even better. When I opened and upended it, glittering jewels cascaded into my palm.

"Holy fuck," I whispered. "Holy fucking fuck! This is enough to set me up for life. Fuck my reputation; I never have to work again."

I flung a look around the dressing room, suddenly paranoid. An assassin always has a place to hide things, but I had to make sure no one was watching me first. I put the jewels back in the pouch, then closed the dressing room door. Once I was assured of privacy, I went to my trunk, pulled everything out, and hit the hidden latch that unlocked the false bottom.

Within the compartment were the few possessions that were priceless to me and my life savings—a Raltven dagger given to me by Fahar when I was inducted into the Wraiths, its corkscrew blade sheathed in a leather tube; the black-gold chain Gren gave me when I completed my apprenticeship, and a leather pouch that contained eight gold, six silver, and twenty-two copper coins in it, most of which was left over from the advance I received to kill Taroc. I put the new gold coins in the leather pouch with the others, placed the velvet pouch beside it, replaced the padding that kept everything from jostling, and clicked the false bottom back in place.

With my wealth secure, I grabbed some fresh clothes and headed into the bathroom to shower. There was an enormous bathtub against one wall, its basin shiny like the inside of a shell, but as much as I would have loved to lay about in hot water for an hour or so, I didn't have the time for that. Instead, I stripped and got into the shower stall, its blue tiles making me feel as if I'd been submerged in the deepest part of the Fresien Sea. I pressed my palms against the wall and bent my head into the spray. The wet heat sluicing over my shoulders loosened my tight muscles. I felt as if I could finally relax, but it had nothing to do with the shower. It was the money. Funny how being rich can take a weight off your shoulders.

When Taroc cast me aside—and he would eventually, no matter how many sweet things he said to me—I wouldn't have to worry about finding work. I could sail off with Teng, go to another kingdom, and build a new life for myself. One that didn't include the Dragon King.

A spear of pain lanced through my chest at the last thought, and I rubbed at my sternum absently. What the fuck was that? Was I . . . ? No, I couldn't be having feelings for him. He was incredibly handsome, undoubtedly the most powerful man in the kingdom, and could fuck like a beast, but he was also a pompous asshole who thought of me as property.

But as soon as I thought those words, I realized they were a lie. Taroc had made it abundantly clear that he didn't think of me as property. Nor had he been a pompous asshole when he confessed that he wanted me to be the one man in his entire fucking kingdom who knew the real him. When I said he had me good now, it had been a subtle confession. So subtle that even I hadn't recognized it. I did have feelings for him. Strong ones.

"Fuck," I whispered. "I think I love him."

Which meant that when Taroc did cast me aside, I wouldn't just need to start a new life, I'd have to deal with the pain of losing him. Yeah, this was gonna hurt. But that was in the future, hopefully a distant one, and I didn't want to waste time worrying about what would or wouldn't happen. If I loved him—and I wasn't sure about that since I'd never been in love before—it was done, no going back. So I might as well enjoy the Dragon King for as long as I could.

A knocking on the bathroom door startled me.

After cursing again, I called out, "Yeah?"

"The King is requesting that you attend him," one of the knights shouted back.

"I'll be right there."

I rinsed, dried off, and dressed as quickly as I could, then sprinted over to the King's bedchambers. He wasn't in them. While I paused in the doorway, I heard voices coming from further down the hallway. I followed them to the dining room and found Taroc at the table, eating breakfast while he spoke with Captain Vettan.

I went to stand beside the Captain to listen in, but as soon as Taroc saw me, he waved me toward a chair across from him where another plate of food had been set. I just stared at it for a second before I realized it was for me. Hesitantly, as if someone might stop me, I went to the chair and sat down. Once I was seated, a servant came forward and poured a cup of coffee for me.

"Thank you," I whispered to the woman. *Holy shit, he really is trying. Did he have feelings for me too?*

"These were the only suspicious items we found, Your Majesty." Captain Vettan set down a piece of paper and a dagger with a nasty glance my way. "The dagger's been cleaned, but I can smell blood on it. Could be nothing, of course."

"Another note?" Taroc asked as he lifted the paper and read it. "What is this? 'Service to be rendered tomorrow night. Please remit payment by midnight tonight or the transaction will be canceled.'"

"Oh, fuck," I whispered.

Taroc focused on me. "You recognize this?"

"I recognize the wording. May I see it?"

The King passed it over to me.

"Yeah, this writing matches Yusef's ledger."

"Yusef wrote this? So this concerns my assassination?"

"I believe so, Your Majesty. A broker doesn't merely arrange jobs, he also ensures payment. Before a job is completed, the broker secures the payment and holds onto it until the kill is verified, then he releases it to the assassin. That way, neither side has to worry about being swindled."

Taroc sat back and stared at the dagger. "Thank you, Captain, that's all for now."

"Shall I have Lord Crushei executed, Your Majesty?"

"Not yet. I need to think about this."

"Your assassin just confirmed that this is proof of Crushei's guilt."

"I said, that's all!"

"Yes, Your Majesty." Captain Vettan bowed and left.

I started to eat.

"You're excused as well, Madeline," Taroc said to the servant.

She curtsied and left.

Ren went to sit beside the door, her stare on the hallway and ears perked.

I kept eating.

"Well?" the King demanded.

"The evidence is considerable."

"But?"

"I don't know. Something feels off to me."

"Any suggestions?"

"Why don't you give it a week? Crushei isn't going anywhere. Leave him in a cell where you can be certain that he has no contact with anyone but your guards."

"And what will that prove?"

"Well, if the murderer is still free, they're going to try again."

"So soon?"

I shrugged. "Maybe not. Maybe they'll have a hard time finding someone to replace Yusef. Maybe they'll have to resort to looking for an assassin themselves. But I figured you wouldn't want to leave Lord Crushei down there for months."

"No, I don't. But I do want to be certain he's guilty before I kill him."

"It would be upsetting to execute him, then have his innocence proven by another assassination attempt."

"Upsetting? It would weigh on me forever, and the Shanba Council would become set against me. Relations with that race would falter, and there could be protests and riots. The wrongful death of one man can topple a kingdom."

"Not in my neighborhood," I muttered.

"Yes, you're right. Many people die every day without anything happening, not even justice. But Crushei is a wealthy wine merchant, beloved by his people, and that makes his death important. It's a harsh truth, but a truth nonetheless. So I must be certain of his guilt."

"Then wait."

"What about your friend? Could he investigate Crushei?"

"I'm sure he could. And he'd probably do a better job than Vettan did with searching Crushei's house."

"Then I want you to hire him for me." He withdrew a gold coin from his pocket and slid it across the table. "Will that be enough?"

"What the fuck?" I picked up the coin. "You just walk around with gold in your pockets?"

"Doesn't everyone?"

"I can't tell if you're joking."

The Dragon King chuckled. "I carry a few in case of emergency."

"In that case, no, it's not enough."

"Why do I get the feeling that I'm being conned?" His smile turned tender as he pulled another coin from his pocket and slid it over to me.

"Because you're not a stupid man." I lifted the second coin. "This one's for me. Finder's fee."

"Uh-huh. I thought as much."

I put both coins in the inner pocket of my jacket. "It's a pleasure doing business with you, Your Majesty."

He suddenly went grim. "Don't tarry, Lock. I'm giving you as much time as you need to speak to this friend of yours, but I won't appreciate it if you abuse my leniency."

"Understood. I'll be as quick as possible."

"Good."

We began to eat in companionable silence and it all felt very unreal. The smart thing to do would be to keep my mouth shut and enjoy the perks he was giving me, but I wasn't that guy. I ate a bit, drank my coffee, then sat back and stared at the King.

"Yes?" Taroc lifted a brow at me.

"This feels strange but good. Thank you."

"We've dined together before."

"Technically, yes, but I've never sat down across from you to eat. I always remain standing."

He frowned, made a few pensive sounds, and said, "I'm sorry. I really have treated you like a pet, haven't I? From now forward, when I dine, I'd like for you to join me. At the table."

I grinned. "Thank you."

Ren whined.

"Ren, I'm sorry, but dogs don't sit at the table," he said.

She whined again.

"That was Lock's entire point."

She widened her eyes at him.

"Oh, very well."

Taroc pulled out a chair, and Ren bounded over and onto it. Thankfully, the King had large chairs, and Ren's fluffy body fit as long as she sat up. Head lifted and tail wagging, she yipped.

I looked from her to Taroc, who was only a few inches taller than Ren with her on that chair, and shook my head. "And I'm back to being treated like the dog."

Chapter Thirty-Six

After breakfast, Taroc and I went below the palace to the subterranean cells where the prisoners were kept. There wasn't a lot of them. As in, there was Lord Crushei. Taroc wasn't big on keeping prisoners, a fact which I found hard to believe since he'd been treating me like one. Yes, I did try to kill him. Fair enough. Still, I was surprised when we reached Lord Crushei's clean cell with its blanket-covered bed and separate bathroom.

"This is nicer than my first home." I waved a hand at the cell beyond the thick bars. "I would have killed for that bed. In fact, I paid for my bed with the proceeds of my first kill, but it's not as nice as this one."

Lord Crushei just stared at me.

"Are you done?" Taroc asked me.

"No, I'll bet his bathroom is bigger than mine too. And I'll bet his water doesn't come out brown before it turns clean."

"You have brown water in your bathroom?"

"There's an easy solution to that; flush the toilet," Lord Crushei said.

"Oh, great! Rich people humor. Yeah, that's really funny. You've never had to worry about rusting pipes a day in your life, have you? Or wonder if the water you're drinking is going to kill you. Or if that shadow moving in the dark is an insect, a rat, or someone coming to kill you and steal what little you have."

Crushei blanched.

"Anyway," I said brightly, "we have more evidence for you to take a look at. A dagger and a note from Yusef, both found in your home."

Taroc held the items up.

Crushei frowned at them. "I don't recognize either of those." He drew closer so he could read the note. "Service to be rendered? That could be anything. Why exactly is this evidence?"

"It's what's done before an assassination is attempted," I said. "The client is advised of when the kill will occur and payment is held by a third party until the death is confirmed."

"I did not hire an assassin!"

"And the blade?" Taroc asked. "This doesn't belong to you?"

Crushei inspected the blade. "That blade is of human make. The wood comes from the Southern Desert of Var. I therefore conclude that it was made by the Wy'Var tribe."

"Something you would know if you purchased it," I said.

"I know the wood because I am a Shanba. And *since* I am a Shanba, I would never buy a dagger of human make. Why would I when I could purchase a superior weapon made by one of my people?"

"Perhaps you bought it just so you could say that when you were confronted with the murder weapon."

"And would this maybe-me have been stupid enough to leave the murder weapon, as you call it, in my home? Or would I throw it in the Vevaren, as everyone else does with things they want to never be found?"

"I agree that the evidence is not enough to prove your guilt," Taroc said.

"But?"

"But I can't be sure. I'm keeping you here for now. If another attempt is made on my life, I'll be certain of your innocence."

"So I must wait here and hope that someone tries to kill you?!"

"That's about it," I said. "Good luck."

"Unless you know of a way to prove your innocence," Taroc said.

Crushei grimaced. "No, Sire, I do not, and it seems as if everyone is against me."

"I am neither for nor against you. I seek the truth, Lord Crushei. You have my word that I will not execute you unless I'm absolutely certain of your guilt."

"Thank you, Your Majesty. Forgive me if I'm not overjoyed by your beneficence."

Taroc laughed. "I'm trying to make you as comfortable as possible."

"Oh! That's why he has a nice bed."

"What is it with you and the bed?" Taroc shook his head at me.

"Asks the man who made me sleep on a pallet."

"Perhaps now is not the time for this conversation, Assassin."

"Fine." I looked back at Crushei. "Are there any members of your staff who might have been persuaded to hide those items in your home?" I asked.

"My staff?" Crushei asked, then frowned. "I suppose anyone can be bribed for the right price but, generally, I trust them. Most came here with me from Tresheha."

"The Shanba city in the Grimcree Forest?"

"Yes, I wanted to export Shanba wine here, but I had to move to Mhavenna to oversee the business. I gave my household the choice to come with me and most of them did."

"I'll speak to them. At the very least, they can vouch for your whereabouts."

"Thank you. Could you tell Alanth to make sure that everyone is paid while I'm here?"

"Alanth?"

"My butler."

"Sure." I nodded.

"If you think of anything that might be helpful to our investigation, ask one of the guards to notify me," Taroc said.

"Thank you, Your Majesty."

We left Lord Crushei to enjoy his nice bed and bathroom.

On the way up to the ground level of the palace, I said to Taroc, "It speaks well of him that his people followed him here."

"And that he wants them looked after while he's

imprisoned," Taroc said. "But you said this was a personal vendetta. A man can be kind to those he favors while still harboring hatred in his heart for his enemies."

"True." We got to the top of the stairs, and I crouched to pet Ren. "Look after our king while I'm gone."

Ren yipped.

"Good girl. I know I can count on you." I stood and met Taroc's stare.

"You're leaving now?"

"If that's all right with you, Your Majesty."

"Look at you; so sweet now that you've gotten your way." He rolled his eyes.

"But have I?" I winked at him and walked away.

"Remember what I said, Assassin," he called after me.

"I will return to you anon, my King."

Chapter Thirty-Seven

On my way out of the palace, I swung by Dr. Chisuren's clinic. As expected, it was modest, with only three beds, all of which were empty, and one nurse. I found the doctor and nurse sitting at a round table in a corner of the room, having tea and reading. Lucky bastards.

"Ah, it's the King's Assassin," the doctor said as he stood. "I attempted to check on you but was unable to locate you."

"There's been some excitement. Would you have time to check on my back now?"

"Yes, of course. This way." He led me to the back of the clinic and through a doorway into an exam room.

A padded table sat along one wall with a stool on one side of it and a chair on the other. The other walls were lined with countertops that had cabinets both below and a few feet above them. Several items sat on the counters but far more could be seen beyond the glass doors of the upper cabinets—neatly labeled jars and boxes of medical paraphernalia. I would have scanned them for any familiar bottles, but I had never gotten a look at the magic potion he used on me. What I did note as the doctor closed the door, was the vast number of bottles there were. There was no way I'd be able to steal all of them, especially not with him there.

"So it's just the two of you?" I asked him.

"The two of us?"

"You and the nurse?"

"Oh! No, there are several doctors and medical assistants on staff here, but we do weekly rotations. This is my week."

"Ah." It was all I could do to hold back a sassy comment about how hard it must be to work a week a month doing absolutely nothing.

"The rest of my month is spent with the Scales," he went on. "The money I make here allows me to donate my time and services to those who desperately need medical help but can't afford it."

Thank the Gods I hadn't opened my big mouth!

"That's incredibly admirable," I said. But I couldn't help testing him. "As a man from the Broken, I know exactly how much your help is needed."

"You're from the Broken?" he asked in surprise.

The surprise wasn't his alone; I was just as shocked that he knew what I was talking about.

"Yes, born and raised."

"I see," he murmured, staring at me as if he were meeting me for the first time. "How amazing it is that you are standing here before me now. I think the Gods favor you."

"If they favored me, I wouldn't have been born in the Broken."

"To make a sword, the metal must be heated and pounded, over and over. The Gods have forged you, Assassin. You should rejoice in their work."

"Oh, I always rejoice in a good pounding." I grinned.

Dr. Chisuren cleared his throat while simultaneously looking disapproving.

"Sorry, Doc. I'm not a religious man."

"Evidently not. But you're right; it is not my place to preach to you. Now, remove your shirt and lie down on the table, please."

"Sure." I took off my jacket, belt, then shirt, laying them in the chair set to one side of the table. "Um, Dr. Chisuren, could I see that potion you used on me?"

He went still. "Which potion?"

"The one that sped up my healing. I'm just curious to see what it looks like."

"Ah, yes, *that* one. Uh . . ." He looked around the cabinets, then went to one and opened the door. The glass bottle he retrieved had a deep blue liquid inside. "This is it." He held it up for me to see.

"Huh, it's a pretty color."

"Yes, very nice." He set it back in the cabinet. "Now, on your stomach, please."

"Yes, Sir." I spun as if to jump up on the table and knocked a jar off the counter.

The jar crashed to the floor between us, shattering to pieces and spilling cotton swabs everywhere.

"Oh, shit!" I leapt back. "I'm so sorry!"

"It's fine." The doctor held up his hands. "Just stay where you are, there's glass everywhere and even though you have shoes on, it could slice through the leather."

"I won't move a muscle."

"I'll find a broom. Shouldn't take me long." He hurried away.

No problem; I wouldn't need long.

I nudged some glass out of the way, took a single step, and opened the cabinet with the potion. There were several bottles of the stuff, but I wanted to be certain I took the right one, so I grabbed the very one the doctor had, then moved one from the back to the front. Done in three seconds, I closed the cabinet, got back into position, and slipped the bottle into my jacket. A quick jerk of my foot put the debris back in place and still, I had a good thirty seconds before the doctor returned with his broom.

"Let me clear the space around your feet and then you can get on the table, out of the way for me to sweep up the rest," he said.

"Sure." I waited for him to sweep a spot clear, then got on the table and laid down. "I'm really sorry, Dr. Chisuren. I should be doing that."

"Nonsense. Accidents happen. There. All done." He left the broom leaning against a counter, guarding the pile of glass and swabs. "When the maids come by to clean later, they can handle the disposal; I just wanted it out of the way." He stepped over and started prodding my back. "Any tenderness?"

"Nope."

"Well, I think this is the fastest check-up I've ever done, but I can see with a single look that you're healed and if you have no internal pain, you should be fine." He tapped my back and stepped away. "Took me longer to sweep." He laughed.

"Thanks, Doc." I climbed off the table. "I thought I felt good, but it's nice to have confirmation."

"No problem. Please, let His Majesty know that I've cleared you and that the, uh, potion has worked."

"Will do." I hurried into my clothes, shook his hand, and headed out of the exam room with him. "Thanks again," I said when we reached the nurse, still seated at the table, then I walked out as casually as I could.

About ten feet away from the clinic, I allowed myself to grin.

Chapter Thirty-Eight

I found Tengven back at the Shrieking Ghost, at his usual table, eating his usual seafood soup, and listening to everyone around him while looking as if he weren't. With a look and a jerk of my head, I indicated that our conversation was better suited to his boat. Teng paid for his meal, and we walked to his ship together, mostly in silence. As someone who made money off the indiscretion of others, Tengven knew when to keep his mouth shut. The only talk was of the safe variety; my health, his crew, his stupid soup.

At last, we were in his cabin, the door shut and the sea wind the only witness to our words.

"I got it." I pulled out the bottle.

"I thought you were going to take all his potions?" Tengven asked.

"Hard to do when he has a collection larger than I could carry. Even harder when I had to steal it practically in front of him."

"You're certain this is the one?"

"I asked him to show it to me first."

"Risky. If he notices that it's missing, he'll know it was you."

I shrugged.

Teng peered at the bottle. "Doesn't look all that exciting." He tucked it in a pocket. "I'll have my guy analyze it."

"There's something else."

"Oh?"

I pulled out the gold coin. "The King would like to hire you."

Instead of looking thrilled, Teng backed away. "To do what?"

"Relax, he doesn't know who you are. I'm playing the role of the hooded man."

"I appreciate that."

"As if I'd ever do anything to put you in danger," I huffed. "I told him you could gather information about Lord Crushei of the Shanba."

"Lord Crushei? The wine merchant?" Teng stepped forward and took the coin. "What does the King want to know about him?"

"If he hired me."

"What?"

"Yasima gave up the hooded man—Lord Yusef Lancarester. Except when we went to arrest him, he was dead. Murdered unprofessionally."

"Well, fuck."

"Yes. That's not all. We found evidence in his home—a log book with the initials of his clients and their targets. He listed the man who hired me as CV."

"Crushei Venlebar. Fuck."

"Yes."

"But there are other men with those initials in this city. I'd wager there's a whole lot of them."

"Yes, but Crushei has a history of butting heads with the King, and we also found a letter in Yusef's desk written by Crushei. It was unaddressed but in it, Crushei asked for help with the King and offered to pay more than the usual rate. And he signed it."

"Who the fuck *writes* to someone about hiring an assassin, then *signs* it?"

"Exactly. It doesn't make sense. When we confronted Lord Crushei, he denied it. He said the letter was one he wrote to the palace steward, Lord Paslan, to request that Paslan arrange an audience for him with the King. Paslan controls the King's public meeting schedule and has been taking bribes to adjust it."

"And why offer to pay more than usual?"

"Crushei just had an argument with the King." I grimaced. "He didn't think the King would agree to see him. Having been a witness to the argument, I'd say he was right to be concerned."

"If Crushei is telling the truth, someone deliberately put that letter in Yusef's desk to implicate him."

"Yes."

"Someone with Crushei's initials."

"Most likely."

"What did the steward say?"

"He admitted to taking bribes and said that Crushei had sent him such letters in the past, but he swore he'd never seen that particular note."

"So, the note was intercepted before it reached the palace."

"Possibly. There's more."

"More?" Teng's eyes widened.

"Once we had Crushei in a cell, his home was searched. They found a dagger with remnants of blood on it and a letter from Yusef. Unsigned, of course, but it was his handwriting, and it advised that the service would be performed the following night if payment was received on time."

"Standard procedure for any kind of criminal work."

"Yes, and pretty fucking damning."

"But you're not convinced."

"Why would Crushei keep that note? And, as he pointed out himself, if the blade is the weapon he used to murder two men, why would he keep that?"

"Two men?"

"A violinist was killed as well, just hours after he told me that he had information about the man who hired me."

"A violinist? Fucking musicians get the best gossip." He grimaced. "Wait, where did you meet a violinist?"

"They had a party at the palace for Ensarena's rite."

"So, the murderer was at the palace for the rite."

"Yes, I believe so. Although that hardly narrows it down, everyone with any bit of money or influence was there. Oh, and the dagger we found in Lord Crushei's house was made by humans. Crushei recognized the wood and swore that he would never buy a human-made dagger."

"As offensive as this may sound to you, Lock, that's not an uncommon attitude among the other races."

"Yes, I know. I'm inclined to believe him, Teng."

"I'll look into him. It could take some time but with this,"—he held up the coin—"I'll have what I need to loosen the tongues that might not otherwise wag."

"And there's another one for you if you succeed."

"Sea serpent shit! Are you fucking with me?"

"Nope. One now, another when you're done."

Tengven laughed. "This is your doing."

"I might have told the King that the other coin was for me." I shrugged. "My finder's fee."

Teng's face softened. "You didn't have to tell me about it."

"I may have stolen some coins from Yusef's safe when the King wasn't looking." I grinned. "I don't need the gold, Teng. I negotiated it for you."

Tengven laughed uproariously. "Always thinking ahead, brother." He hugged me, slapping my back. "Well done. So, you've got a plan for when he's done with you, eh?"

"As if I'd rely on the kindness of Dragons." I snorted.

Teng chuckled. "My offer still stands. You can sail with us the next time we take the Lu-Ken out."

"I may just take you up on that, but I'm hoping it won't

be anytime soon."

"Enjoying yourself, eh?"

"He's got a big dick, and he knows how to use it." I grinned. "Yeah, I'm enjoying myself."

Teng laughed again. "I wish you the best with him, brother." He slipped the coin into a pocket. "In the meantime, I'll find out everything there is to know about Crushei Venlebar."

"Thank you."

"Fuck, you've already paid me ten times what I would have asked a stranger for. I should be thanking you. How about a drink before you go? I've got some Hesian wine."

"That's twenty times what you would have asked," I shot back with a smirk. "And the King gave me leave to take all the time I need. Pour the wine, brother."

Chapter Thirty-Nine

Despite what I'd said to Teng, I only stayed an hour. I'd promised to be back soon, and I didn't want to ruin this new accord I'd formed with Taroc. However, an hour with a Neraky pirate and his stash of Hesian wine was more than long enough to get me tipsy. Maybe a bit more than tipsy.

I staggered off the ship and headed to a busier street to hail a carriage. It was still daylight so there would be some drivers brave enough to enter the Broken. Thoughts swirling in the alcohol soup of my brain, I went from contemplating Taroc's rare smile to the asshole who wanted to make sure he never smiled again. Then back to Taroc. Then my money—I had so much of it now! Then Taroc. Then oh, look, is that a bird? That thing better fly the fuck out of the Broken before some starving kid hits it with a rock.

To say my senses weren't at their sharpest, would be an understatement. So, I didn't hear the footsteps that would have warned me of someone coming up behind me. I only felt the blow to the back of my head, some brief pain, then everything went black.

Eventually, a rough hand yanked me out of unconsciousness, shaking me awake.

"What the fuck?!" I shoved my attacker away as I blinked my eyes open. Then I saw who it was. "Taroc?"

The King grabbed me by the front of my tunic and hauled me to my feet. With a shove toward his carriage, he growled, "Get the fuck inside."

I caught myself on the doorframe and climbed in, stumbling toward a bench. Ren moved out of the way, jumping up onto the seat across from me.

"Hey, girl," I mumbled and collapsed onto the cushion.

Taroc stormed in, slammed the door shut, and smacked the roof. The carriage lurched forward, sending me tumbling and Ren jumping to the floor. The King caught me and shoved me back onto the seat.

"I trusted you," he growled. "And this is what you do?"

"What the fuck are you talking about?"

He wrinkled his nose and turned his head to the side. "You reek of wine."

"Yeah, I had a bottle with my friend." I rubbed at my head, but there wasn't even a tender spot. I was certain I'd been hit.

"You had a bottle? A fucking bottle of wine while you were supposed to be hiring him to investigate Crushei?"

"I did hire him. Then he offered me some wine. Fuck, Taroc, someone hit me over—"

He cut me off with, "Did you steal a bottle of medicine from Dr. Chisuren?"

I winced. "All right, yes, I took a bottle of that magic potion he used on me."

Taroc's face squished up, his eyes twitching and his skin turning pink.

"My friend wanted it. I told him what it did for me, but he'd never heard of such a thing. He asked me to get him a bottle so he could have someone analyze it."

"I trusted you, sent you out on your own, gave you gold, and you steal a precious potion from my physician, then get so drunk that you pass out in an alley?"

"I didn't pass out!"

"Oh, and what would you call it?"

"Someone hit me over the head!"

He scowled and looked me over. "Were you robbed?"

"Fuck!" I patted my pockets and found the few tools I'd brought with me. Then, with a sigh of relief, I pulled out the gold coin. "No. It looks as if they just bashed me over the head and left."

"Sure. Someone saw you and thought, 'hey, that man looks like someone I need to hit,' and they knocked you unconscious, dragged you into an alley, and left you there for the fun of it."

"Fuck you, Taroc! I just got assaulted and you won't even believe me?"

"I found you reeking of wine in an alley."

"And I'm telling you that someone put me there."

"That's really fucking convenient."

I made a huff of amazement and shook my head. "You're willing to believe Crushei, but you won't believe me?"

"I'm willing to *investigate* Crushei's claims, and you are not in jeopardy of being executed."

"Well, that's a relief," I muttered.

"Is that some kind of twisted human humor or did you really think that I'd kill you after taking you as my lover?"

"I don't know what to think now." I waved a hand at him. "Something horrible happens to me, and you act as if I'm the villain."

"You are the villain! You're a fucking assassin and now you've proven to be a thief too!"

"You weren't complaining about my thieving skills when I opened that safe for you. And what happened to your whole, 'I'm a Dragon, I'm a killer too?'"

"That was before I learned that in humans, it's an indication of nefariousness."

"Nefariousness? Really? Dragons can kill and it's honorable but when humans do it, we're automatically nefarious?"

"You take money to kill people. That is the very definition of a nefarious deed."

"Oh, fuck you. Yes, I kill people for money, but I make it quick and painless, can you say the same about the people you've killed?"

"I killed to become king!"

"And I killed to eat!"

Ren whined.

"Silence, Ren!" Taroc snapped.

"Don't yell at her for being upset when you act like a fucking madman!"

"I'm the only rational one in this carriage!"

"I can't do this," I whispered suddenly, my whole body deflating. "I'm done."

"What?"

"I can't be with you anymore," I said while something inside me shattered. "You tell me that you're going to treat me better, then the very next day you're back to acting as if I'm scum. I'm done, Your Majesty. I'll be your assassin but not your lover. Find another asshole to take your shit." I paused, replaying that last line in my head, and snorted a mirthless laugh. "Not literally, of course."

Taroc stared at me for five long seconds. During those seconds, the carriage stopped. We were back at the palace.

"You're dismissed from my service, Assassin."

"Excuse me?"

"Report to Captain Vettan when your friend completes their work for me, but that is the last I want to do with you. Gather your things and get the fuck out of my palace." With that, he climbed out of the carriage.

Ren whined at me, then jumped out after her master.

I got out, stared at Taroc's back, and said, "With pleasure, Your Majesty."

He flinched but kept walking.

Chapter Forty

I could barely process what was happening. I went to the guest room I'd been using, packed a few changes of clothes, and left the rest. I carried my trunk out to find Captain Vettan waiting for me in the corridor, a smirk on his face.

"So, you've shown your true colors at last, Assassin."

"Fuck you, Vettan." I brushed past him. "I've always been honest about who I am."

He turned and followed me out of the royal suite. A group of knights waited outside. I thought maybe I'd get thrown in a room and beaten before I left, but they only escorted me to the front gates as if I might steal something on my way out. Then they stood there, barring the way back.

I hailed a carriage, got in, and as I was shutting the door, I called out, "Good luck keeping him safe now, assholes!"

I shut the door on their furious faces and the carriage headed off toward the Broken. Only then, in the quiet of the carriage, did I really start to think.

What if the attack had been an attempted murder? Sure, it had been the middle of the day when I'd been assaulted, but in the Broken, that wasn't so shocking. That being said, if they had hit me over the head and dragged me into an alley to finish me off, then a group of people happened by, my potential murderer would probably have abandoned me. Conclusion, I may be in danger.

The problem was that I had this constriction in my chest that demanded all of my attention. If I let up on it just a fraction, I suspected I would start screaming and never stop. So I wasn't afraid; I was in too much pain for that. But I still had some sense left in my head.

I leaned out the window and said to the driver, "Change of plans. Take me to the Enchanted Swan."

"Yes, Sir," his tone and the loosening of his shoulders expressed his relief of being saved from entering the Broken.

The carriage slowed and turned in the direction of a much nicer part of the city. The Enchanted Swan wasn't the best hotel in Mhavenna, but it was close. Fancy enough that they had their own security. Plus, I doubted anyone would expect me to be there.

The carriage stopped before the immaculate stone steps of the Enchanted Swan and a uniformed man came down from its gilded doors to open the carriage door for me.

"Welcome to the Enchanted Swan, Sir," he said as I stepped out.

"Thank you. I have a trunk on the seat."

"I will fetch it." He leaned in, pulled out the trunk that I had refused to strap to the outside of the carriage for obvious reasons, and carried it up the stairs for me. At the top, he set it down so he could open the door. "Keth will see you to the front desk, Sir."

He waved another man over, and that man took my trunk.

"Thank you." I followed Keth and my luggage to an expanse of polished wood where a human woman waited to check me in.

I'd learned enough in my time at the palace to fit in there and now, I had enough money to afford it. I secured a room, received a key, and Keth took me upstairs to a modest suite. I may be wealthy now, but I'd been poor for too long to spend frivolously.

Keth set my trunk in the closet, and I gave him a copper for his effort. That appeared to be the proper procedure because he nodded his thanks, advised me that one pull of the service cord would bring one of the staff to my door, then left. With the closing of the door, I plopped down on the bed, laid back, stared at the pretty moldings on the ceiling, and willed myself not to cry.

Turns out, my will isn't that strong.

When I was done with that, I sniffed and replayed it all in my head. Everything we'd said and the way Taroc had looked. He had been so determined that I was in the wrong. He wouldn't even entertain the possibility that I was telling the truth. Yes, I stole the medicine, but so what? It was a bottle of medicine. I'm suddenly nefarious because I palmed a potion? What the fuck? And who the fuck uses the word nefarious?

"Fucking Dragons," I growled as I sat up.

Then I realized that I was free. And rich. And fucking free. Taroc had let me go!

I looked around the luxurious room. There was absolutely nothing for me to do there besides sleep, eat, and bathe. Basic things, but I hadn't been able to fully enjoy them in a while. Yes, I'd had a meal with Taroc, but that was one meal. All the others had been spent on my feet, and I couldn't remember the last time I'd bathed or slept without being prepared to jump to the King's defense. Yeah, a bath sounded amazing.

The bathroom wasn't as nice as His Majesty's, but it was mine for the time being, and no one would come pounding on the door telling me that the King had summoned me. I was out of it, all of that mess. No more worrying about finding whoever hired me. No more worrying about what Taroc would do with me after we did. Or if Taroc really wanted me. Or if Taroc were going to cast me aside. Taroc, Taroc, Taroc. I'd been so focused on him that I'd lost sight of me.

Me time.

I ran a bath. Because I fucking could. I'd never had a bathtub before, not unless you count a bucket, and I'd never had the time to use the one in my guest room at the palace. It was amazing. Sheer bliss. I lounged in that hot water, rubbing expensive soap over my skin until I was wrinkly and as relaxed as I could get after being cast aside.

Hold on, I was the one who had done the casting, not Taroc. He'd thrown a temper tantrum about it and kicked me out of the palace, but I had ended our relationship. There was a certain satisfaction in that, although it didn't do much to ease the ache in my chest. Still, it was something. Freshly bathed, I got out of the tub, dried off, and wondered what rich people did when they were bored.

"I could eat," I said to my reflection in the gilded mirror over the bathroom sink.

After putting on one of the outfits the King had bought me, I locked my hotel room and went downstairs. I could have ordered some food brought to my room, but I needed to be around other people. Eating in solitude would not alleviate the clawing ache in my chest. I needed to find a distraction. Once downstairs, I wandered around the lobby. Well-dressed people were coming and going, paying me no mind, but their presence alone was calming. I wove my way through them, then edged along the perimeter where a few small shops sold fancy, rich-people things like expensive perfume and frilly hats. There was also a restaurant.

I hadn't eaten anything since breakfast, but all that drama with Taroc had suppressed my appetite. I began to rethink my decision to eat, but then a mouthwatering scent wafted out of the restaurant's open door. My stomach rumbled, my appetite returning with a vengeance, and I headed inside eagerly.

A lot of white greeted me. White table linens, white furniture, white flowers. It would have been blinding if they hadn't kept the lights low. As it was, it was perfectly lit, the color alone adding a certain amount of illumination. The place was nearly full, but a waiter greeted me at the door immediately, showed me to a small table, and discretely removed the other place setting. He left me with a menu and a promise to return shortly.

I sat there, staring at the empty chair across from me for a moment, then mentally slapped myself. This was my first time in a nice restaurant where they covered the tables in cloth, set out silverware, and had crystal glasses for water. For water! I wouldn't let Taroc ruin it for me.

The King didn't know it, but he had released me from his service, fully prepared to enter the upper class. I was one of them now, thanks to Yusef's money and the manners I'd learned by watching the courtiers. I couldn't stay in Mhavenna, someone would eventually recognize me and out me as an assassin, but if I laid low and didn't speak to any of those rich assholes, I could blend in with them for a while. Then I'd sail off with Teng. In another kingdom, I could use my wealth to become whoever and whatever I wanted.

"Are you ready to order, Sir?" The waiter was back.

"Uh." I looked at the menu. Half the items I didn't recognize and the other half had names I couldn't pronounce. "This is my first time here, and I'd like to sample your best dishes. What would you recommend?"

The waiter beamed at me and rattled off about if I preferred meat to fish and so on. It would have bored me if I hadn't needed the guidance so desperately. I chose the meat option and the appetizer he recommended, declined a salad, but let him pick a bottle of wine for me. The man hummed as he left, he was so damn pleased with himself.

"You made his day," a man at a nearby table said.

I looked over at him. He was alone (which made me feel a little better about myself), human, blond, handsome, and young. Oh, and physically fit. Very fit.

"Why is that?" I asked.

He shrugged. "Most of the people who eat here are..."

"Dicks?"

The man laughed. "Yes, dicks. I doubt they ever ask his opinion on anything, much less follow his recommendations."

"Honestly, I was baffled by the menu."

"It's like reading another language, isn't it? With some dishes, it really is another language. I mean, why can't they write everything in Seraian? We all speak it, for fuck's sake. Why do they think that giving a dish a Parsanian name makes it more appealing? There aren't any Parsans in this city; those humans hate everyone, even other humans. I certainly don't want to eat their food."

I burst out laughing.

He grinned at me. "I'm Greven."

"Locrian," I said. "Uh, would you like to join me?"

"Yes, actually, I would." Greven motioned at the waiter, who came hurrying over, then told him he was moving to my table.

The waiter moved Greven's place setting over to my table as if such requests were made all the time. After everything was laid out perfectly, he inclined his head to us and went to lay fresh place settings on Greven's abandoned table.

There went the whole laying low idea. But fuck it, Greven was hot and into me. I could tell by the way he leaned forward and kept looking at my lips. We finished the bottle of wine I ordered—that would be my second of the day, but who the fuck cared?—and then he paid the bill. I didn't try to dissuade him. As I've said before, I may be rich now, but I'd been poor too long to spend frivolously. If someone wanted to buy me a meal, I'd take it.

And since he'd been nice enough to pay for me, I decided to go for it. There's nothing like a good fuck to get you over an old lover. I tried to think of a come-on line a rich person would say and went with, "Would you like to see my room?"

It did the trick.

"I absolutely would."

We went upstairs and before we reached my door, Greven had taken my hand. Grinning, we went inside, closed the door, and attacked each other.

"Hold on," I broke away from his lips to say. "Are you a top?"

Greven went still. "No, I prefer to receive."

"Fuck." I let him go.

"You too? I thought you had a more..."

"Top attitude?" I asked. "Nope. I like to take the dick, not give it."

"Well, we could always suck each other a bit and tongue each other's assholes. I'll finger you too if you like."

"I *do* like." I grinned and started to strip.

With a laugh, Greven stripped as well, revealing a slim, tight body. His cock wasn't all that impressive but since he wasn't fucking me with it, what did I care? Less for me to gag on.

"Nice dick," he said as we crawled onto the bed. "Bring it here."

We laid on our sides, heads to cocks, and as I moved closer to his, an image of Taroc bloomed in my mind. His eyes were glowing, his magnificent body bare, and his cock hard. I jerked back.

"What's wrong?" Greven asked. "Oh, great Gods, do I smell bad?"

"No." I chuckled. "Sorry, just a muscle spasm."

"Oh, all right." He grinned and moved toward my cock again.

I rolled away from him in a spasm, my body acting all on its own, almost as if I'd touched fire.

"What the fuck? Are you playing with me?"

"No, I—" Taroc's face filled my mind again, and I slammed my hands against my temples. "Fuck!"

Greven rose onto an elbow to look at me. "Damn it all! You just broke up with someone, didn't you?"

I lowered my hands, grimaced, and admitted, "Yeah. Today."

"What the fuck? Really?"

"A few hours ago."

"Shit." He sat up, sighed, and smacked the bed beside him. "Sit down. Let's talk it out."

"Talk it out?" I laughed.

"Yeah. You tried to fuck him away and that didn't work, did it?"

"No."

"So tell me what happened. Maybe you just need someone to listen."

I sat down beside him heavily. "I don't fucking know what happened."

"Tell me what you do know."

"He's a really important man, and I'm, well, not."

"That's a bunch of shit, but go on."

"I went out this morning to see a friend. I told my lover that I wouldn't be that long, but he said to take all the time I needed."

"Hold on, did he control where you went and who you saw?"

"Not in the way you think." I waved my hand. "That's a long story, and I don't want to get into it."

"All right. So, you went to see your friend."

"Yeah, and we had a bottle of wine."

"Uh-huh."

"He has a boat at one of the east docks."

"You've got some interesting friends."

"Yes, well, since you seem familiar with that part of town, I don't have to tell you that it's not the safest place to walk around when you're drunk."

"Oh, fuck, did you get robbed?"

"No, that's the weird thing. Someone hit me over the head and dragged me into an alley, but they didn't take my money. And I had gold on me."

"Now that is very interesting." Greven drew up a knee and propped his arm on it. "Tell me more."

"I woke up to the ... *him* shaking me. He was really mad. He thought I had passed out, drunk. We got into a horrible argument, and it felt as if he had already made up his mind about me before he'd even found me. He wouldn't listen to anything I said. Scorned me for trying to tell him that I was hit over the head."

"Did you show him the injury?"

I grimaced. "I didn't have one. It's odd. I was hit hard enough to black out. There should have been something."

"That is odd. But you said you were drinking; it wouldn't have taken much to put you out."

"That's a good point."

"And I'm sorry to say this, but I can see why he didn't believe you if you didn't even have a bump to show him."

"Yeah, I guess."

"However, as your lover, he should have taken you at your word."

"Thank you!" I said with a huff.

"Unless you've given him a reason not to trust you."

"Ugh, you were doing so well, Greven."

He laughed. "I'm trying to help you see what happened as accurately as possible. It's hard to be unbiased when you're involved, but even harder when everything is so fresh. You need a neutral perspective."

"And what does your neutrality think?"

"Well, regardless of what he should or shouldn't have done, the whole attack has made me suspicious. You said he's an important man. Would he have enemies or maybe an ex-lover who would want to break you up?"

I went still. "Holy fuck, I've been set up. I thought maybe someone was trying to kill me, but what if their goal had been for him to find me passed out in that alley, just as he had?"

"You said that it seemed as if he'd already made up his mind," Greven reminded me. "That sounds to me as if someone prepped him."

"Prepped him?"

"They got him worked up about you before he went looking."

"Shit. You're right."

"Do you know anyone who would do that?"

I rolled my eyes. "I could write a list as long as my dick."

He snickered. "That's a nice-sized list."

"Shit, I'm sorry about this." I waved at our nudity.

"Don't be. This is still a lovely night for me."

"Night?" I glanced at the window. "Shit. Now, I'm losing track of time."

"Are you sure you don't have a head injury?"

"Yeah, I'm sure."

"Any nausea, blurred vision, or dizziness?"

"No. Really, I'm fine. This Neraky doctor injected me with a magic healing potion the other day when I, uh, fell and hurt my back. I think maybe it's still having an effect on me. That would explain why there was no bump on my head."

"A magic healing potion?" Greven laughed.

"Yeah, I had the same reaction, but an injury that should have taken weeks to heal was gone in less than a day."

Greven went still. "First of all, I still find that hard to believe. I'm a doctor, Locrian, and I have never heard of a Neraky healing potion. Second, that is the second injury you've mentioned to me. How exactly did you fall?"

"It was just an accident."

"Uh-huh. Was his fist involved in this accident?"

"No." I held up my hands. "It's not like that. I don't do abusive relationships. Life is abusive enough as it is."

Greven snorted. "Ain't that the truth." Then he looked me over. "So, what are you going to do?"

"About whoever set me up?"

"Yes."

"Fuck if I know. Frankly, if it was so easy for him to believe them over me, I don't think I want him back."

Greven nodded. "Still, doesn't he deserve to know that someone deliberately broke you up?"

"Maybe."

"And with that, I'm going to leave so you can cry." He got up and started getting dressed.

I burst out laughing. "You don't have to go."

"I think I do. Why don't you take a bath and try to relax? The urge to scream will pass."

"Holy fuck, you're good."

"I've been there." He put on his pants, tunic, and boots, then hung his jacket and belt over his arm. "If you want some company for breakfast, I'll be taking mine in the restaurant tomorrow around nine. But I won't hold it against you if you don't show."

"Thank you. I don't know if I'll be up by nine, I'm planning to get really drunk tonight, but if I am, I'll be there."

Greven chuckled. "Good luck, Locrian. If I were you, I wouldn't let some scumbag break up my relationship and get away with it, regardless of what I wanted from my ex. But you won't feel up to doing anything for a while, and that's all right. Just be kind to yourself right now. And if you do experience any kind of unusual symptoms like those I mentioned, I'm in room 203, just down the hall. Or see another doctor, but don't take chances with a head injury."

"Yes, Dr. Greven." I grinned. "It was nice to meet you."

"You too, Locrian. Goodnight." With one last glance at my dick and a disappointed shake of his head, he left.

"Goodnight."

After he left, I stared at the door. I wasn't the kind of man to let someone get away with fucking me over either, but Greven was right; I also wasn't up for dealing with that shit at the moment. Instead, I crawled under the covers and cried, just as the doctor predicted.

Chapter Forty-One

I let myself wallow another day, holing up in my hotel room with good food and a lot of wine. I didn't even have to fetch the food and wine. I simply pulled a cord, someone came to my door, I told them what I wanted, and they brought it to me. Being rich was spectacular. But there was only so much wallowing I could do. I'm just not that guy.

Despite the ache in my chest that hadn't lessened one single bit, I got up the next morning, showered, dressed, and pulled the cord to request that breakfast be delivered to my room. I'd gotten lucky with Greven, but I wasn't about to risk showing my face in that restaurant again. After breakfast, I went downstairs, and the doorman hailed a carriage for me. The driver looked surprised when I told him to take me to the east docks.

"That's a bad part of Mhavenna, Sir," he said.

"Yes, I'm aware. Thank you for your concern, but I'll be fine." I climbed into the carriage.

"It's your funeral," he muttered as he closed the door.

I chuckled to myself, wondering what he'd say if I told him I'd been born in the Broken. He probably would have kicked me out of the carriage.

Since it was still early, I went to the Lu-Ken first. There was very little activity on the main deck when I arrived, some of the sailors smoking their first pipe of the day with a cup of coffee while others lazed in the sun. The Neraky loved to sunbathe. When I boarded, no one stirred beyond waving a greeting at me.

"He's in his quarters," one of them called out.

"Thanks." I waved and headed to the captain's cabin. I knew better than to barge in unannounced, especially at that time of day, so I knocked and waited.

After several minutes, a gruff, "What the fuck d'ya want?" came through the door.

"Teng, it's Lock."

"Lock? Shit. Give us a minute."

Us. Right. I moved back and flattened myself against the wall. A few minutes later, the door opened and three women slipped past me—an Argaiv and two humans—all smiles, pretty perfume, and fluttering fabric. They pulled their cloaks tight around themselves and hurried up to the deck. And not a single one of them was a whore. Teng was magical with the ladies. Three was a slow night.

"All clear?" I asked as I poked my head around the door.

Teng was stretching and yawning in bed, still on his back amid the rumpled sheets. "Yeah. Shout for some coffee, will ya?"

I leaned out into the hallway again. "Coffee!" Then I shut the door and went to sit at the small dining table. "I left him."

Teng jerked upright. "What did you say?"

"Fuck, Teng. I think I was set up."

He closed his eyes, rubbed at them, then climbed out of

bed naked. Although Teng had a beautiful body, I looked away; you don't ogle your friends. He stumbled over to a pile of clothes, found his pants, and pulled them on. Then he fell into the seat across from me.

"Could you please start at the beginning, then work your way to the middle before getting to the end? You know, as a normal person does."

"Sorry." I grimaced. "I'm a little fucked up right now."

"No shit. It's too soon for me to have anything on Crushei, so I hope you weren't expecting—"

"No, I just needed a friend. And I have another job for you." I pulled out Taroc's remaining gold coin. "Here, you can have this now."

"Lock." His expression went concerned, but Teng will always be a pirate before anything else, and his hand automatically took the coin and pocketed it. "What happened?"

I told him everything, in order, as requested. "I need you to ask around the docks and find out if anyone saw the guy who assaulted me."

"It happened on the docks?"

"No, but nearby. Hursa Lane."

"Shit, they waited until you were just out of sight of the ship."

I nodded. "It's gotta be one of Taroc's courtiers or maybe even a soldier. I wouldn't put it past Captain Vettan. In fact, he was smirking at me when he escorted me out of the palace, looking really fucking pleased with himself."

"The fucker." Teng shook his head. "You got it. I'll have a

name for you in a few hours."

"Shit, that's fast."

"It's the east docks, Lock. Someone must have seen the attack and everyone down here is willing to talk for coin."

"Thank you."

"I can't believe he let you go."

"Me either."

"And I can't believe *you* broke up with *him*."

I made a face at him.

"Well, he is the King. I thought you'd hold on to His Majesty's cock until he pried your fingers off it."

"He was such a fucking asshole, Teng. I couldn't handle the ups and downs anymore."

"I don't blame you."

A knock came at the door. "Coffee!"

"Enter!" Teng said.

One of the younger crew members came in with a tray of coffee and some Neraky breakfast items. Some of those items were still wriggling. I sighed when I saw the plate of seafood. Of course, for the Neraky, it was simply food.

"Thank you," Teng said as he helped the boy get everything off the tray. He made sure to put the plate of wriggles—I mean nibbles—on his side of the table.

"Captain, the alchemist is here to see you," the boy said.

"Already?" Teng perked up. "Send him in."

"Yes, Captain."

"The alchemist?" I asked as the kid left.

"The man who I hired to analyze that magic potion you gave me." Teng grinned. "We're about to find out exactly what's in it."

"Whatever it is, it's incredible stuff. I didn't even have a bump after I woke up in that alley. I'm sure it's because of that potion."

A man suddenly strode in, no knocking. He was dressed well and groomed—not at all how I imagined an alchemist would look. *Weren't they supposed to wear robes and have a beard?*

He strode up to the table in a huff, smacked the bottle of potion down, and glared at Teng. "Is this supposed to be a joke?"

Scowling, Teng stood and faced the man. "What do you mean?"

"That is a bottle of srapa venom."

"No, there's venom in it, but I was told that's a magical healing potion," I said.

The man affixed his razor stare on me. "I assure you, there is nothing but venom in that bottle. Whoever told you this is a magic potion is a charlatan, and you are a fool for believing him." He swung his stare back to Teng. "Do not waste my time again, Tengven." With that, the man turned on his heels and left.

I stared at the bottle.

Teng went to shut the door behind the alchemist, then came back to the table and sat down, his expression pensive.

"Do you think the doctor deliberately showed you the wrong bottle?"

"I don't know. Something feels off about all of this. It's like I have all the pieces of a puzzle but don't know where they go."

"Do you think your healing has something to do with the attack?"

"Yes, but I can't figure out what."

"Assassination attempts, magical healing potions that aren't magical, a possibly innocent Shanba lord, and you, left in an alley to be found by your lover like a common dock drunkard."

I leaned forward. "Taroc knew about me stealing that potion too. He might have believed me if I hadn't done that."

"I'm sorry, Lock."

"No, don't be. It wasn't a big deal. He knew I was capable of theft. I opened Yusef's safe for him."

"Yes, but he didn't know that you were capable of stealing *from him*," Teng said gently.

"I didn't steal from him; I stole from his . . ." I blinked and leaned back in my chair. "Oh, I see."

"Yeah." Tengven grimaced. "I feel responsible."

"Don't. It was my decision." I scowled. "Do you think it was the doctor?"

"Who attacked you? I doubt it, but I suppose anything is possible."

"Why wouldn't he show me the potion he used on me?"

"Unless that was the potion he used on you." Teng stared at me.

"But it was only srapa venom. How did I heal so fast?"

"That might be the question you really need to be asking."

"What the fuck is going on?!"

"I don't know, but I've got this tickle in my gut, Lock."

"No!" I pointed at him. "No, Teng, no tickle. I'm not ready to run. Yes, I will sail with you. I will go somewhere else and start over. But first, I need to know what happened here. I'm involved in this, Teng. Someone has fucked with me, and I can't let that stand."

"Then I will help you, brother."

"Thank you."

Teng nodded and poured me a cup of coffee. "Here. Drink this while—damn it." He set the coffee pot down and snatched up something that had wriggled its way off his plate and was making a run for it. Or a squirm for it. "Gotcha!"

I stared forlornly at the squirming thing, feeling a strange kinship with it. When Teng popped it in his mouth and began to chew, I hoped it wasn't a sign that I was headed for the same fate.

Chapter Forty-Two

Teng was right; we had an answer within an hour. The problem was that the person who had attacked me had been cloaked and masked. All we got on them was that they were tall. Could it have been another assassin? Sure. It could have been anyone over six feet.

"That's it!" I stood up. "I'm a fucking assassin; most of my work is surveillance. I'll find out who fucked me over on my own."

"How?" Teng asked.

"The same way I prepared to kill the King. I'm going to spy on the palace."

"Good luck."

"If you find out anything, either on my attacker or Crushei, send a message to the Enchanted Swan."

Tengven let out an impressed whistle. "You're staying at the Swan? Well, la-dee-da. Someone has grown accustomed to the finer things."

"Someone wanted to be as safe as possible."

Teng nodded. "You always have a bunk here, brother."

"Forgive me, but I'd like to put off swaying in a hammock in a room full of farting Nerakians for as long as possible."

Teng laughed. "We can't help it, it's the fish. It gives us nasty farts."

"Yes, that's my point." I waved goodbye and left.

Half an hour later, I was back at the Swan, getting dressed in black. I fastened on my assassin vest and suddenly felt better. I had a plan, an action to perform, and it was something I was good at.

I waited until it was full dark and left the hotel. I didn't hire a carriage. Instead, I walked to the palace and strolled around the back. Some work had been started on capping the walls, but it hadn't been completed yet. I was betting that was the case for all the changes I recommended. When I made it over the wall unseen, I was both relieved and annoyed at how easy it was. There was a guard posted at the top of the back tower, but he never even glanced my way. Unbelievable. I had to resist the urge of shooting him with an arrow.

First, I went to the King's garden. I had no intentions of spying on Taroc, he'd probably be fucking someone else, but the garden shed was a perfect place to stow my cloak as I roamed the grounds. Cloaks are great for hiding within but not so good when you're going to be sneaking about amid plants and scaling walls.

I climbed onto the roof of the shed, slipped out of my cloak, and pulled up the lower half of my mask. Black, of course, and made of stretchy fabric, it was a tube that covered me from just below my eyes to the base of my neck where my tunic took over. A rigid panel over my nose and two small holes beneath kept the material from smothering me. For times like this, when I went without the cloak and its hood, I had another piece that fastened over the lower one, covering my hair and forehead so that only my eyes showed. I put that into place as well.

Granted, I could have left the cloak behind the shed, or even behind a bush, but leaving it on the roof ensured that no one happened upon it. I was about to climb down when the lights came on in His Majesty's bedroom. I paused, my back to the room. Shivers ran down my spine and my muscles locked up. Looking was a bad idea. Nope, not going to do it. I crouched and grabbed the ledge, preparing to leap.

A roar rent the quiet night and spun me around.

As I gaped behind my mask, the Dragon King proceeded to tear apart his bedroom. My view was limited to the windows to either side of the balcony doors, but it was enough for me to see that the King had lost his fucking mind. Ren ran into the hallway, remaining within sight of her master but out of the combat zone. Things shattered, wood and stone included, and debris went flying. I dropped onto my ass, staring at the scene in shock.

"What the fuck?" I whispered.

Claws tipped Taroc's hands, and he used them to shred wooden furniture as easily as he did the bed linens. His tunic caught on something, and he tore it from his body with another roar, arching backward and shaking his head so that his hair tossed about him. Muscles bunched and veins stood out on his throat as he lowered his head and bared his teeth. I'd never seen him in such a terrifying state. It was as if he were facing off with an invisible opponent.

Then Taroc lifted the remains of the bed and chucked it through the balcony doors.

"Holy fuck!" I jerked back.

The doors exploded in all directions as a chunk of bed frame tumbled to the garden below. With my new unimpeded view, I watched Taroc fall to his knees, cover his face with his hands, and start to cry. From terrifying to pitiful in three seconds. Hunched forward, hair hanging around his face, his whole body shook with his sobs.

Breath ragged, loud in the sudden quiet, I got to my feet. Every instinct I had shouted at me to go to Taroc. To climb up to that balcony, walk inside, and wrap my arms around him. Tell him I was back and I wasn't leaving ever again. But then Ren ran forward and licked his face.

Taroc shuddered, one arm going around the dog to pull her close, then just sat there and cried into her fur.

Maybe this wasn't about me. I was being a fucking narcissist to think it was. Taroc would never cry over me. No, this had to be something else. Maybe it was everything; the assassination attempts, Crushei's possible innocence, and my leaving. I was the pebble that tumbled the rock pile. Nothing but the impetus that brought him to this.

Yep, that's what I was going to tell myself.

I climbed down and walked determinedly away from the sobbing king. Did a part of me feel glad that he was upset? Yeah, I sure as fuck did. My insides were being torn apart by his pain, but there was still a seed of smugness in there. A little fuck you to the man who had tossed me out on my ass for daring to say no to him.

What really pissed me off was that no one came running at the sound of the disturbance. A patrol should have at least checked on Taroc from the garden but even as I crept around the palace wall, no one appeared. I made it all the way to the east wing unseen, and the further I got, the more annoyed I became.

The fact of the matter was, I should never have made it onto the palace grounds. Not ever. These were fucking Dragons with heightened senses and military training. It was bad enough that I had made it past them once, but for me to breach their defenses several times, after I'd specifically pointed out the weaknesses that I had made use of, was fucking stupid. And it wasn't only me who had gotten past them. I'd told them again and again what to do to secure the palace, and they had appeared to listen to me. Yet, there I was. It was beginning to feel purposeful. As if someone were deliberately making things easier on us assassins.

I stared up at a dark window. "Fuck, could it be him?"

Unlike the rest of the soldiers, the Captain slept in the palace—one of the perks of being in charge. In charge of all those patrols who never caught anyone and the lookouts who didn't see anything. In charge of capping the walls and changing the locks. Fuck, if it was the Captain behind all of this, it would explain a lot. The way he'd looked at me as he escorted me out of the palace, that smirk on his face, had been nagging at my mind. There was something in his eyes. Or maybe a lack of something.

"Motherfucker, if it's you, I'm going to take great pleasure in revealing your treachery to Taroc."

After strapping on my climbing claws, I scaled the wall, just another shadow in the night. I reached Vettan's window and peered inside. The Captain wasn't there. The fucker was probably off trying to look busy while doing absolutely nothing. I used the tip of a claw to try the window and found that not only did it have an old, worthless lock, but that lock wasn't engaged. The fucking window was open.

"What an arrogant asshole," I muttered as I eased it open and slithered inside.

I slipped off the claws, slid them into a pocket, and searched the room. It didn't take long. The Captain had a large room but very little in it. A bed, a side table with a lamp, a worktable with a few weapons laid out for cleaning, and that was it. There was a bathroom and dressing room attached but neither held any secrets. No false bottoms in his dresser drawers, no hidden safes. Not even a book. The man was utterly boring.

I went back to the bedroom and glared at the single piece of personality in the place—a painting of the Captain with another man. It didn't look romantic. In fact, the other man bore a family resemblance to the Captain. I was betting it was a brother or father. It could even be his grandfather. It was impossible to tell with immortals.

A click came as the door handle turned.

I didn't have enough time to put my claws on and with very few options, I dove under the bed. Yes, I know, it's the dumbest hiding place of all, but the Captain didn't have a reason to search his room for assassins. I mean, the man hadn't even changed the lock on his window; he wasn't worried about intruders. I suppose that was a sign in his favor. If he were behind the assassination attempts, he would have at least protected himself, wouldn't he? I mean, a fresh lock on his window, while every other window was ignored would have been damning evidence. But he'd left himself just as vulnerable. Fuck.

Scooting back against the wall as far as I could, I slowed my breathing to an inaudible level. The lights came on and two men walked in.

"Shut the door," Vettan said.

"What the fuck is wrong with him?" I recognized the voice as belonging to Hersk, one of the knights.

"It's that fucking assassin! The King is pining for him."

"For a *human*?" Hersk said the word in a tone one might use to describe a cockroach.

"I tried to warn him. That bastard assassin is as lowborn as they come, and the lowborn are never loyal. They smile and bow and say the right things while inside, they plot against you."

"At least he's gone now."

Vettan grunted. "Fucking thief. Even knowing that he was scum, I was still surprised when he stole from the King. That fucking piece of shit. I'll bet he's known all along who hired him and just kept it to himself, waiting for a chance to share it with the King and look like a hero."

Well, shit, my theory was looking less and less likely.

"You don't think it was Crushei who hired him?"

"No. I did at first, but now, I'm not so sure. He hasn't wavered, not once. A guilty man *always* wavers."

"Then what do we do? If Crushei isn't the one who hired the assassins, then that person is still out there. We need to guard the King, but how do we do that when he's in a rage?"

"The man who brokered the assassins is dead. Hopefully, that will give us enough time to find our enemy before he finds another assassin to do his dirty work."

"Fucking coward," Hersk hissed.

"Indeed. He must be from one of the other races; a Dragon would never hire someone to kill for him. If for no other reason than he'd want the satisfaction of doing it himself."

"It's a human. Only a human would think that a human assassin could kill a Dragon."

Vettan made a mirthless laugh. "True. Unless the broker didn't tell his client that the assassin was human."

"I didn't think of that. You're right. With something so shady, they probably weren't allowed to know anything about the assassin."

"Probably not. This means we can't exclude the other races."

"So, what are your orders, Captain?"

"For now, I need you to take a team into the royal gardens and watch over the King as best you can from a distance. I'm going to try to speak to him."

"Good luck, Sir."

One set of footsteps left the room. I assumed they belonged to Hersk.

I waited, but Vettan didn't leave, so I risked a peek with a spy mirror. Extending its telescoping rod, I slid the tiny mirror just beyond the edge of the bed. Vettan was standing before the painting, staring at it intensely. He whispered something, but all I caught was the word, brother. Then he squared his shoulders and left.

I crawled out of my hiding space and grimaced at the door. I had really wanted Vettan to be the bad guy.

"Aw, fuck."

Chapter Forty-Three

I crept about, peering through windows and listening in on conversations for the next few hours. The palace never slept, not fully. Someone was always wandering about. I had learned long ago that patience pays off. Still, I heard nothing incriminating, nothing even interesting, until I found Dr. Chisuren.

He was having a drink with his nurse in one of the side gardens. I'd been making my way slowly around the palace when I heard them speaking and crept closer.

"—should have told him the truth," the nurse was saying.

"I couldn't. I was under orders not to."

"Then you should have kept your mouth shut about the theft. He wouldn't have taken it if you hadn't told him it was magical!"

"I didn't force him to steal! The theft had to be reported. And I could have gone to His Majesty, but I didn't."

"Telling the Captain was nearly as bad, maybe even worse. You know he ran straight to the King. He probably hummed a tune as he went."

"Not my business."

"His Majesty is in love with that man, and you just tore them apart!"

"You don't know that and if he is, then it's even more imperative that he knows the man he loves is a thief."

"All you have to do is see them together to know it's true. Everyone in this damn court knows it. Those fucking Dragons were shaking in their boots, thinking he'd become the King's —"

"He would never."

"Well, not anymore. It was one stupid bottle of srapa venom. You couldn't have just turned a blind eye?"

"He made me feel foolish!" The doctor crossed his arms. "Stealing right under my nose. And after we had such a nice conversation."

"You ruined the King's happiness because of some hurt feelings?" The nurse shook her head and stood. "You are a healer, not a Talon of the law." She took her drink and left. But she looked back once to add, "Now we shall all pay for it."

The doctor sighed, slumped, and stared into his drink.

I left him to it, caught up in my own thoughts. But before I could take a single distracted step, I mentally slapped myself. I couldn't afford to get caught there, and if I wasn't careful, I would. Vettan had sent men to the royal garden. I'd have to abandon my cloak and leave via another route. I turned, veered around the doctor, and went to the nearest wall. There would be plenty of time to wonder over his words later.

#

Chapter Forty-Four

After dropping to the ground on the city side of the palace wall, I yanked my lower mask down and braced my hands against my knees, panting and processing. I needed a fucking drink.

I could have gone anywhere for a bracing beverage, even at that time of night. The city had shaken off the modesty of the day and slipped into something a bit more comfortable. More sultry. Far more dangerous, even in the best parts of town. But I didn't head toward a bar in a nice part of Mhavenna. I didn't want to sit among the well-bred assholes spewing their bullshit. I wanted to go home.

I hailed a carriage and had the driver drop me on Bracken Road. At that time of night, even the bravest of carriage drivers wouldn't go past Bracken. But that was all right; I was good with walking. Most people in the Broken knew me and even those who didn't, knew enough to stay away from me. I made it to the Shrieking Ghost unmolested. I almost wished that hadn't been the case; I could have used a good fight.

Once I was inside the Ghost, I felt instantly at ease. I nodded at the Raltven I knew as I wove past the regulars. The whores knew to stay away from me as well as the pickpockets and thugs; they drew out of my way politely. Too politely. I looked around and caught several people quickly averting their eyes. Right, I wasn't just Locrian anymore. Now, the whole fucking city knew what I did for a living.

Running with the Raltven Wraiths had earned me a certain amount of prestige and notoriety in the Broken, but an assassin was a different kind of beast. People feared the Raltven gangs, sure, but the gangs functioned under their own laws. Unless you wronged them or got in their way, they wouldn't fuck with you. An assassin, however, didn't live by any laws. I was a wild card now. An unknown threat. And people in the Broken had enough known threats that an unknown was a type of god. A dark god who demanded sacrifices, but a god nonetheless. And this god had stood at the King's side.

"Rum," I said to a passing waitress.

"Sure thing," she said breathlessly and scurried away.

I found a table in the back, sat down, and began to replay the events of the night in my head. This was only the beginning, surveillance took time, so I wasn't concerned about how little I'd learned. In fact, I was impressed that I'd overheard so much on my first foray. Taroc . . . no, I couldn't deal with that yet. Let's move on to Vettan.

The Captain may not be the man who hired me, but he was the one who betrayed me. I didn't hold a grudge against the doctor; I'd stolen from him, and he reported it. Fair enough. But Vettan must have taken that information and twisted it into a devious tale in which I played the villain. He had been the one to turn Taroc against me. It was his words that had convinced the King that I was trash before he'd found me in that alley.

Had Vettan been the one who bashed me over the head? Possible. He could have waited for me to leave the palace, had me followed, then come for me when I was vulnerable. As the Captain of the Palace Guard, it would have been easy enough for him to leave the palace without raising suspicion. Then, once I was comatose, he'd have the time to scurry back to the King and spew his vile in His Majesty's ear.

His Majesty is in love with that man, and you just tore them apart! I flinched at the memory.

Right on its heels came a vision of Taroc tearing apart his bedchambers. His brutal body had seemed even larger than usual and perhaps it had been. He had appeared to be on the verge of shifting. I admit that was something I'd love to see. City Dragons rarely shifted into their creature forms; there just wasn't the space for it. They'd have to take to the sky and that might cause a panic. So although I lived in the royal city under the rule of a Dragon, I'd never seen one of them in their dragon form.

"He's probably gorgeous," I whispered.

"What's that?" the waitress asked as she set down my drink.

"Nothing." I handed her a silver coin. "Bring me the bottle, would ya, sweetheart?"

Her eyes widened at the coin, then she snatched it, and quickly shoved it down her bodice before anyone else got a look at it. "You got it, Locrian. Anything you need, you let me know."

That's another thing about the Broken, money could get you just as much respect as fear, more even, but only if they feared you first. Otherwise, all it got you was dead.

I set to brooding over Taroc's temper tantrum and how fucking beautiful he was even when he was acting insane. Was it wrong that watching him toss his bed through those doors had turned me on? Oh, who the fuck cared? He wasn't mine anymore. Never had been. I suppose what I should say is that I wasn't his anymore, but that didn't feel accurate either.

"Here you go, Lock." the waitress set down a fresh bottle of rum, still corked, a loaf of even fresher bread, and a pot of butter. When I lifted a brow at the bread, she said, "You need a good foundation for that rum. How about a bowl of stew too?"

"No, thank you. This is good for now."

"All right, Lock. You let me know if you change your mind."

"I just need some time alone with this bottle."

"You got it. I'll make sure everyone leaves you the fuck alone."

"I appreciate it."

That last bit alone was well worth the silver and came with the added perk of helping someone in the Broken who was trying to make an honest living. Honest was the hardest living to earn there. The Gods know I'd tried.

I was a quarter down the bottle when someone made it past my guardian waitress.

"Lock!" Tengven grabbed my arm.

"Whoa!" I held my glass away from him. "Watch it, you almost spilled my drink."

"Fuck, how drunk are you?"

"Only a little, but don't worry; I'm persistent. Give me another hour and I won't be able to stand."

"Gods damn it!" He grabbed my glass when I tried to lift it to my mouth. He started to set it down, then got a whiff of it and lifted it to his lips instead. After shooting it back, he muttered, "Damn, I never get served rum this good."

"Have you ever given the waitress a silver?"

"No rum's worth a silver." Teng slammed the glass down. "Lock, I know who hired you."

"What?" I sat up straight.

"I sent someone to investigate Crushei, and they found a witness who works across the street from him. That person swears that they saw the Captain of the Royal Guard at Crushei's house the day he was arrested."

"Yes, I know." I slumped back into my seat. "He was sent to arrest Crushei and then returned later to search his house."

"Alone?"

"What?"

"The witness saw Vettan arrive hours *after* Crushei was arrested but several minutes *before* a group of knights."

"Hold on. You're saying that Vettan went ahead of his team to search the house?"

"Yes."

"That's a little suspicious but it's not proof of anything. I heard him talking to another guard last night. He's an asshole, and he's definitely the one who told Taroc that I stole the medicine, but he doesn't sound as if he wants the King dead."

"I'm not finished." Teng poured himself another drink and shot it back. "I thought that was odd, so I started asking around about the Captain. That's when I found another witness, this one connected to Yusef."

"Yusef?"

"Yeah, one of Yusef's servants."

"What did this servant say?"

"That he heard a sound in the early morning, long before it was time for him to wake up. He got up and crept downstairs to check on Yusef."

"Holy fuck. Did he see the murderer?"

"Yes, but he didn't recognize the man."

"Fuck."

"Not at first."

"Gods damn you, Teng, just get to it already! Who murdered Yusef?"

"He said the man was wearing a coat with gold buttons, that's all he remembered because he was so horrified by the murder. He snuck back to his bed and stayed there until he heard shouting several hours later. He went downstairs, and *that's* when the servant saw the murderer again."

Shouting. Shouting hadn't happened until Vettan sent a servant up to check on Yusef. And the murderer wore a coat with gold buttons. Fuck me. The image of a gold button bloomed in my mind. A button, according to the King, that was drenched in Vettan's scent.

"No fucking way," I whispered.

"It's Captain Vettan. The servant swears to it. And he couldn't report it because—"

"Vettan was the one who interviewed the servants."

"Exactly. The poor man had to sit there and tell his master's murderer that he had no idea what happened and had heard nothing."

Captain Vettan. CV. It had been staring me in the face. Literally smirking at me. Yes, I had overheard him saying that he didn't know who was behind the assassination attempts, but he'd been speaking to one of the palace knights. Of course, he'd play innocent with them. What a fool I'd been.

"Son of a bitch," I whispered. "I was so sure of his loyalty. Why? Why would he do this?"

"Now that, I don't know. But, Lock, isn't he the man in charge of the King's security? And if he's the one who turned you in for stealing the medicine, he did it to get you out of the way. He's probably the one who attacked you and dragged you into that alley. And now he's alone with the King."

"Fuck!" I lurched to my feet.

All conversations stopped, and everyone stared at me as I went running out of the Ghost.

"Lock!" Teng ran after me. "You can't face him alone!"

"I just need to warn Taroc." I clasped Teng's shoulder. "Thank you, brother!"

"How the fuck are you going to get past the knights? They're all under Vettan's command."

"The same way I did it earlier tonight." Then I remembered that Vettan had assigned men to the royal garden. With my luck, they'd remember to look up or those men in the towers would look down. "Shit. Vettan just upped the security."

"You need a distraction." Teng nodded at the shadows and several of his men stepped out of them. "We've got your back."

Chapter Forty-Five

We managed to find a carriage on the other side of Bracken Road and had the driver drop us forty feet from the palace. We split up at the back wall; the Nerakians heading for the front gate while I went to the stretch wall I'd scaled earlier—the one I had used to leave. Dropping back into the side garden where I'd eavesdropped on the doctor, I went still and listened a moment to make sure no patrols were about. Then I made a mad dash to the royal gardens. No time for creeping now.

As I ran, I heard shouting. I flattened myself against the palace wall just as a unit of knights ran past me. That was yet another issue I'd failed to address; when something went wrong, every knight left their post and headed toward the disturbance. Sloppy, but again, I was grateful for it. Teng and his men would hold everyone's attention long enough for me to get to Taroc.

Once the knights had passed by, I made another sprint for the royal gardens. The gardens were empty, the remnants of the King's rage already removed. A glance up showed me that the doors had been hastily repaired and the windows were dark. The King was finally at rest.

I fastened on my climbing claws and scaled the wall. Within seconds, I was on the balcony, casting aside my claws in my haste to reach the King. The temporary doors weren't much more than wood panels with hinges. No locks, nor was anything wedged against them. I just pushed one open and slid inside.

"Taroc?" I automatically widened my eyes to adjust to the dark, but that was unnecessary; I could see. Colors were muted, but other than that, my vision was good. I would have wondered over that, but I was too worried about the King. And then I saw the dog lying to my right. She was on her side, tongue hanging out of her open mouth and eyes closed. "Ren?" I shook the animal, but she didn't stir. "Fuck!" I looked up and sought the King. He was stretched out in a new bed. "Taroc!"

"Lock?" the King's rough voice came seconds before the fireplace sparked and the wood there caught.

"Thank the Gods," I whispered when I saw him sit up. "What's wrong with Ren?" I knelt and shook her again. "Ren?"

"What the fuck did you do to her?" Taroc snarled as he climbed out of bed. Once on his feet, he stumbled, shook his head, and scowled at me. "Fuck, there's something wrong with me."

Just as I was getting up to help him, the bedroom door opened and Captain Vettan strode into the room.

"Your Majesty!" Vettan rushed toward Taroc.

"Stay away from him!" I shouted at them both as I also ran for the King.

"What?" Taroc looked from me to the Captain. "Captain, how did—"

The Captain grabbed the King's bicep with one suddenly clawed hand and swung at him with the other. Taroc turned toward Vettan, his eyes widening. Then I barreled into him, taking him to the ground and away from Vettan's claws.

"Taroc, focus!" I slapped his face.

"Lock," he murmured. Then his hands clenched in my clothes. "Lock, you're really here!"

"I was going to let you live, Assassin," Vettan said as he ambled over to us. "I did you a courtesy by leaving you in that alley. But you couldn't stay away. Foolish. Very foolish. Now you will die with your lover."

"Vettan?" Taroc narrowed his eyes at the Captain.

"I'll be right with you, Your Majesty," Vettan said as he reached for me. "Just as soon as I kill your assassin."

"What the fuck?" Taroc shook his head again as if trying to clear it.

Vettan grabbed me by the throat and lifted me as if I weighed nothing more than a pillow, easily breaking Taroc's hold on me. I didn't have my lightning gloves on, but I did have a few options within reach. An assassin is always prepared for murder, whether it be his target's or his. Even as I strangled, I carefully withdrew a slender dagger from my vest and, with a swift, downward strike, stabbed Vettan through his forearm.

Vettan howled as he let go of me. I landed on the ground in a heap as the Captain lifted his forearm and glared at the blade skewering it.

"Heal that, motherfucker," I said.

"Lock!" Taroc cried.

Drawing in ragged breaths, I stumbled to my feet and pulled two, far more substantial daggers from the sheaths in my boots. I could have gone for my gloves, but they were dangerous in such close quarters. He could grab me and then I'd be frying along with him. So, I went with the daggers. Settling into a balanced stance in front of Taroc, I stared down my enemy at last. Or rather, I stared at him, finally knowing that he was my enemy.

"You're right; I am a fool, *CV*," I said. "I didn't see it. It was right there in my face—your initials in that book. It never even occurred to me that Yusef was using titles, not just names. Assassin Locrian, His Majesty the King, and Captain Vettan. You needed someone with the same initials to take the fall for you. Did you plan for that? Is that how you had Crushei's letter ready to *find* in Yusef's desk? I assume you took it when it was delivered to the palace. It never reached Paslan."

Vettan laughed. "And then the King sent me to search Crushei's house. All I had to do was hide the note Yusef sent me and the dagger I'd used to kill him in Crushei's house, then pretend to discover them in front of the other knights. Setting him up couldn't have been easier."

"The button was a mistake, though," I said. "Yusef must have grabbed it while you were killing him. Did you have to dispose of your clothes? Is that the real reason you changed them? They must have been covered in blood."

"No. I know how to kill without dirtying my clothing."

"Or your hands. What was it that you called a man who hired an assassin? Oh, yes, a fucking coward. Hold on, no, that wasn't you, that was Hersk. You only agreed with him so he wouldn't suspect you."

"Human filth!" Vettan hissed and lunged for me.

I sprang onto the bed and kicked at his face. Unfortunately, although I outclassed the Captain in clean killing, he was better at brawls. He grabbed my foot before it made impact and wrenched it in a direction it wasn't meant to go. I screamed as I lost my footing, falling from the bed to hit the ground hard.

"Lock!" Taroc shouted.

"Shh, Your Majesty. Your guards are busy at the gate with some drunken Nerakians—friends of your little fuck-boy, I assume. They won't hear your shouts."

While he was taunting Taroc, I dove for Vettan's legs. Once he was down, I lifted my blade—the only one I'd managed to keep a hold of—and aimed for his crotch. Hey, desperate times.

Vettan kneed me in the face, cracking my teeth together and sending me tumbling backward. I lay on the floor with my legs twisted half beneath me, and gasped past the pain. Blood ran down my throat, both inside and out, and my eyes watered. I couldn't see Vettan as he came for me, but I heard his heavy footsteps.

"Stupid little pig," Vettan hissed as he picked me up again. "You've walked right to your slaughter.

My chest suddenly burned. I looked down to see his claws in my belly, angled up toward my heart. They hadn't quite reached it yet; he was taking his time. Making me watch and writhe in agony as he sliced his way closer and closer.

"No!" a roar came from my left and then I was falling, Vettan's hand wrenched free of me.

I gasped, spat blood, and clutched at my belly. Blood gushed between my fingers, but my stare was locked on the two men. One of them wasn't entirely a man anymore.

King Tarocvar Verres stood four feet taller than he'd been just moments before. The shorts he'd worn to bed were hanging from his bulging body in shreds and his skin gleamed with the gloss of crimson scales. Curving up from his temples were ebony horns, his hands had become talons, and a pair of enormous, black wings swept up from his back.

In the grip of those royal talons, Captain Vettan struggled. "Why can't I shift?!" He swiped at the King's wrists, but his claws only clicked and skidded across those ruby scales. "You're the one who's drugged. You shouldn't be able to shift, not me!"

"There was poison on that first blade," I wheezed, then laughed. "You're already dead, Vettan."

The Captain's wide eyes went to me.

"And nothing can keep a Dragon from shifting to save his mate," Taroc snarled. "Not even a traitor's drugs."

He broke the Captain's arms and tossed him to the ground. Powerful feet tipped in claws came down upon Vettan's legs and the resounding cracks added bass to his screams. As soon as he was disabled, Taroc rushed over to me.

"Lock?" The King eased me gently onto his lap.

"Taroc," I whispered as I stared up into his strange face.

Covered in tiny scales, he shone as if made of glass, those teal eyes so bright beneath his heavy, ridged brow. Small horns had emerged from his cheekbones in diagonal lines, leading up to, and going back into his wild hair. His lips had thinned to almost nothing, and they parted to reveal sharp teeth.

"Don't speak." His hand went to the wound in my belly.

"I have to tell you something."

"Tell me later. Just rest for now, Lock."

"Taroc, I'm human; I won't survive this."

"Yes, you will. You're going to be fine."

I smiled at his lie. "I shouldn't have left you. I'm so sorry. It was my stupid pride."

"Don't be sorry. It's all right now. You came back to me. It's all right. It's going to be all right. I've got you now."

"Taroc, stop." I took his hand and wet my lips. "Just let me say this before—"

"You're not dying, Lock." His stare went to the blood that seeped between his fingers and tears began to well in his eyes. "You *can't* be dying."

"I'm sorry, Your Majesty, but you'll have to make do without your assassin."

"Lock." He met my stare.

"Let me see your other face one more time."

Taroc shifted in seconds, the scales, horns, and claws withdrawing as his body shrunk. The fullness returned to his lips, his teeth blunted, and then, at last, the wings vanished.

"You're beautiful either way, but I wanted to say goodbye to the you I fell in love with."

"Lock, no. Don't go. Don't you leave me again."

"It was worth it. *You're* worth it. I have no regrets." Despite my brave words, a tear slipped down my cheek.

"He's a murderer!" Vettan hissed.

"I will fucking tear you apart if you don't shut the fuck up!" Taroc roared even as he held me tenderly.

"You killed my brother!"

The room went silent for three heartbeats.

Then Taroc asked, "Who the fuck is your brother?"

"Emellen Haden."

Taroc blinked. "I fought Emellen for the throne. It was a fair, witnessed fight. Part of the crown tourney. I won, and he lost. That is not murder."

"You cheated," Vettan whimpered. "You cheated. I know you cheated. Emellen was unmatched. No one could beat him. He was the rightful king."

"For fuck's sake, I did not cheat! You can't cheat in a crown tourney; there are no rules for the fights. And that was over a century ago."

"I've been waiting for my chance at you. I came here and slowly put my plan into motion, and I nearly had you. If only I hadn't let that fucker Yusef talk me into—"

"Oh, fuck off and die, you gods-damned idiot," Taroc said and refocused on me.

I made a huff of amusement, it was all I could manage without pain. Then, with the last of my strength, I lifted my hand to Taroc's cheek. "I love you."

"Lock," he whispered and bent his head to mine. Against my lips, he said, "I love you too, Assassin."

I closed my eyes, fully expecting to never open them again, and kissed my lover goodbye. It was romantic and beautiful and bittersweet. Or at least it would have been if Vettan wasn't spouting hateful things at Taroc the entire time.

With a snarl of frustration, I sat up, pushing Taroc up with me, and snapped, "You heard your king, shut up and die, asshole!" Then I blinked and looked down at my chest. "What the fuck?"

Taroc tore the material of my tunic apart, wiped at the blood with a bit of the fabric, and revealed angry, red skin. *Whole*, angry, red skin. And that's when the King began to laugh.

"What the *actual fuck* is happening right now?!" I shrieked.

Taroc cupped my cheek and kissed me. "I told you, love, you're not dying."

"But *why* aren't I dying? *How* am I not dying?"

"Because he mated you, you fucking moron," Vettan said.

Taroc and I swung our heads toward him but before we could say anything, the Captain closed his eyes and finally did as ordered.

"What an asshole," I said. "All of that because his brother is a sore loser?"

"Well, it was a fight to the death. Don't you remember? I told you about the men I killed to win my throne."

"Oh, that's right. But you said it's an honorable tournament, all legal and shit."

"Yes, it was all legal and shit," he said with a grin.

"Then it was a dumb vendetta."

"It was indeed, and it cost him his life."

"But that last bit was interesting."

"You mean the part about me mating you?"

"Yup. That would be it. Care to explain why that explains this?" I waved at my stomach. There wasn't even a mark anymore.

"I told you, Dragons share their immortality with their mates."

"Yeah, I get that, but when exactly did you perform this immortality sharing ritual? Because I don't remember it, and I would think something like that would stay with me. So would a mating ceremony, for that matter."

"The immortality sharing comes with the mating, and it's not a ritual exactly. It's a process. Usually, it starts as an instinctive reaction. The Dragon's body recognizes its mate and produces the mating hormone. Then—"

"Taroc, I swear to the Gods, if you don't fucking tell me, right the fuck now, how you made me your mate without me knowing or even fucking consenting, I'm going to headbutt you!"

Taroc chuckled. "I had to give you some foundation to the procedure, or you'd think I was teasing you."

"Why? What's the procedure?"

"The bonding magic is delivered through sexual release."

"Come again?"

"Precisely."

"What?"

"It's in my cum. I claimed you that very first time we were together."

"In your . . ." I gaped at him. In my mind, a picture formed of Taroc angling his cock at me. Coming all over me. Rubbing it in. "Holy fucking shit! The tingles! That was magic?"

"The tingles?"

"Your cum made me feel tingly. And it absorbed into me.

I thought that was just a Dragon thing."

"It is a Dragon thing." Taroc grinned. "But only when a Dragon is claiming his mate."

I frowned. "How do the females do it?"

Taroc grimaced. "Trust me, you don't want that image in your head."

I laughed and yanked him into a hug. Then I shoved him away and punched him in the gut.

Taroc grunted, hunching with the punch, then gaped at me. "What the fuck?"

"That's for not telling me! Or even fucking asking me!" Then I remembered the potion and what I'd overheard Dr. Chisuren saying. "Holy fuck! This is why I healed that stab wound so fast. It wasn't a magic potion. You lied to me and then made the doctor lie to me too!"

Taroc flushed. "You weren't ready to hear the truth."

I jumped to my feet. "You motherfucker! You fucking asshole!"

Ren suddenly whined, and both Taroc and I rushed over to her.

"Ren!" I cried.

"Ren?" Taroc picked her up and carried her to the bed. "Hey, girl."

"He must have drugged her too," I said as I stroked Ren's head. "You'll be all right, sweetheart. Looks as if it's wearing off. You're fine." Then I remembered that I was mad. "But you!" I pointed at Taroc. "You . . . ugh!" I threw up my hands and headed for the door. "I can't even look at your gorgeous face right now. I wanna fucking punch it!"

"Lock! Lock, don't you walk out when Ren is like this!"

"Ren will be fine."

"Fuck! Hold on, Ren. I'll be right back."

"No!" I swung around and pointed a finger at him. "Don't you fucking follow me. I need to think this shit over."

"Lock, please. I'm sorry. I didn't know how to tell you. I tried to ease you into it, but then you got mad at me."

"You treated me like . . . well, I'm not sure what you treated me like but it wasn't like your mate."

"Can't you see that this was hard for me too?" Taroc snapped. "You think I wanted to mate a human?"

"Oh, fuck you, you elitist prick."

Taroc growled and rolled his eyes. "For fuck's sake, you know what I mean by that. It's a tough match. And I'm not an elitist just because I acknowledge that my race is superior to yours. That's a simple fact, Lock."

"Oh, it's a fact, is it?"

"We rule the planet; I think that says it all."

"You're stronger and can turn into giant beasts. That doesn't make you superior."

"Fine!" He tossed up his hands. "We're not superior. Nonetheless, I had to work past my issues with our mating before I told you about it."

"Have you then?"

"Have I what?"

"Have you worked through your issues, Taroc?!"

"Yes, of course."

"Is that what you were doing last night?"

He went still. "You saw that?"

"I was investigating. Trying to find out who had set me up."

"And I was a part of your investigation?" Taroc grinned.

"Oh, fuck off," I huffed and walked away.

"Lock!"

"I'm staying at the Enchanted Swan. You can come by tomorrow, and we'll talk then."

"I can *what*?"

"You heard me. And set the Nerakians free; they helped me get in so I could save you."

"What Nerakians?"

"The ones your knights arrested at the front gates."

"What the fuck is happening right now?" the King muttered.

I chuckled under my breath as I walked away from him. Tarocvar Verres. My mate.

Chapter Forty-Six

I wasn't leaving without Teng and his men. No fucking way. Luckily, I didn't have to look very hard for them. I found them sitting in a line along the palace wall just down from the guard shack, all of them in manacles and under the watchful eyes of Sir Hersk, who stood nearby. Tengven started to grin when he saw me.

"The King is well?" Teng asked.

I nodded. "Thanks in part to all of you."

"Assassin!" Hersk strode over to me. "How the fuck did you get inside the palace?"

I gave him a sympathetic look. "Were you born this slow?"

Tengven and his men burst out laughing.

Hersk snarled, bared his teeth, and started for me.

"Hold!" Sir Drasik called from the palace's main doors.

"What the fuck?" Hersk pulled up short and glared at Drasik.

"The Captain just tried to kill the King," Drasik said as he ran over to us.

"What the fuck?" Hersk repeated in a whisper.

"The Assassin helped to save His Majesty's life." Drasik grimaced. "And the King has announced that he's his mate."

"*Who's* his mate?"

"The Assassin!" Drasik waved at me.

"The Assassin is Captain Vettan's mate?"

I shook my head and drawled, "Again, I ask, were you born this slow?"

"Fuck," Hersk muttered. "He really mated a human?"

"Yes." Drasik waved toward Teng's group. "And the King has ordered that these men be released; they helped his mate save his life."

Hersk looked as if he might throw up and then stare at the stuff, wondering where it came from.

"I swear, if you start that who's-who stuff again, I'm going to smack you," I said to him. "Let my friends go."

Hersk looked at Drasik.

"I saw the Captain's body myself," Drasik said. "He drugged the King and his dog."

"*Drugged* them?"

"Look, watching you process this is very entertaining, but I just made a dramatic exit, and if the King comes out and finds me still here, it's going to ruin it. So, release my friends, we'll leave, and then you can continue this idiocy without us."

"That is the last time you call me an idiot, Assassin!" Hersk went for my throat.

Drasik grabbed him and yanked him back. "Do you have a fucking death wish?! The King will tear you apart if you touch his mate."

I smirked at Hersk and while Drasik had him restrained, removed the keys from his belt. "I'll just do it myself then, shall I?"

I sauntered over to the Nerakians while Drasik and Hersk had a heated discussion behind me. I had just finished unlocking Teng's manacles when Hersk strode over.

"Let me do that," Hersk said gruffly as he took the keys from me.

Drasik stood behind him, staring at me as if I were a rare creature he'd never seen before.

"Thanks for helping me with him," I said to Drasik.

He bowed to me. Fucking bowed.

Teng laughed his scaly ass off.

"Shut up," I hissed at him. "I'm important now."

"What the fuck do you think I'm laughing about?"

"Asshole." I grinned.

"Dragon mate," he shot back. "What does that mean exactly? Are you going to be a second king?"

"No," Drasik and Hersk said at the same time, Hersk a little more emphatically than Drasik.

"We don't know what the King will decide to give Locrian for a title," Drasik added, "but there can only be one king. The Assassin will be his mate."

"*If* I decide to forgive him," I said.

"If?" Drasik gaped at me.

Hersk stood from unlocking the last set of manacles and joined the other knight in his gawking.

"Come on, guys," I said to the Nerakians. "We deserve a nice breakfast, and I know just the place. My treat."

Chapter Forty-Seven

I didn't have to hide anymore. The bad guy had been found and dealt with. I could be exactly who I was and do exactly what I wanted to do. What I *needed* to do was sleep, but I was too excited for that, too baffled and shocked, and the Nerakians were just as ramped up after their escapade. So, I took them to the Enchanted Swan's restaurant for breakfast.

The look on the face of the doorman as we strode past him was priceless. And that was only the start. For some of the staff and guests, it was probably the first time they'd been within forty feet of a Neraky pirate, much less six of them. But the Swan was known for its excellent service and these Nerakians were in the company of a guest. That made them guests by extension. So, they were treated with respect—a fact that both impressed me and endeared the staff to me.

"This is nice," Ry said as he looked around the restaurant. "A bit white, but nice. Everything is so fucking clean."

"Don't steal anything," Teng said.

Ry grimaced. "I wasn't gonna."

Teng just stared back.

Ry pulled a silver salt shaker out of his vest and set it back on the table.

"They're being very nice to us, and that is something I did not expect," Teng said sternly. "We're going to be respectful in return."

"Fuck that," I said. "I mean, yes, be nice to the staff and don't take anything, but I brought you here so we could enjoy ourselves, not feel awkward. This is a thank you breakfast so, please, make yourselves comfortable."

Grei, one of Teng's men, grinned at me, leaned back in his chair, and started to lift his foot.

"Not that comfortable!" Teng snapped.

"Just testin' the waters, Captain," Grei said, still grinning.

"Here you are," the waitress said as she set a pot of coffee and another of tea on the table, then placed delicate teacups in front of the pirates. "You fellas look like you had a fun night."

"We stormed the palace," Ry said with a charming smile. "And saved the King."

"Did you now?" She grinned at him, then lifted the coffee pot.

"Oh, no, you sweet thing!" Ry took the pot from her. "Don't you worry about that. We can pour our own drinks." He handed the pot to Grei. "Here, pour the coffee." Then he swiveled his smile back at her. "Would you like a cup of coffee, darlin'?"

The waitress giggled and held her tray to her chest. "No, thank you, Sir. I'd best get back and check on your food. It's still early, so yours are the only orders the chefs are working on. They should be ready soon."

"If we're the only ones here, then surely you can have a quick cup of coffee?" Ry made to get up and offer her his chair.

"Ry, sit down and leave the girl alone," Teng said. "Can't you see that she's worked all night? We're probably keeping her from leaving."

"Oh, not at all, Sir," she protested. "I'm happy to have one last table to wait on before I go home. I usually have to sit around doing nothing this last hour, and I work mostly for tips."

"I figured as much," Teng said, sliding a sexy look her way. "And we'll make it worth your while, but you'd best hurry off now. My men are used to tavern wenches; they don't know how to behave around real ladies."

The waitress blushed, did a quick bob, and went back to the kitchen.

"Damn it, Teng!" Ry snarled once she was gone. "I was halfway down her drawers, and I'll bet they're real pretty, silky things too."

You were nowhere near her pretty underthings. That's a good girl right there."

"Yeah, and good girls like bad boys." Ry waggled his brows, and the other men laughed. "And I would have been *really* bad for her."

"You'll get a few more chances," I said. "Best work on your next line before she returns."

"In other words, shut the fuck up, you man-whore!" Lue, another of the pirates, said.

We all started laughing but our laughter was cut short by the arrival of a group of palace knights, who came marching into the restaurant as if it were under siege.

"Aw, fuck, I thought we were good with the King?" Ry asked me.

And then the King walked in with Ren at his side.

"We are," I said softly, my gaze locked on Taroc.

"Holy fuck," Tengven whispered. Then he surged to his feet and motioned at his men. "Get up, you fucking idiots. That's the King!"

I got to my feet a bit slower, lifting my brows at Taroc as I did. When he came to a stop in front of our table, the other men bowed. I did not.

"What the fuck are you doing here?" I asked.

The palace knights who stood behind Taroc made various sounds of affront.

"You said to come and see you here tomorrow," the King said. "This is tomorrow."

"Barely." I gave him my *what's-wrong-with-you* look. "We've only just sat down to breakfast."

"Well, I'm here now. Are you going to introduce me to your companions?"

Ren yipped.

"Your Majesty, may I introduce Captain Tengven Wei, his first mate, Ry, and sailors, Grei, Lue, Henshen, and Ju. Everyone, this is His Majesty King Tarocvar Verres and his dog, Renraishala."

"Your Majesty, it's an honor to meet you." Tengven bowed, then shifted his head to the side and glared at his men.

"Your Majesty," they murmured and bowed.

"Please, sit down, gentlemen." Taroc looked at me pointedly.

"What?"

He looked at my chair, then at the men who were still standing—because *he* was still standing.

"Oh. Sorry, I didn't realize that part of my duties as your mate included chair fetching. *Allow me, Your Majesty.*" I went to another table, grabbed a chair, and set it behind him with a flourish.

"Thank you." Taroc sat down.

The rest of us did as well, including Ren, who sat beside her master.

"I've been told that you assisted my mate this morning," the King said to the pirates.

"We merely served as a distraction so that Lock could get past the guards," Teng said.

"Then you six helped save my life. Thank you."

"It was our pleasure and an honor, Your Majesty," Teng said.

"Are you the friend Lock has told me about?"

"That depends. Did he say nice things?" Tengven grinned.

Taroc chuckled. "He didn't say much beyond you being the only man he trusts."

"The *only* man he trusts?" Tengven looked at me. "Aw, Lock, I'm touched. A little sad for you, but touched."

"Fuck you, Teng," I said.

"I'll forgive that since I'm the *only* man you trust."

"What about me, Lock?" Ry asked. "I'm hurt."

"Oh, I'm sorry. Fuck you too, Ry."

"Thanks!" Ry beamed.

"Um, excuse me," a feminine voice said. "Oh, my. Um."

"Pardon me, Your Majesty, but I must assist my future wife." Ry shot up and wedged between the knights. "Move aside, can't you see that a lady's trying to get past? Allow me, sweetheart." He took the massive tray from the waitress, balanced it on one hand, and offered his free arm to the woman. "Would you like to meet the King?"

"Um." Her wide eyes went to the back of the King's head. "Yes?"

"Right this way." Ry led her to Taroc, handed the tray to Lue, and presented the waitress as if she were a visiting princess. "Your Majesty, this is our beautiful waitress, uh . . ." He looked at her.

"I'm Marissa, Your Majesty." She curtsied deeply. "I'm so sorry to interrupt. May I bring you something to eat or drink?"

"Thank you, Marissa. Yes, I'd like some coffee and a plate of whatever meat you have available."

"We have bacon, sausage, ham, or steak, Your Majesty."

"Yes," he said.

Marissa blinked, then nodded, curtsied again, and hurried away.

"My sweet, you've forgotten your tray!" Ry called after her.

She stopped in her tracks and came back.

"Hurry up and pass out the food!" Ry hissed at Lue.

Lue shot him an annoyed look as he set the last dish down, then slapped Ry's chest with the tray.

"Thanks." Ry grinned, spun around, and presented the tray to Marissa. "There you are, my lovely one. I told you we saved the King. You thought I was teasing, didn't you?"

"I did." Marissa blushed again. "Thank you." With another look at the King, she fled.

"I apologize for the antics of my crew, Your Majesty," Teng said. "They are just humble sailors."

A few of the humble sailors snickered at that.

Teng shot them a silencing look before adding, "I imagine you'd like to speak to Lock alone."

"Not at all. I'm enjoying this. Please," he waved at them, "continue as if I'm not here."

"Yeah, as if they can do that," I muttered.

"Would you like me to leave, Lock?" Taroc asked, his expression shifting into careful neutrality.

I sighed. "No, I don't want you to leave. But, fuck, Taroc, I wanted at least a few hours to calm down and maybe take a fucking shower before I spoke to you. I needed some time to think about everything."

"You can shower after breakfast. I'll wait for you in your room."

"Wonderful." I rolled my eyes.

Ren yipped again.

"I'm happy you're all right, Ren" I said, then handed her a piece of sausage from my plate.

As she ate, Taroc eyed my food.

"Do you want a piece of sausage too, Your Majesty?" I drawled.

"Maybe just to tide me over until my food comes."

I snorted, speared a whole sausage with my fork, and handed it to him. "You came straight here once you had the palace settled, didn't you?"

"They had to clean my chambers anyway." He took the sausage from my fork and started munching on it happily.

"Yeah, I'm pretty hungry too." I started to cut into my breakfast pastry but, suddenly, there was a sausage in my face. The very sausage that I'd just given to Taroc. I leaned back and asked him, "What are you doing?"

He was staring at me with an odd expression. "You need to eat. I shouldn't have taken this from you."

"I was *about* to eat when you shoved your sausage in my face."

The pirates snickered again. Teng smacked Ry before he could comment.

Taroc lowered the sausage.

"Is this really happening or is this another cava hallucination?" Wei whispered.

"I'm ninety-nine percent sure this is real," Lue whispered back.

"And this is why you should have waited to come by." I waved at the pirates.

"I couldn't wait," Taroc said. "I've waited too long as it is. The beast inside me is unsettled without you. You saw what

I did to my chambers. That's what happens when a mated Dragon rejects his mate; he goes wild. I need you *now*, Lock."

"Taroc, I'm really mad at you for not telling me about this."

"I know, and I'm so sorry."

"You should have asked me before you did all that. I should have had a choice in this."

"I didn't even have a choice."

"What the fuck does that mean?"

"I told you, my dragon recognized you as my mate. I reacted instinctively, without any conscious decision. Lock, I claimed you *before* I fell in love with you. Honestly, I was shocked by it. I wasn't trying to take away your choice."

"What?" I whispered.

"Mating is magical. A gift from the Goddess. She chooses who is right for us. I suppose I could have tried to fight my instincts, but I trust in Ensarena. And she has proven, yet again, to be worthy of that trust. You are the man I want to spend eternity with."

Under the intensity of Taroc's eyes and words, I forgot to breathe. Suddenly, my body took over, and I inhaled deeply, taking his scent into me. Something inside me clutched at that smell and shivered. It recognized the truth of what Taroc said and the importance of it. Plus, it was the most romantic thing anyone had ever said to me.

"You still should have told me. And you should have believed me when I told you how I ended up in that alley. Instead, you listened to that asshole. You didn't even try to work things out with me."

"You ended our relationship, Lock, not me."

"And you kicked me out of the palace."

"Yes, I did. I was angry and hurt. I'm sorry. I've made a lot of mistakes with you, but I want to correct them. Tell me how to make this up to you."

Pirate eyes darted back and forth from Taroc to me.

"Promise me it won't happen again. From here forward, you tell me *everything*, especially if it has to do with me. And you trust me above everyone else."

"Will you trust me in return?"

"Of course, I trust you, you asshole."

Taroc grinned. "Then you have my trust and fidelity; I swear it."

"All right." I took a bite and chewed.

"All right?"

"Mmm-hmm," I said with my mouth shut.

"You'll come home with me?"

"Mmm-hmm."

"And be my mate?"

I swallowed. "Yes, Taroc. Can I eat now?"

Taroc lurched up, yanked me out of my chair, and kissed me. I fully expected the pirates to make some kind of commentary or even just funny kissing sounds, but, thank the Gods, they stayed silent. I shared a sausage-flavored kiss with my mate, finally shedding all the weight on my heart and shoulders. I hadn't just needed this time to calm down and forgive him, but also to process and accept what was happening. I was still in a bit of a daze, but the kiss helped. The zinging thrills it sent through my body told me this was real. He was real. *We* were real.

I was the immortal mate of the Dragon King.

Holy fucking shit.

When we eased apart, the scent of roasted meat wafted up between us. We both looked over to see Marissa standing nearby, holding an enormous platter of meat.

She curtsied. "Your meat, Your Majesty."

I burst out laughing.

Chapter Forty-Eight

Dragons don't get married. Mating was final; once a Dragon was mated, that was it. No other lover for him or her. Not ever. Marriage was meaningless in light of that. That being said, there was a ceremony performed. After Dragons chose their mates, they formally presented themselves to their dread, or dreads if they came from different ones. The dread—a group of united Dragons, like a clan or tribe—would either accept or reject the mated pair.

It was the possibility of the latter that made me nervous.

"They will not reject us," Taroc said as he stepped up behind me and met my stare in the mirror.

He, of course, looked fucking amazing in his presentation robe. Midnight silk flowed over his broad shoulders and down to the floor. It would have been somber if not for the crimson and gold embroidery that stiffened the edges. Beneath the robe, leather pants molded to his legs and impressive manhood, with matching boots that rose to his knees. Over that, he wore a black tunic, topped by a resplendent tabard of gold links. Chain mail for a king. His hair was loose, the thick locks glossy beneath his crown—a simple, gold band with rubies the size of my thumbnails evenly spaced around it.

I, on the other hand, looked like someone's idea of a joke. My hair wasn't dark enough to go with Taroc's, nor light enough to make a nice contrast. Just somewhere in the middle, a drab brown. My eyes were no match for his either, again, a boring brown compared to his startling teal. The rich clothing he insisted I wear seemed to mock this and my plain face, making my complete inferiority obvious.

"I don't think you see what I see," I said as I transferred my stare back to my reflection.

"Who the fuck are you?" Taroc scowled.

"Excuse me?" I turned to look at him.

"Where's the cocky assassin I claimed? The man who stood up to me when no other dared. The man who tried to kill me, then told me I was boring in bed. That man wouldn't give a shit about the opinions of a few Dragons."

I chuckled. "You said that there are over four thousand Dragons in your dread."

"As I said, a few." He grinned.

"I'm ugly."

Taroc burst out laughing.

"Hey! You're not supposed to laugh at that!"

"It's ridiculous, so I'm laughing." He took my face in his hands. "You are beautiful, and I love you. Get over yourself and then pull yourself together, Assassin. You're about to meet the Racul Dread."

"Yeah, that makes me feel so much better." I rolled my eyes.

"Come, Mate." Taroc took my hand and led me out of my dressing room—he'd had the guest room turned into the mate's chambers—and then out of the royal suite, Ren walking proudly beside us.

The entire palace guard stood at attention outside the suite doors, one line to either side of the corridor. They bowed as we passed, then smoothly fell into line behind us, as if the King's magnetism pulled them along in his wake. Drasik had been appointed the new Captain and stood at the head of the group, hand on the pommel of his sword. I just hoped he did a better job than his predecessor. Not that Vettan had set a high bar.

Our massive parade made its way to the ground floor of the palace. When we reached the double doors of the throne room, most of the Royal Guard split off from us, going to stand to either side of the doors and forming lines that disappeared down the corridors. Only an honor guard formed of Captain Drasik and five others continued into the room with us.

An aisle had been formed by a narrow, red carpet and the guests. Their sharp, Dragon eyes focused on me, analyzing me critically. More than a few snarled when I passed by, hand-in-hand with their king. Despite their fine clothes, every single one of them looked as if they might shred me to bones in seconds. Perhaps that was because I now knew what they could become. Or at least one of the things they could become. Only the strongest Dragons could do a partial shift as Taroc had, most only had two forms.

I steeled myself and recalled Taroc's words. No, I shouldn't care what these people thought of me. But they were like Taroc's family, the only family he had since his parents had died without producing any siblings for him. So, yeah, I wanted them to like me.

We made it to the dais where a smaller throne had been set beside Taroc's. I may not get crowned, but mating Taroc meant that I got to sit beside him on the royal dais and it also made me a noble; I was now a duke of the Racul Dread. That is,

325

if the dread accepted me.

Taroc and I went to the thrones, then he let go of my hand, and we turned to face the room together, him before his seat and me before mine. We didn't sit, not even Ren. Instead, we waited as a woman separated from the crowd and climbed the steps of the dais, stopping one step below the top. She was tall, sturdy as all Dragons were, and had a rope of golden hair trailing down the back of her gleaming robes.

The woman bowed to Taroc—bowed, not curtsied—and then spoke, "Greetings, King Tarocvar Verres. The Racul Dread is here at your command, eager to meet your mate. Is there anything you'd like to say on his behalf before we start the presentation?"

"Greetings, Yarena, honored Vas. Yes, I have something to say." Taroc reclaimed my hand. "Racul Dread, I rejoice to see you standing before me in your entirety. You are my dread, the very blood in my veins, but this man beside me has become my heart. Sent to kill me, he has instead, become my life."

Several Dragons growled at that last bit. So many that Taroc had to hold up his free hand to silence them.

"Yes, he was hired to kill me, but he failed, and I claimed him as *my* assassin," Taroc said. "Locrian made a vow to protect me and find my enemy, and he fulfilled that vow. This man has saved my life and uncovered the traitor who not only lived in my palace but also led my knights."

That lifted a few brows. Taroc must have stopped the news of Vettan's betrayal from spreading to his guests.

"Captain Vettan framed another man for his misdeeds, a man who I imprisoned, and then he placed Locrian under suspicion as well. I cast out my mate, believing Vettan's lies over his truth, and I did so without telling Lock who he was to me."

Many of the Dragons gasped at this, surprising me yet again.

"Yes, I betrayed my mate and our Goddess, who sent him to me. For that, I will never forgive myself. But despite the way I treated Locrian, when he learned of Vettan's deception, he rushed back to my side. Vettan had drugged me, leaving me vulnerable and in a daze, unable to shift."

Another gasp.

"This human fearlessly defended me against a Dragon when I could not defend myself, and although Vettan was stronger, Locrian proved wiser. His first strike was made with a poisoned dagger. He knew Vettan would die, but not how long it would take. So, Locrian fought on, protecting me until the poison set in, knowing it would likely mean his death. When the inevitable happened, and Vettan overpowered Locrian, the mating bond finally roused me, and I was able to join the fight. Together, we defeated the traitor." Taroc looked around the gathering, meeting the stares of his dread. "I was shocked by the Goddess's choice of mate for me, as shocked as I assume all of you are, but now I see the wisdom in it. Now, I *rejoice* in it. Locrian is my match. Brave enough to fight for me but also to speak the harsh truths I need to hear. He helps me see this world and my kingdom from another perspective. My mate makes me a better king, and I know he will be just as good for our dread. Just as ferocious in his loyalty to you as he is to me."

Then Taroc looked at me.

Oh, fuck, he wanted me to say something? What could I possibly say to convince a roomful of Dragons that I was a good match for their king? Maybe I shouldn't try to convince them. Maybe I should take Taroc's advice and be the man he fell in love with.

"Accept me or not," I said, lifting my chin. "I love him, and no one on this planet is going to take him from me. Not even an entire dread of Dragons."

Lips twitched, many even stretched into smiles, and one of those smiles was on the face of my king.

Yarena turned to face the dread. "Our king and his mate have spoken. Step forward and give them your decision."

The Dragons glided into a line that flowed up the steps to us. The first man approached, his gaze unreadable. He inclined his head to Taroc, then moved to stand directly in front of me. Taroc had refused to give me any details, so I was prepared for anything. These were Dragons; they'd surely do something dragony, right? Acceptance might mean a ball of fire thrown in my face and denial could be—shit, that could be truly horrible.

I met the man's stare, bracing myself for the worst.

"Welcome to the Racul Dread, King's Mate," he said and shook my hand.

I blinked. "Thank you."

That was it?

The woman following him did the same, repeating those words exactly, and the Dragon after her as well, and so on. I didn't relax, no matter how many of them gave me their approval, called me King's Mate, and went back down the steps. Because the one thing Taroc had told me was that in the case of a non-Dragon mate, acceptance had to be unanimous. If even one Dragon disapproved of me, one of the thousands, we would be cast out of his dread. Taroc would have to give up the throne or me.

Fuck. How could he look so damn calm?

Sweat rolled down my back as I shook hand after hand

and tried to keep my gaze steady. As the line shortened, I began to hope. Then I told hope to fuck off because isn't that always when things go bad, right when you start to hope?

But nothing went bad. The Dragons of the Racul Dread accepted me. Even Hersk, though that was a bit awkward. Then came the last Dragon. Yarena moved to stand in front of me and stared at me for a long moment. The other Dragons watched her carefully, waiting.

"Our king is very precious to us," she said to me at last. "He's our strongest warrior but also wise. In all but this."

I nearly passed out. Was I about to be rejected after standing there for hours, accepting everyone else's welcome? I looked over at Taroc and saw a crease between his brows. Fuck.

"King Tarocvar says that the Goddess chose you for him, but that is only partially true. The Goddess sends us those who she approves of, but she does not decide for us. Your mate doesn't understand that although he has not chosen you with his mind or even his heart, his soul made the decision to claim you, and your soul has chosen him in return, Locrian. A mating bond cannot be completed without the full consent of both mates. You judged each other worthy, and I find your judgments to be sound. You are a fine addition to our dread." She held out her hand. "Welcome, King's Mate."

The Racul Dread roared in celebration as I shook Yarena's hand.

Chapter Forty-Nine

The celebration went on long into the early hours of the morning, but Taroc and I made our rounds and left after a few hours. The only Dragon whose name I remembered was Yarena, but she was formally introduced to me as the Vas. I waited until we were leaving the dining hall to ask Taroc about it.

"What's the Vas?"

Taroc, more carefree than I'd ever seen him, swung his smile my way. "The Vas? You met her."

"No, I mean, what is her title mean?"

"It's a very old Draconian word that means a lot of things—protector, guide, gatherer. Basically, she's a type of mother, a role that's part hostess and part mediator. To put it simply, the Vas organizes meetings, but she does so much more than that. With Dragons, every meeting runs the risk of turning violent. The Vas ensures that they don't."

"Is it always a woman?"

"Yes, women are better at it. We've tried males in the very distant past, but they often made things worse. Thus, females, and thus, the title of Vas."

"Interesting."

"There's a lot about my culture for you to learn. It's your culture now too." He lifted my hand and kissed it. "I told you it would be all right, Assassin."

"It felt as if it could have gone either way."

"It could have. But I had faith that you would prevail, and, as usual, I was right."

"Of course." I rolled my eyes toward Ren. "It's about him. It's always about him."

Ren yipped.

"I'm glad you've accepted that," Taroc said. Then he nodded at the guards who opened the doors of the royal suite for us.

We went into the royal bedchambers, fully repaired now. The new balcony doors that I'd requested had been installed. They had glass panels, so no one could sneak onto the balcony ever again. A fire was burning in the fireplace across from the bed, and Ren immediately found a spot on the rug before it. The new bed, slightly larger than the last, was draped in ruby velvet and silk to celebrate my induction into the Racul Dread. Around the room, candles flickered in silver holders, so Taroc didn't bother to light the overhead chandeliers.

He also didn't take me to bed as I'd expected. Instead, the Dragon King led me out to the balcony and up to the railing. He breathed in deeply, his eyes closing with it, then stared up at the stars.

"My entire life, I've had this knot in my chest. An ache that compelled me into action, an anxiety that drove me to the throne. I kept grasping for more and more but nothing eased that knot." He turned to look at me. "Until tonight. When my dread roared for you, that knot unwound, and I knew that it was you who my soul has been reaching for. All this time,

I've felt incomplete. Eager for something I didn't have. But it wasn't a thing or a goal; it was you. I needed *you*."

"It's been a long time since I've had a family, the closest I came was with a pirate captain."

Taroc scowled. "Tengven is a pirate?"

"Huh?" I blinked. "What? No, of course not. What I'm trying to say is that *you* are my family now. You and the Racul Dread, but, mainly, you." I grinned. "I love you, Taroc. My life began the day I tried to take yours."

Taroc laughed brightly and pulled me into his arms. "That was a good day for me as well, Assassin. And now we start our life together."

Then his lips were on mine and his hands roaming my body. We stripped each other right there, standing in the moonlight, the sound of revelry a soft hum in the background. There would doubtless be a patrol coming through the garden soon, now that they were actually following my instructions, but I didn't care. I dropped to my knees and lavished love on my mate.

But my mate had other plans.

Taroc lifted me and sat me on the railing. My legs went to his waist, but he moved them between us, straightening them so that my feet hooked over his shoulders. The position pushed me back, and I had to grab his arms so I wouldn't fall. But I wouldn't have fallen, my mate had me. His hand gripped my hip, moving me down so that the curve of polished stone served as the perfect support for my arched back. And that's when I felt his wet cock nudge me.

Gently, slowly, he moved into me, both of us groaning and trembling with need. I clutched at his thick biceps as he went deeper and deeper, working that hard flesh into my yielding channel. Ripples of pleasure ran through me as my mate and I became one.

"I love you," Taroc said, a bold statement instead of a whispered endearment. "And now, we have forever, Lock."

"Forever." I pulled his face down to mine and kissed him, showing him what forever with him meant to me until his passion became too wild for kissing.

"Lock," he panted as he pumped rapidly.

"I've got you, Taroc. I've got you."

The Dragon King growled in pleasure. "Yes, and I've got you."

What eternity would hold for us, I didn't know, and I didn't care. I had him, and he had me. The Dragon King and his assassin. The future didn't stand a chance.

A Special Look

Keep reading for a special look into the next book in The Dragons of Serai Series:

The Dragon Prince and the Necromancer

Chapter One

I've never been a physically powerful man. Some might call me effeminate, but they would do so for only a short time. I may not have the physical strength of some men, but I am still powerful. I learned how to use weapons to make up for my lack of muscles, becoming proficient in bow and blades, and as a Raltven, I can transform my body into an almost translucent form, blending into the shadows to creep up on my enemies. Those skills assisted in making me the man I am, but it was my magic that brought me here.

I stared across the undulating sea at the shores of Erimbar, the capital city of the Zaru Kingdom. Domed roofs were sprinkled among the flat-topped buildings, the largest of those belonging to the royal palace, perched upon a hill in the center of the city so that there was no doubt of its dominance. For a city in a desert region, Erimbar was surprisingly lush. Greenery overpowered the boring beige of bare stone. But in the distance, beyond the city walls, the green was spotty at best, swallowed by a sea of sand.

"Have you ever been to Erimbar?" the Dragon Prince asked me.

He had asked many questions of me during our journey from Racul. It seemed as if the more he asked, the more he needed to know. And I found myself wanting him to know. I'd even ventured to ask a few questions of him.

I glanced at Prince Racmar. Many Dragon males had a presence that demanded attention and, in his case, respect. They were all physically and magically powerful, but, as it was in any race, some more so than others. Racmar's power was great enough that I could sense it hovering about him, could almost smell the smoke of the fire he commanded. But it wasn't his power I was drawn to. Nor was it his stunning face that bore the sharp lines of his race, a jaw that could crack stone, and eyes the color of Spring leaves. His hair was dark, golden blond. Not metallic, but a glossy antique gold, precious and ancient. He wore it long, often braided as it was today, but even that crowning glory didn't sway me. I'd seen many beautiful men. Had several of them.

But there was something more than power and beauty here. Perhaps it was simply the fact that I knew the Prince of Zaru didn't want to like me. He needed my help, but he didn't trust me. Not because I'm a necromancer, but because I'm a Raltven. This wasn't surprising, most of the races of Serai distrusted my kind. It didn't help that many of us who lived in the integrated cities became criminals. Nor was it our fault that the Gods had given us forms that fit unlawful work so well. Just as it wasn't my fault that I'd been given control over the dead.

Prince Racmar had been sent by his brother, King Saric, to the Kingdom of Racul to enlist the aid of its king. Zaru was having a problem with their dead; mainly, they wouldn't stay that way. They had tried a necromancer from their kingdom, but she wasn't a Raltven, and my kind make the best necromancers. We are, after all, a step away from being spirits ourselves. So, as I said, the Prince needed me.

At first, that rankled him. Especially since he was also attracted to me—a fact that became obvious the instant we met. He was both attracted and horrified by his attraction. Because of this, I added a condition to my acceptance of this mission. I demanded his support. I would be entering a foreign city alone, and although there would be Raltven there who I could call upon in an emergency, they would not be of my clan, and so I needed a champion. Not necessarily a friend, but an advocate to speak on my behalf. Someone who would be on my side. I made him promise to be that man for me, and he did. He swore that no one would disrespect me without consequence, not even the King of Zaru himself.

I believe it was this promise that prompted the Prince's questions. He wanted to be certain of the man he had made such a vow to. At least, that's what I assumed all those questions about my people, family, and me were about. I don't think he expected my answers to affect him, but they did. My words drew him closer. I've always been good at that—drawing men to me, making them feel at ease—and that's what I had done with Racmar. Two weeks at sea had gone by swiftly and with it had gone the Prince's wariness.

But not mine.

"No, I've never been to your kingdom before, Your Highness. The city looks lovely."

Prince Racmar grinned. "But the land beyond is bleak, right?"

"I cannot make that determination with one, far-off look."

"Nicely said." He turned his bright green gaze back to his home. "The desert can be daunting but also beautiful."

"I'm sure it can be."

Racmar grimaced. "When it's not full of walking corpses."

I chuckled. "I will do my best to change that."

He sighed as he leaned onto his forearms. "I hate feeling powerless."

I glanced at him in surprise. Although he demanded information from me, Racmar rarely offered anything of himself in return. He did answer when I asked, but often vaguely, and never anything that could be construed as weakness. This glimpse of vulnerability made him less princely, more real, and I liked that. It was a good sign.

We'd been dancing around a sexual relationship for the past two weeks. Put in such close quarters, it was difficult to avoid his hot looks and "accidental" touches. I'd nearly given in several times, but as much as the confinement of a ship gave rise to desire, I knew it could just as easily kill it. A new relationship is a fragile thing. It needs space to grow. I sensed that having sex with him on that ship would lead to annoyance and regret. We'd be over before we had begun, and I didn't want that.

I wanted more from the Dragon Prince. Much more. Which meant that I had to remain as rational and aloof as possible. As contradictory as that sounds, I knew that becoming too attached to someone is the surest way to lose them. And I had no intentions of losing the Prince of Zaru.

"You are not powerless," I said. "You found me. That was what you needed to do. Now, you will support me through my task and, in that way, help your kingdom."

Racmar chuckled. "You sound like my brother."

"Too cocky?" I grinned.

"No. Cocky implies unreasonable arrogance. You have made it clear that until you know what is causing the dead to rise, you cannot promise me results, and yet, you are confident in what you *can* do. That is not cockiness; that is wisdom and self-awareness. And I like that."

I went serious. "I hope that I can help your kingdom, Your Highness. But if I can't, I will do all in my power to find someone who can."

"Thank you. I know you will." He smiled and it lit his eyes, taking his harsh features and turning them into something sublime.

Oh, fuck.

Pronunciation Guide

Argaiv: Are-guy-iv

Balahar: Bahl-are-har

Bracaro: Back-cah-row

Crushei: Crew-shay

Drasik: Drah-sick

Locrian Mahvis: Lock-kree-an Ma-viss

Mikbal: Mick-bahl

Mhavenna: Muh-ha-vehn-nah

Neraky: Nah-rah-key

Paslan: Paws-lahn

Racul: Rah-cool

Raltven: Rahl-T-vehn

Ricarri: Ree-car-ree

Serai: Sir-rye

Shanba: Shan-bah

Tarocvar Verres: Tear-rock-varr Vare-riss

Tengven: Tayng-vin

Vettan: Veh-tahn

Vevaren: Veh-vahr-rehn

Yuref: Yer-reff

More Books by Amy Sumida

The Godhunter Series (in order)

Godhunter
Of Gods and Wolves
Oathbreaker
Marked by Death
Green Tea and Black Death
A Taste for Blood
The Tainted Web

Series Split:
These books can be read together or separately
Harvest of the Gods & A Fey Harvest
Into the Void & Out of the Darkness

Perchance to Die
Tracing Thunder
Light as a Feather
Rain or Monkeyshine
Blood Bound
Eye of Re
My Soul to Take
As the Crow Flies
Cry Werewolf
Pride Before a Fall
Monsoons and Monsters
Blessed Death
In the Nyx of Time
Let Sleeping Demons Lie

The Lion, the Witch, and the Werewolf
Hear No Evil
Dark Star
Destiny Descending
The Black Lion
Half Bad
A Fey New World
God Mode

Beyond the Godhunter
A Darker Element
Out of the Blue

The Twilight Court Series
Fairy-Struck
Pixie-Led
Raven-Mocking
Here There Be Dragons
Witchbane
Elf-Shot
Fairy Rings and Dragon Kings
Black-Market Magic
Etched in Stone
Careless Wishes
Enchanted Addictions
Dark Kiss
Shame the Devil

The Spellsinger Series
The Last Lullaby
A Symphony of Sirens
A Harmony of Hearts
Primeval Prelude
Ballad of Blood
A Deadly Duet
Macabre Melody
Aria of the Gods

Anthem of Ashes
A Chorus of Cats
Doppelganger Dirge
Out of Tune
Singing the Scales
The Devil's Ditty
A Shattered Song
—completed series—

The Spectra Series
Spectra
A Gray Area
A Compression of Colors
Blue Murder
Code Red
With Flying Colors
Green With Envy
A Silver Tongue
A Golden Opportunity
—completed series—

The Soul Stones
The Hawk Soul
The Lynx Soul
The Leopard Soul
The Fox Soul
The Wolf Soul
The Falcon Soul
The Eagle Soul
The Lion Soul
The Tiger Soul
—completed series—

Tales of the Beneath
The Ghosts of War
A Leopard Changes His Spots
Heart of Stone

Fairy Tales

Happily Harem After Vol 1
Including:
The Four Clever Brothers
Wild Wonderland
Beauty and the Beasts
Pan's Promise
The Little Glass Slipper

Happily Harem After Vol 2
Including:
Codename: Goldilocks
White as Snow
Twisted
Awakened Beauty

Erotica

An Unseelie Understanding

Historical Romance

Enchantress

About the Author

Amy Sumida is the Internationally Acclaimed author of the Award-Winning Godhunter Series, the fantasy paranormal Twilight Court Series, the Beyond the Godhunter Series, the music-oriented paranormal Spellsinger Series, the superhero Spectra Series, and several short stories. Her books have been translated into several languages, have won numerous awards, and are bestsellers. She believes in empowering women through her writing as well as providing everyone with a great escape from reality. Her stories are full of strong women and hot gods, shapeshifters, vampires, dragons, fairies, gargoyles... pretty much any type of supernatural, breathtakingly gorgeous man you can think of. Because why have normal when you could have paranormal?

Born and raised in Hawaii, Amy made a perilous journey across the ocean with six cats to settle in the beautiful state of Oregon which reminds her a lot of Hawaii but without the cockroaches or evil sand. When she isn't trying to type fast enough to keep up with the voices in her head while ignoring the kitties trying to sabotage her with cuteness, she enjoys painting on canvases, walls, and anything else that will sit still long enough for the paint to dry. She's fueled by tea, inspired by music, and spends most of her time lost in imaginary worlds.

Connect with Amy

Amy's Social Media Links

For information on new releases, detailed character descriptions, and an in-depth look into the worlds of the Godhunter, the Twilight Court, the Spellsinger, Spectra, and the Happily Harem After Series, check out Amy's website:

Amy Sumida's Website

Want a free book? Sign up for her newsletter and get a free ebook as well as the latest news on Amy's releases, parties, and giveaways:

Amy's Newsletter

Want more free books? Grab the first books in the Godhunter and Twilight Court Series for free: Godhunter and Fairy-Struck

Read more of Amy's books:

The Godhunter Series
The Twilight Court Series
The Spellsinger Series
The Spectra Series
The Soul Stones Series (Gay Romance)

Printed in Great Britain
by Amazon

83796095R00200